"Major! Major Bannister. Wait. Please."

Ace considered walking faster, then reluctantly slowed his steps and let her catch up. "Call me Ace," he said. "Instructors aren't formal when there are no cadets around."

Meredith frowned. "What's your real name?"

"Ace sounds real enough to me."

She tapped a fingernail on his name tag. "It says A period, C period. That does not spell Ace."

Ace crossed his arms defensively. What A.C. stood for sure as hell wasn't something he'd share with Captain West Point. "Guess I was never good at spelling," he snarled.

She didn't let his rudeness deter her. "No? So what *was* your best subject? Annihilation 100?"

"Excuse me. I think I've lost the thread of this conversation. Who did I just kill?"

Dear Reader,

In the days when my husband first entered the military, a common saying was that the Marine Corps builds men— the implication being that they came into the service boys and left boot camp men. Strong men.

No doubt the word *strong* means different things to different people. To the great fraternity of military men it spelled strength of mind, body and spirit. Then with the advent of women joining our armed forces, the old guard who considered West Point and the regular army barracks strictly *men's territory* suddenly came up against a new, unique force. *Heart.* He-men who climbed out of the trenches found themselves butting heads with social change. Some laughed. Some balked. Some learned and grew stronger—like Major Ace Bannister. His story is about change. A process that's sometimes funny. Occasionally touching. Often exasperating. But never easy. Especially when I've given him a group of rascally ROTC students to make his road even rockier.

But underlying the framework is heart and hope, because I've always admired the real-life men and women who ultimately find a way to love and laugh and soldier, all at the same time. It takes a person of special strengths to succeed.

My best always,

Roz

Roz Denny Fox

Major Attraction

Harlequin Books

TORONTO • NEW YORK • LONDON
AMSTERDAM • PARIS • SYDNEY • HAMBURG
STOCKHOLM • ATHENS • TOKYO • MILAN
MADRID • WARSAW • BUDAPEST • AUCKLAND

ISBN 0-373-70649-9

MAJOR ATTRACTION

My thanks to the following people, who generously
provided information about Baltimore, West Point,
military social workers, officers and the ROTC:
Carolyn, Diane, Donna, Greg, Jim,
Ken, Pete, Scott, Steven and Tom.
(The mistakes, if any, are mine!)

CHAPTER ONE

LARGE, FAT WATER BALLOONS suddenly rained from the men's residence, striking two men walking below. Major A. C. Bannister covered his head to ward off what he realized were exploding condoms and sprinted toward his campus office at the U.S. Army Reserve Officers Training Corps. He saw that the friend with whom he'd been chatting, U.S. Air Force Lieutenant Colonel Frank Loudermilk, had cut toward the building housing the culprits. As if they'd wait around. Ha! ROTC had done a good job teaching them the principle of attacking first and clearing out fast.

Once out of range, the major slowed to a jog. These pranks, army against air force and vice versa, were getting tedious. More so when, like today, the little charmers hit on the brass. Last week it had been cayenne pepper in the minestrone soup, courtesy of the army kids. Frank had been hell-bent on retribution ever since.

By the time the major reached his office, the water had seeped through to his skin. He stopped just inside and stripped off his wet shirt.

Joel Sutton, the craggy master sergeant who served as the major's clerk, leapt to his feet and gasped, "What happened, sir?"

"Loudermilk's new batch of fly-babies happened."

Sutton shook his head. "God, the LC will march everyone's butt off for this. Water balloons are so...so juvenile."

Major Bannister yanked his T-shirt off over his head. "They used condoms," he said dryly, "although I doubt half this batch of cadets knows what they're really for. Some of these kids should still be home playing with GI Joes." A sigh softened his grumble. "There's always a consequence. You'd think they'd learn."

"Don't you remember how it was at that age, sir?"

The major paused, one hand inside a closet where he kept extra uniforms. Did he remember? No. He'd grown up on the back streets of San Antonio, where only the tough survived. Horseplay had never figured in his youth. It had taken him a while to thank the bighearted cop who'd wangled him a hitch with Uncle Sam, instead of three to five in Huntsville prison.

"It wasn't easy climbing up through regular-army ranks, Sutton. And I damn sure didn't win this gold oak leaf throwing water balloons at the enemy."

"I know that, sir." The sergeant's tone instantly changed to respect. "A Bronze Star and a Distinguished Service Cross during Desert Storm." His gnarled hands shuffled a pile of papers. "Me, I broke both legs in parachute training and never made it to 'Nam. What's it like, earning citations in combat?"

The major scowled into a small mirror he was using to try to tame his wet, unruly hair. "I only did my job. No man likes the taste of fear. Be glad you didn't get to 'Nam."

Before Sutton could reply, the door opened and Colonel Wylie O'Dell, commandant in charge of the army's ROTC program at South Oakes University, strode to the major's desk and slapped down a manila folder.

Both men in the room snapped to attention.

"At ease." The colonel pointed a stubby finger at the folder. "Ace, m'boy, we've got ourselves a snafu."

The major felt a ripple of tension. Not because of the colonel's familiar use of his nickname—no one used his birth name. It was because he'd learned that when Colonel O'Dell, who was mere months from retirement, tossed out his favorite World War II acronym, Ace—as second in command—was about to get dumped on royally. "Snafu" meant "situation normal, all fouled up." Though military men usually substituted the other f-word. Either way, O'Dell's snafus were never normal.

"What's the problem, Colonel?"

"Someone in the Pentagon decided we...er, *you* need an assistant." O'Dell lifted his hat and wiped sweat from his brow.

"An assistant?" Ace finished tying his tie and slid the knot up so fast it almost choked him.

"Yep. According to this fax, our new captain's due here today. I faxed back—asked who's allocating funds for a staff person we really don't need. Typical of those guys on the hill to dump on the ones who do the work. If my schedule wasn't so full, Major, I'd handle this placement myself. You know I would."

Ace knew no such thing. The headaches always fell to him. And this must be a doozy for the old man to come out in ninety-five-degree heat. "As we are fully staffed," Ace began, seeing the need to tread lightly, "where would you suggest I put another professional instructor, Colonel?"

"Somewhere safe. Those orders came from high up. Very high, if you get my drift." So saying, the colonel departed, leaving behind a room rife with tension and the pungent lime scent of his after-shave.

Bannister stared at the file. *An assistant*. Did someone up the ladder think he wasn't doing his job? He gave
a careless shrug for the sergeant's benefit.

Sutton had begun to mutter. "What's his schedule full
of, I'd like to know. Tiddledywinks? Golf?"

Ace let the remark pass. Perching on the edge of his
desk, he cautiously opened the innocuous-looking file.

The sergeant tried to peer over his shoulder.

"Son of a bitch!" Ace exploded.

Sutton jumped back. "Sir?"

The major reread a sentence that said Captain Meredith Marshall St. James had graduated with honors from
West Point. The next line indicated the captain had rid-
den out the Gulf War at a safe post near Baltimore,
Maryland.

Not everyone had served in the Gulf, Ace knew. But
most able-bodied officers had. He traced a finger down
to the block marked Age. Twenty-seven. That certainly
sounded able-bodied to him.

"What is it, sir?" the sergeant prodded.

"A damned ring polisher, Sutton. And listen to this
moniker." Ace singsonged the name. "Meredith Marshall St. James."

"A mouthful, all right," the sergeant agreed. "Why
us? Does it say?"

Ace groaned. "Jeez! This dude's got two degrees. One
in *social work*. What in hell am I supposed to do with
some fancy-pants do-gooder when we already have our
hands full turning mama's boys into men?"

Sutton merely grunted as his boss punched the air with
his forefinger. "Don't those guys upstairs know how
tough it is putting backbone into cream-puff college
kids?" Ace snorted. "Did I ever tell you about Spicer
Van Brocklin III?"

The old sergeant shook his head.

"He was a spit-polished West Point lieutenant I met in ranger training. Creases just so. Absolutely would not get his hands dirty. What'll you bet our new captain starches his underwear?"

"Who cares about his underwear? Where'll we put his desk?"

"Not here. Uh-huh. No way am I sharing an office with some preppy pain in the ass. I don't care if his orders came down from God."

The sergeant wrinkled his brow. "With a name like Meredith, sir, it could be a woman."

"A woman?" That notion threw Ace a curve. "The only Meredith I've ever met is a man." Ace flipped the page. "It figures. Damned fax paper—can't read that square." Glancing up, he said, "I've never been stationed with a woman out of the Point. Have you, Sutton?"

"One, sir." The sergeant flopped down in his chair, shaking his head.

The major tugged at his right ear. "Bad, huh?"

"Well, you know, sir. Men didn't want women at the academy. Some still do rotten things to wash the women out. Only the toughest get through."

Ace formed a mental picture of a woman who might "get through." "Great," was his only comment.

The sergeant returned to the issue of where to put the new person. "Man or woman, they'll need a desk, sir. ROTC had to fight for this space. The college will never approve another office."

Ace was still considering the possibility of a woman. "We know how Ron Holmes hates men out of the Point. Might not be the hassle squeezing a female in next door with him and Captain Caldwell."

"Even if there was room over there, sir, which there isn't, do you really see Cap'n Holmes making room for an Amazon queen?"

Swearing roundly, Ace threw the folder back on his desk, snatched up his hat and headed for the door.

"Where are you going?" Sutton bolted upright. "Colonel said the captain's due in today."

"I'm feeling bum, Sarge. I need medicine. The kind they dole out at the O-club," he said, referring to the officers' club at nearby Fort Freeman.

"Before 1700 hours, sir?" Sutton sounded genuinely shocked that Ace would consider such a thing before five in the afternoon. "Normally when O'Dell drops a bomb like this, sir, you run the track a lap or two. That's what you did when Buddy Watson flunked out and O'Dell sicced Buddy's mama on you."

"Yes, well, a social worker out of West Point warrants a marathon. And frankly it's too damned hot to run."

"Yes, sir," the sergeant mumbled. "What should I do when Captain St. James shows up?"

"Call and get him—or her," Ace hastily corrected, "set up temporarily in the BOQ." Returning to the Rolodex, he pulled a card and tossed it on his clerk's desk. "Wouldn't hurt my feelings if the bachelor office quarters you call happened to be in Alaska," Ace said pointedly.

"We know the captain's single?" Sutton's hand hovered over the phone.

Ace went to his desk and opened the folder. The square behind Captain St. James's name was marked with a bold black S. "That we do, Sutton. Single and a blue blood. Tell me this is just a bad dream."

"I can see where it'd be hard for somebody who came out of the trenches to be assisted by a West Pointer. Guess I don't blame you for going to the pub, sir."

The major's growl resembled that of a wounded animal as he slammed out the door. Backing out of the parking area, he suddenly felt the loneliness that often accompanied command. Another good reason for going to the O-club. What he needed was some camaraderie, a few laughs and a few drinks. Although, compared to some who hung out at the club, Ace wasn't a big drinker. Nearby Fort Freeman had no official ties to the ROTC program, but access to the officers' club was considered a perk for army and air force instructors assigned to teach military science. The companionship of other military folk might assuage the loneliness of his rank and his position at the college. On impulse, Ace decided to stop and invite a woman he knew to join him.

He had met Ruby Tindall, an attractive divorced redhead, on a previous post. Last year, after she got smart and dumped her drunken philandering husband—a lieutenant Ace knew only by reputation—they'd begun dating. On occasion Ace had heard Ruby talk about the same emptiness in her life he often felt. Although what she talked about most often was her kids. She spent a lot of time discussing whether or not to take them back to the small town in Oregon where she'd grown up.

Ace tried never to offer advice in areas he knew nothing about. He certainly didn't see himself as inducement for her to stick around here. He and Ruby were friends. They'd never shared a bed, mostly because he'd returned from the Gulf with a changed view of permanence. Life was about more than physical gratification.

So tonight, as on their usual Friday dates, Ace wanted nothing more than a smooth glass of bourbon, and the company of a friend. Maybe that would help him forget the colonel's latest snafu. Namely, Captain West Point.

ACROSS TOWN, Captain Meredith St. James had just completed a long, tiring flight. What should have been a four-hour jaunt from Baltimore had taken eight on military standby. The last leg was spent on a noisy chopper that had made a stop at the civilian airport ten or so miles from South Oakes University.

Cabs weren't exactly plentiful, and that caused yet another delay. When at last all her bags were loaded into one, the captain had one window free to look out at the unfamiliar countryside. Culture shock for someone who'd spent the better part of twenty-seven years in and around the historic city of Baltimore.

The sun beat down mercilessly on the cab, and dust rose from beneath the wheels to hang on an invisible wind. As far as the human eye could see, flat reddish earth blended with low-growing scrub. What trees there were had small ruffs of green atop squat dark trunks.

And it was *hot*. Captain St. James was positive hell could not be any hotter than this plot of ground in west Texas—even though, technically, it was spring. In Baltimore, cherry blossoms were popping out and other flowers had begun to color the landscape. If she had to be transferred from her comfortable assignment in Baltimore, almost anyplace in the universe seemed preferable to Texas.

It only added to the day's frustration when, after walking two blocks in the unholy heat to locate the army ROTC office on campus, Captain St. James was informed that, yes, Major Bannister knew the captain was due in today, but he'd gone to the O-club anyhow.

"Colonel O'Dell faxed that I should report to the major on my arrival." The captain's voice rose in disbelief. "I've released my cab. Do you have someone free to take me to him?"

"That might not be such a good idea," the sergeant muttered.

"What?" Captain St. James arched a pale eyebrow.

"I said, that might not be such a good idea, *sir*," the sergeant repeated more loudly.

"Let me be the judge of that," she snapped. "Now, if you'll get that driver—"

"Yes, sir. Right away, sir." Sutton grabbed the phone.

On the short drive from the campus to the fort, Captain St. James garnered a passable description of Major Bannister from the youthful driver. But even without it, the major wouldn't have been hard to spot. The only gold oak leaf in the club blazed from a jacket thrown carelessly over a chair.

Captain St. James studied the dark-haired man in the corner with some misgiving. His military record might be impeccable, but his deportment was not. His tie hung loose and his sleeves were rolled halfway to the elbows in flagrant disregard of the army's dress code.

Having spent a lifetime in the company of officers, the captain knew every syllable of the code. Three generations on both sides of the family had graduated from West Point, where dignity and decorum were tantamount to godliness.

Suppressing scorn, Captain St. James marched across the dimly lit, thickly carpeted room and saluted smartly. "Major Bannister, sir! Captain St. James reporting as directed." Both form and salute were near perfect. Chin in, back arched, heels touching.

Ace peered up. Ruby was cloven to his side, and even then he was having trouble hearing her over the music. Given the lack of light, it took him a moment to locate the person who'd interrupted—although the cultured-sounding inflection of her voice left Ace in no doubt that he was looking at Captain Snafu.

He felt his jaw go slack. Perhaps, for the first time since he'd become an officer, Ace Bannister failed to return a salute.

Before him, hat in hand, stood a wisp of a female whose great golden eyes reminded Ace of aged cognac—mellow on the surface, covering a sharp bite below. Magnificent eyes that clearly showed disapproval. Of him.

That in itself made Ace sit straighter. Not that he was one to brag, but it was a rare woman who dismissed him on looks alone.

Yet she had—this lady captain, whose pale blond hair was cut nearly as short as his, except for a few longer strands that blew about her face like dandelion fluff, thanks to the lazily churning fan overhead.

This was Captain St. James? Captain *West Point* St. James?

Ace felt his teeth come together like a rubber band suddenly snapped. Dazed, he closed his eyes and shook his head. Only then did he collect himself enough to manage a passable salute. Even so, he neglected to say, "At ease," and the captain remained as she was, chin up, back ramrod-stiff, nose tilted just a bit as if she smelled something bad.

"Major Bannister."

Ace noted that her smoky voice masked her irritation well.

"Anxious as I am to discuss incorporating my curriculum into your ROTC program, it's plain to see that you are...otherwise occupied. Perhaps it would be best if we met in your office tomorrow. Will 0800 hours suit you...sir?"

An unspoken rebuke lurked just below the surface of her words, asking if he would be...what? Sober?

Ace didn't like her attitude. It was barely short of insubordinate. And he hadn't drunk so much that he couldn't figure out that somewhere along the way, Little Miss Uppity Britches had picked up a powerful mentor. Very powerful, judging by her manner.

Hell, he didn't fault her for having a mentor. He'd had a few himself. All tough, brilliant officers. Good soldiers, who saw something in him that made them think he was worth sticking their necks out for. But a social worker? *Give me a break.*

"Miss St. James," he said tightly, scarcely able to force her name through his lips.

She drew herself up taller, twin spots of color on her cheeks the only sign she had heard his insult. Heard it and didn't like it.

"It's *Captain* St. James." She enunciated each syllable. "At your service...Major."

Ace flushed. He had never insulted an officer, or a woman. Not in his entire military career. Until now.

Deciding the wisest move would be to leave before he said something unforgivable, he bent and whispered his intention in Ruby's ear. She giggled.

Ace didn't think his request was funny. Now, unwinding himself from Ruby in front of those condemning golden eyes was embarrassing. Come to think of it, though, he didn't give a damn *what* the snooty captain thought about him. Or his companion.

Captain St. James heard the major's date snicker. Presumably he'd said something snide about *her*—the jerk. Through narrowed eyes, she watched the pair slide out of the booth as though they were joined at the hip. Something deep inside her wanted to dump the amber contents of the glasses over their heads. But of course she wouldn't. A St. James never acted out of petulance, and certainly not in public.

What she did was press her fingers tighter to her sides and command her elbows not to waver. If Major Bannister thought he could break her by leaving her to stand at attention, he was mistaken. She had lived through more rigid discipline at home—meted out in military fashion by a man who, although he controlled every aspect of his life, had not been able to command the birth of a son.

And she'd survived worse at the Point. Meredith Marshall St. James had learned early to separate her ego from the whims of male officers. She could stand like this until hell froze into little ice cubes if the major so desired.

It wasn't easy to watch him uncurl a six-foot frame from the dark booth. Meredith tried not to blink as he towered over her. It was downright humiliating when he dropped a twenty-dollar bill on the table, looped a well-muscled arm around his lady friend's neck and, just before they walked off, said oh-so-casually, "Have a drink, Captain—on me."

And he left without placing her at ease. When she realized her mouth was gaping, Meredith shut it and allowed only a sliver of her gaze to follow Major A. C. Bannister's progress. He sauntered out in a way that defied description, even for someone as articulate as herself.

Who does he think he is? she fumed silently. He might be good-looking, but she'd certainly seen good-looking men before.

He might have the body of an athlete, but if he made alcohol a habit he certainly wouldn't keep it long.

His eyes.

What derogatory thing could she say about silver-gray eyes, fringed with lashes so long most women would kill for them?

Meredith dragged her thoughts off that path.

Rude. He was rude, inconsiderate and tactless. Nothing attractive about that. And it was obvious he thought he was God's gift to women.

Well, if she'd been unclear as to why her father had pulled strings to have her sent here—after he went out of his way to belittle her field of expertise—it no longer mattered.

South Oakes ROTC was the perfect place to begin honing the rough edges of fledgling officer candidates. Not only that, Major Bannister, top professional instructor in charge of the poor impressionable kids, had more rough edges than steel wool.

Frankly Meredith didn't think her tour here would be long enough to even *find* them all. But now that she had a focus, now that she knew what needed doing, she could hardly wait for morning.

CHAPTER TWO

WHEN MORNING rolled around, Ace wasn't in the best
shape. His mouth tasted of stale whiskey and his head
felt like a target used for tank bombardment. He could
barely crack his eyelids enough to look in the mirror.
Just the thought of his regular five-mile run sent his
stomach into a tailspin.

Damn! He clung to the shower wall by the tips of his
fingers and let first hot then cold water hammer feeling
into a body not accustomed to overindulgence.

If only he'd gone to Ruby's for coffee as she suggested, he might not wish he were dead right now. Or
maybe if his own house hadn't seemed so empty when he
came in after dropping her off, he wouldn't have opened
the bottle of Jack Daniel's—a Christmas gift from a few
years ago he'd been saving for a special occasion.

Ace shut off the water, reached for a towel and
groaned. Captain West Point's arrival wasn't exactly the
occasion he'd had in mind. He shut his eyes and wished
for deliverance from the pounding in his temples. He
didn't have the strength to dry off. Instead, he draped
the towel around his torso, hoping it'd suck up water
droplets on its own.

Visions swirled behind his eyelids. Sherry gold eyes,
cotton-puff hair and skin that gleamed like silk. He
threw himself naked onto his king-size bed, and when
the room stopped spinning, he stared at the ceiling.

Maybe he'd conjured up that scene in the O-club. Maybe St. James was hatchet faced, with skin like shoe leather.

And maybe the earth would open and swallow him, bed and all.

But he wasn't that lucky. Painfully, Ace worked his way to the closet and with a great deal of effort got dressed. His tie took three tries, but he made it. Shoes on feet—a greater accomplishment.

He made his way to the kitchen for coffee and waded through a stack of dirty dishes, old tuna cans and microwave containers, looking for the coffee tin. Empty. Fate's worst blow yet. He started to chuck it across the room, then considered what the noise would do to the top of his head.

Damn! His first class met at 1000 hours today. It was already 0900. Well, he could always hope Sergeant Sutton had brewed a pot of coffee that didn't resemble axle grease.

Ace donned dark glasses and collected his hat. He took one last look at his messy kitchen and left, vowing he'd tackle putting the room in order tonight. The way he'd let things go lately made him wonder why he'd ever thought owning a house was the secret to happiness. Well, no, the answer to that was actually easy—it was because he'd never *had* a real home. But he'd begun to see that a roof and siding didn't guarantee the love and warmth he'd envied in the homes of married friends. What did all this really mean? That he needed to find a woman and settle down? Lord, he hated getting sentimental.

And what if he turned out to be as unreliable as the man who'd fathered him? That was a risk he'd have to consider.

Still, it was a damn good thing his house was close to campus, because if he had to drive another mile he'd probably stop and propose marriage to some stranger on the street—just so he wouldn't have to be alone again tonight.

God, it even hurt to laugh.

As he parked and climbed out, his spirits lifted. Inside, he'd share the usual male camaraderie with the other instructors. Surely that would erase these odd feelings. Oh, the guys would razz him about his hangover. But they'd understand. That was what he needed today. Understanding.

Ace pushed the heavy office door open, stepped inside and tripped over his own desk, which had somehow gravitated into the center of the room. Surprised, he ripped off his sunglasses, then cringed at the harsh light.

Sergeant Sutton was on his knees filing a pile of manila folders into a third desk. A desk behind which sat none other than Captain St. James.

She looked up, saw Ace, slammed her center drawer and came to attention like a shot.

Ace felt the noise from the roots of his still-damp hair all the way down his face to his teeth, which clenched in self-defense. "Owww..." He suffered further when Sergeant Sutton dropped his files and sprang to his feet.

"At ease," Ace breathed, groping behind him for a place to lean. Failing to find one, he clutched his head and glared at the captain. All this was her fault.

"Are you an alcoholic, Major?" Iced-sherry eyes made an unfriendly assessment of his condition.

"Jeez," he muttered. "You don't pull any punches. What happened to 'good morning, sir'?" He straightened. "More to the point, what in hell are you doing here? This is *my* office, St. James. All mine." Ace winced. If that didn't sound childish, he didn't know what did.

She arched a feathery brow. "Avoidance is more telling than denial, Major. I'd be happy to offer some type of counseling for staff. My master's is in substance abuse."

The sergeant broke in. "The major isn't normally like this, Captain."

"Thank you, Sutton—but I don't need defending." Ace followed the edges of his desk, hand over hand, until he reached his chair. He sat before he realized it placed him facing her—and her bright lamp. Ace was sure his head would explode if he didn't close his eyes. But she already thought him some sort of damned degenerate. He'd die before he'd give her the satisfaction.

"Look at you," she said softly. "Your tie is wrong side to, and your eyes look like road maps."

"Sergeant?" Ace said evenly, trying not to blink those telltale eyes. "Is that coffee I smell?"

"Yes, sir. It's fresh and hot. Captain St. James said mine looked like the Mississippi River, so she threw it out and made a new pot. I'll get you a cup." The older man hurried into an adjacent anteroom that served as both kitchen and workroom for Ace's office, as well as for Captain Holmes and Captain Caldwell next door— two other instructors in the ROTC program. Their office was even smaller than his, or Ace would have moved St. James there PDQ.

He'd love to refuse her coffee. Was nothing safe from this woman? he wondered, snatching up the telephone to punch in a number from memory. "Colonel," he growled when O'Dell answered. "Get me a transfer. I'll take leave until the orders come through." It gave Ace a little kick in his conscience to see the captain flush and look away. But at least he could close his eyes now and avoid her killer lamp.

"What do you mean, why? I just do, is all," he mumbled, reluctant to spell it out with her in the room. "Call it burnout."

Ace listened a moment. "Yes, the captain arrived. Yes," he said, lowering his voice, "that's part of the reason. It isn't going to work, Colonel." Ace didn't want to sound desperate, but he was afraid he did.

Again he fell silent and watched the captain gnaw her lip. If she didn't quit, dammit, she'd have it bloodied. His attention was suddenly pulled back to what Colonel O'Dell was saying. "...and her father's aide called today. General St. James didn't have time himself, because he's lunching with the president."

"So, let him have lunch with the Almighty," Ace snapped. "What does that have to do with my transfer?"

He thought he saw the rigid set of the captain's shoulders slip a bit, but he wasn't sure. A father at the Pentagon explained a lot.

"You say General St. James serves on the advisory council to the Joint Chiefs? I don't see... Yes, sir. But how does that... Yes, sir. No transfer?" Ace straightened and glared at the captain. "Yes, sir! I do indeed understand." He slammed the phone back into its cradle, then winced as the sound ricocheted inside his head.

Sergeant Sutton returned, carrying a steaming mug. As he placed it on the desk, he reminded Ace that it was almost time for his first class.

Ace nodded. He had a few questions for the captain. Such as why a powerhouse like her daddy didn't pluck her a plum from one of the Pentagon's choice trees. But that could wait, he decided. It wasn't his style to grill officers in front of noncoms. And since it didn't seem that a transfer was forthcoming, he'd have plenty of opportunities.

Ace took a swallow of coffee. He had to admit it was far superior to the stuff Sutton brewed. "This is good, Captain," he said, not begrudging her the compliment. He sipped again. "Any chance you can teach us?" His gaze strayed to his clerk. "Just because we have a woman on staff, Sergeant, doesn't mean she'll pull all the domestic duty."

Captain St. James glanced at him in surprise.

Ace nearly missed it in making sure his clerk got the message. He knew he could count on Sutton to pass the word.

Rising, Ace took a last swallow before he picked up the materials for his class. Then he set the lot down, walked over to the mirror and retied his tie. This time it was perfect.

Captain St. James rose, too. "I'm sorry we didn't have a chance to discuss my curriculum this morning," she said. "Since we didn't, maybe I'll tag along and sit in on your class."

That caught him off guard. "It's tactical maneuvers," he said. "Advanced. By the book. No need for sociological input. But I'll tell you what. Captain Holmes teaches military courtesy at 1100 hours. I'll tell him you'll be sitting in."

Meredith picked up her purse, settled her cap on her head and joined him at the door. "Major Bannister, the world is changing. The new army, especially future officers, must be sensitive to change in *all* areas. Not just in social situations."

Ace stopped outside the entrance. "What *new* army?"

Meredith pursed her lips and closed the door. "I doubt even you are immortal, Major. We're training our replacements here. Hopefully these men and women will be dealing with a more humane world. A higher level of consciousness. They need to be prepared."

Ace slowed his steps and indicated they'd be entering a building on her right. "You might feel differently, Captain, had you served in the Gulf. What precisely were you doing that you managed to escape?"

"Managing Personal Affairs."

"I beg your pardon?"

She stiffened. It was, of course, the reaction she'd expected from him. "It's a broad heading for our department," she explained. "Our office helped families cope with the difficulty of having loved ones abroad. We notified them of injuries and casualties. Substance-abuse counseling and benefit assistance fell to us, as well as myriad other tasks. Surely you know the air force has used social workers for some time."

"Yes, well, the air force fights a different style of war, Captain. Things are different when you're on the ground face-to-face with your enemy."

Meredith followed him up the steps and through the door to the classroom. His attitude was par for the course. But she'd never argue with him in front of students. There'd be time later to make her point.

His class had approximately thirty students. The men outnumbered the women by four to one, Meredith calculated. All of them looked terribly young.

The moment they saw the major, the entire group jumped to attention so smartly their childish chins quivered. Meredith tensed. Was it fear of retribution? Was the major such a taskmaster that he'd scream and yell at them for a small thing like uneven rows?

Very likely. That was how it'd been at the Point. People dishing out verbal abuse because they knew they could get away with it. Or because it was expected. Required, even. Again her lips tightened. Those were some of the things she hoped to change. In her opinion, no war would be lost because the men and women sworn to protect the rights and privileges of freedom showed they were human. Unfortunately many leaders, including her father, thought hard-core discipline won wars.

Meredith wouldn't have stayed in the army after getting her bachelor's had she not believed that somehow, some way, she might be able to make a difference. So she'd gone on to get her master's. As she sat in the major's classroom now, evaluating his teaching, Meredith couldn't help wondering what her father would say if he knew he'd unwittingly dumped her into the perfect proving ground for her theories.

Ace introduced his guest, then asked two of his best tacticians to conduct the class. He didn't often shirk his duty, but last night's calamity had left him edgy, as had this morning's encounter with Captain West Point. He sauntered down the center aisle, took a seat in the last row, folded his arms and pretended interest in every word his cadets said as they quoted from the book. Ace wished he could close his eyes. Impossible with the captain watching, so he watched her, instead.

What had gone through her head a minute ago, he wondered, to cause such an array of emotions to cross her expressive face?

Ace forced his attention back to what the students were saying. It simply wouldn't do to start analyzing the woman beneath that West Point veneer. There was an ocean between officers coming out of the Point and men like himself who were lucky enough to make their way up out of the trenches. And Ace counted himself lucky. He could easily have died on the streets at the hands of fellow hoodlums, or he could have rotted in prison. Still, he didn't kid himself. A man with his background would never have made it to West Point Academy. It took pull to get into that place, either family or congressional. Or both. Captain St. James had both. Look at her. Regal as the queen of Sheba presiding over her minions. His head began to ache again.

When class was over, Ace tried to sneak away. Let the lady from West Point put some of her path finding skills to good use getting back to the office. A man could only tolerate so much superiority in one short morning.

Ah, good! A few of the young women cadets had her cornered. Ace quickly left the room and didn't realize he was holding his breath until he let it out.

"Major! Major Bannister. Wait. Please."

He considered walking faster, then reluctantly slowed his steps and let her catch up. "Call me Ace," he said. "Instructors aren't formal when there are no cadets around."

She frowned. "What's your real name?"

"Ace sounds real enough to me."

She tapped a fingernail on his name tag. "It says A period, C period. That does not spell Ace."

Ace crossed his arms defensively. Every day of his life he tried to forget that the initials A. C. represented two towns on a rodeo circuit where the jerk who'd fathered him had won silver belt buckles in bronc riding. Worthless and tarnished, the buckles had long since been buried with his mother—a pretty but fragile woman who'd never learned to cope with life, or with the fact that her son's father didn't have the decency to marry her. Which sure as hell wasn't something he'd tell Captain West Point Mile-long Pedigree.

"Guess I was never good at spelling," he snarled.

She didn't let his rudeness deter her. "No? So what was your best subject? Annihilation 101?"

"Excuse me. I think I've lost the thread of this conversation. Who did I just kill?"

She shrugged off his sarcasm. "Not literally. Figuratively. It's what you've taught those students. Didn't you hear them? Did you see their faces when they spoke of the enemy? As if one's enemy isn't human."

Ace placed his hands on his hips and leaned toward her. "When did the Point start turning out bleeding hearts? Last time I dealt with the enemy, he was not your basic nice guy. My tactical-maneuvers course is designed to keep the white hats alive as long as possible. That's us, St. James."

"Thinking of one's enemy as human makes him more threatening?"

"More dangerous, you mean? You bet it does. Feelings of any kind give the enemy the edge, which makes him more dangerous."

Meredith was so angered by his archaic way of thinking she could have spit. But getting angry only played into his hands. That whole process she'd witnessed was set up to brainwash young men and women into performing tasks by rote. She'd known, of course, that making inroads wouldn't be easy.

Slowly she relaxed, although an emotional barrier had gone up between herself and the major. "If you have no objection," she said tightly, "I think I'll acquaint myself with the layout of the campus."

Ace prided himself on maintaining control of his temper. However, Captain St. James cut the bonds that held it in check faster than anyone he'd ever met. "That sounds like an excellent idea," he said coldly. "I should have arranged a tour for you, but unfortunately your arrival came as a surprise. Oh, here comes Cadet Larson. I'm sure she'll be happy to show you around."

He was right. Betsy Larson took charge as he knew she would. Having grown up on a cattle ranch two hundred miles south of town, the middle child of eleven brothers, she was one resourceful kid. According to her best friend, Betsy wrangled, roped and branded with the best cowboys. Ace smiled to himself. Maybe St. James wouldn't be such a maverick when she returned.

On reaching his office, Ace placed another call to his superior. "Colonel, if a transfer's out," he said, "could you at least find St. James some office space? We're packed in here like green olives."

Ace sat back, loosened his tie and put his feet on the desk. "Very funny, sir, but I don't *want* to think of her as a pimiento. If anything, she's more of a pit."

Ace noticed Sergeant Sutton grinning as he typed. Fashioning a paper airplane out of a memo from the air force that accused his army cadets of stealing six sets of expensive dress blues and nailing them to telephone poles throughout campus, Ace put a paper clip on the point and looped it toward his clerk's head.

But the front door opened, and Captain St. James took the glider to the chin, instead.

Sergeant Sutton leapt to his feet and came to attention.

Ace did the same, although he was the ranking officer. "I hear you, Colonel. When it comes to the academic ladder, we're in the basement. I'd consider a broom closet, sir. Uh, gotta run, Colonel. Something's come up."

"Hey, I'm sorry." He moved around his desk toward the captain. She laughed, a throaty sound that did funny things to Ace's stomach. Then she bent and picked up the model, adjusted the paper clip and sent it on its way. It nose-dived before reaching its destination. "Not a prototype of an army missile, I hope," she teased.

Ace stopped just short of her. He was pleasantly surprised to find she had a sense of humor. And yet, that small scratch on her chin was his fault. He gave her high marks for not making an issue of it.

"I really am sorry," he said again. "I know it must have hurt." He frowned as he studied her face. "You're so little, it might have hit you in the eye."

"Short. I'm short, Major. Not little."

Ace smiled. So she was touchy about being what—five one or two? He measured her with a sweep of his eyes and noticed that it brought color to her cheeks. "Er, that couldn't have been much of a campus tour," he said. "Did Betsy have a class?"

"No." Meredith shook her head. "We crossed a dorm parking lot and I spotted a compact car for sale. I need a vehicle, but I don't know anything about mechanics." She drew her lip between her teeth and cleared her throat. "I wondered if either of you could recommend someone to check it out for me."

Ace felt another punch to the stomach when she turned those sherry eyes on him again. "I . . ." He swallowed and looked away.

Sergeant Sutton spoke. "The major's your man. Nobody knows cars like he does."

Now it was Ace's turn to flush. "I have to go look into a complaint from the fly-boys. A pretty serious charge." It was as if he needed to justify his refusal.

"That's okay," she said. "I don't want to impose. Maybe I'll just go to one of the car dealers in town."

Sergeant Sutton glared at the major.

Ace felt like a heel. He supposed he was being petty. Had any other officer asked for his help, he wouldn't have hesitated. "Come with me," he said. "It won't be any trouble to swing by and check the car after I see Colonel Loudermilk. But I'm surprised you didn't ship your own vehicle."

"I don't have one."

"No wheels? How do you get around?"

She laughed. "Public transportation is very good in Baltimore. Also, I have a ton of relatives. If I needed a car, I borrowed one." She opened the door and led the way into the sunshine.

Ace paused at Sutton's desk. "Call and assure Frank that I'm working on the problem." He went back for his sunglasses, then followed her out.

So, he thought, she wasn't mechanically inclined. Knowing that made her seem less a West Point paragon somehow. Feeling slightly smug, Ace placed his hand on her back and guided her toward his jet black Firebird.

"Is this yours?" She squinted up at him and ran a finger lightly over the wings of the golden eagle that graced the hood. "I saw it earlier and thought it belonged to some hot-rod kid."

Ace looked abashed as he dug in his pocket for his car keys. With anyone else, he might have joked that there was more under the hood than a kid could handle. Not with her. "Where are your shades?" he asked to change the subject. "West Texas sun is murder on the eyes."

"Um, I suppose I'll need to get a pair. I have some in my household goods, but I don't know exactly when they'll arrive."

"You're not planning to stay in the BOQ, then?"

Easy laughter wrinkled her nose, and he noticed a smattering of freckles across the bridge. "Not on your life," she said. "Oh, by the way, Cadet Larson mentioned an apartment for lease near her dorm. I plan to check it out right after I see about the car. If you don't mind," she added quickly.

"I don't mind. Take whatever time you need to get situated." Ace rounded the car and slid under the wheel. Funny, but out here with just the two of them, he felt more relaxed—had room to be magnanimous. "How did you get in from the fort this morning?"

"I called a cab. But the weather's so nice, tomorrow I may walk."

He frowned. "Don't. It's not safe."

"Major, I'm a city girl. What's not safe in a town this size? I didn't see a soul out this morning."

"Read the paper. We have a couple of street gangs who get their kicks picking on women." Ace knew about gangs. In his youth, he'd done some wild things. But even he was appalled by the atrocities they committed today.

Meredith glanced out at a serene campus and shook her head. "It's so peaceful here."

"Peaceful," he snorted. "You see that telephone pole?"

She twisted in the seat to look. About seven feet up, someone had nailed air-force pants, jacket and hat. The hat sat atop a balloon head on which had been drawn a face with glowering eyebrows and a short mustache. "A work of art," she offered around a grin.

"Work of art, my foot," Ace snorted. "Do you have any idea how much those jackets cost? A hundred bucks at least. I understand we have six of these sets hanging around the campus.''

She laughed. ''Be thankful it's not the college president hanging in effigy. Goodness, how will you find out who's responsible?''

''I have four creative geniuses in my corps of cadets. I saw a cartoon one of them drew of Colonel Loudermilk the other day. A remarkable likeness, too.''

''Oh, no. You mean that's meant to be a real person?'' Meredith saw him nod as he climbed out for a closer look. She joined him at the pole and soon realized that tall as he was, the major couldn't begin to reach it to tear it down.

As Ace considered how best to handle things, he happened to see one of his advanced cadets strolling across campus. ''MacMillan,'' he yelled. The youth stopped at once and turned. ''On the double, Cadet,'' Ace called.

''Is he the artist?'' Meredith murmured. ''He doesn't look old enough to be in the program. I think he's even shorter than me.''

''He didn't do it,'' Ace was quick to say. ''But he'll know who did, and don't let his size fool you. Mac is into everything. He'll pass the word.''

The cadet maintained his innocence with a straight face, even as Ace suggested the boy assemble the corps in front of his office at 1600. ''I'll be making a circuit of the campus at 1530, Cadet. I don't want to see one decorated pole.''

''Yes, sir!'' MacMillan saluted and raced off.

Ace calmly ushered Meredith back to the car.

''What are you going to do to them?'' she asked suspiciously. ''Sixteen hundred is the hottest part of the day.''

Ace climbed in and lifted his sunglasses. "I don't intend to *do* anything. Other than let *them* know that *I* know who's responsible." Their gazes locked.

When she didn't seem mollified, he added, "One of our local charities has a project going this weekend. They fix houses for people who can't afford to do the work themselves. I'll merely suggest our cadets volunteer."

"And will they?" She sounded skeptical.

"They will. Because they know I'll be there to see who shows up."

"Very good, Major." Meredith sank against the leather seat and chuckled.

Ace felt the music of it clear to his toes. He thought it the most bewitching sound he'd heard in a long, long time. Yet some unnamed apprehension coiled tight as a watch spring in his stomach. "Where's that car?" he asked gruffly, retreating behind his glasses as he gunned the Firebird's engine.

Meredith heard the change in his tone and witnessed the demise of his good mood. She reacted the way she did when her father walked into the house and made demands—by folding her hands in her lap and retreating into silence.

"Well?" he said after a moment. "I'm not a mind reader, Captain."

"Look, this is obviously putting you out. Let's just forget it, okay?" Her jaw tensed and she turned to look out the side window.

"It's no trouble. Even if it's not the car you want, don't let me hear that you walked to work. I believe Captain Holmes lives near you. When we get back, I'll arrange for you to ride in with him."

"No. I, uh, no. I'll call a cab if you think it's necessary." She pointed. "The car is by that tall dormitory."

Ace found the street she indicated and also picked up on an undercurrent in her voice. "You've met Captain Holmes?"

"Yes, and Captain Caldwell. Captain Caldwell seems friendly."

"Did Holmes give you a bad time?" Ace knew how Ron felt about officers from the Point. While Holmes had served in Saudi, his fiancée had dumped him and married a lieutenant fresh out of the academy. Still...

"He was, uh... I, uh... No, he didn't say anything out of line." Meredith pretended to find something of interest outside. Truthfully, she'd run into plenty of men like Captain Holmes—men whose lips spouted polite chitchat while their eyes undressed her.

Ace vowed he'd have a talk with Ronnie-boy. None of the instructors would be overjoyed to have St. James thrust on them in midyear. It was fine if they wanted to argue doctrine; she could hold her own on that score. But he'd heard some vague gossip among the women cadets regarding Holmes—and it had nothing to do with doctrine. Maybe he should keep an ear to the ground.

"There it is," she said suddenly. "The powder blue one on the end."

"An import," Ace muttered, ripping off his sunglasses to eye it as they drove by. "Rotary engine," he informed her after he'd made a U-turn in the middle of the block and come back to park beside it.

"Is that bad?"

"Depends."

"On what?" She turned to face him.

"On whether you don't mind driving a car that sounds like an electric eggbeater when it starts." Mischief was back in his eyes.

"Oh. Is that all? I probably wouldn't care, as long as it didn't leave me to beat it on foot." She wrinkled her nose.

His breath stalled. "Uh... if this car belongs to Joe College, it may well do just that." *Focus,* he told himself. "Daddy sends Joe off with a good car. The kid drives it into the ground, then sells it before Dad wises up."

"I see." She stared at the car without blinking.

Ace opened his door and climbed out. "Let's go take a look. Get the info off the window. We'll pick up the key and give it a shakedown. It's the only way to tell."

He pressed his nose to the side window and peered inside as Meredith wrote down the dorm and room number of the owner. "It's four on the floor."

"Stick shift?" She stopped writing.

He straightened. "What's the matter, Baltimore? Don't city folks drive stick shifts?"

She shrugged. "It's not my preference. My father claims I ride the clutch." Her brow furrowed. "You've been very helpful, Major, but I won't take any more of your time. I'll walk to the town house from here. Thanks, anyway. I'll worry about a car later."

For some reason, every time her father's name came up, she closed down. This was about the third time Ace had noticed it. Maybe this transfer was at *her* request. He'd been without family so long he automatically assumed people with parents were lucky. He was always surprised to find that wasn't always the case.

"Do you mind if I tag along?" he asked. "I watched them build those units and never had a chance to look inside."

"You're welcome, of course. Housing here is so different from what's in Baltimore. You may see something I'd miss."

They opted to walk, and both were sweating by the time the manager let them in. The cooler temperature indoors was such a relief they sighed in unison. Eyes meeting, they laughed.

"You and yor *woe man* been hare long?" drawled the manager as he singled out Ace. "I noticed rat off—she talks funny."

Meredith stopped. Her cheeks flamed. "I, uh, don't... I'm not..." She didn't know what to defend first, her virtue or her accent. Ace winked at her and clapped the paunchy, bald-headed man on the shoulder. "You won't hold it against her, will you? Can't everybody be born in God's country. By the way, she's not my *anything*. The lady lives alone. She's an officer in the U.S. Army. I'll vouch for her."

Meredith fairly sputtered when the old man looked at her and said he "'lowd as how she was willin' to defend flag and country, so she must be A-OK."

If the place hadn't been everything she wanted, she would've walked out. But it was perfect, so she buried her irritation and wrote a check. After they were out of earshot, she exploded. "He thinks *I* talk funny. He slaughtered the Queen's English. Or *Ainglish,* as he'd probably call it."

Ace tried not to laugh as he guided her back to the car, but as he climbed in and fastened his seat belt, he lost the battle.

She shot him a heated glare, then recognized the humor and joined his mirth. "I can't believe you managed a straight face. Or that he believed you were serious."

Ace's laughter subsided into a rumble in his chest. "I wish you could have seen yourself. You wanted to call both of us chauvinists so bad."

"Pretty transparent, huh?" She shook her head. "It's so different here. Last night when I went to dinner at a steak house in town, a group of cowboys trooped in." Her voice faltered and she took a deep breath. Letting it out slowly, she said, "I imagine I'll get used to rustic—eventually."

Ace knew that even if she didn't, she was homesick. He'd been down that road. Oh, the army had taught him that men weren't supposed to get homesick, but he recalled a time when his longing for home—for Texas—had been so acute he'd awakened expecting to see mesquite and sage in place of those endless, damned sand dunes. "Tell you what," he said impulsively. "You need wheels and I know cars. Why don't I pick you up later and we'll hit some car lots downtown? After you look at a few, we can grab a pizza somewhere and narrow your choice."

"No." She had a strict rule about not dating fellow officers. True, he hadn't mentioned *date,* but how could she be certain car shopping was all he had in mind? He seemed changed suddenly, and she'd never been good with casual man-woman encounters. The last thing she'd ever entertain was a relationship with a military man. Not that her record with civilians was all that good, either. Her one romantic interlude had been with an accountant and had ended in disaster. Granted, he was a two-timing louse, but Meredith knew that, for her, liaisons with army officers would have more serious, longer-lasting effects.

Ace read her hesitancy as something else entirely—that he wasn't from the Point and therefore wasn't good enough for her. "Forget I brought it up," he said, unable to completely hide his reaction to the perceived slight. "It was a bad idea."

Meredith realized how abrupt her refusal must have sounded. And she really didn't want to spend another long evening alone. Trying for businesslike, she murmured, "On second thought, how well do you know cars, Major?"

His lip curled. "By the age of eight I was stealing any car part that wasn't nailed down. At fourteen, I moved on to wholesaling entire cars. So, aren't you surprised to see me in this uniform, instead of one with pretty stripes?"

Ace was nearly as shocked by his uncharacteristic outburst as she. He'd never shared that part of his life with any other woman, and he couldn't think why he had now, except that he wanted to shock her right back on her neatly pressed little West Point skirt.

Meredith stared at him for a long moment, wishing she could see behind the glasses that hid his eyes. By the time they reached the ROTC office, it was abundantly clear he wanted her out of his car.

She opened her own car door and made up her mind. "I doubt I'll find anyone who knows cars as well as you do, Major. Shall we say 1800? I'll be outside the BOQ. Unit thirty-one." She slid out slowly, waiting for his refusal.

Ace sat, absorbing her words. Then he smiled. The lady captain was unpredictable, and he liked that. "You got yourself a horse trader," he said, bending to see her—to make sure she wasn't regretting anything. "Eighteen hundred hours." He checked his watch. "Meanwhile, would you corral some thirty cadets while I make a run by those telephone poles?"

Feeling a need to hide her delight, she snapped off a salute. "Yes, sir," she said, as she stepped back and slammed the door.

His head nearly flew apart. "Damn!" he exclaimed as he drove off. "With all the great minds at the Point, you'd think they could teach 'em how to close a door right."

CHAPTER THREE

THE TELEPHONE POLES were as clean as wishbones ready for pulling. Ace had expected it. Still, this group of cadets was very creative, as well as full of the old nick. They had surprised him before, which was why he drove around the entire campus, paying close attention to the poles near the air-force ROTC offices. If Frank Loudermilk walked out and recognized one of the balloon likenesses, he'd pop a blood vessel.

Ace worried about Frank. They used to play handball together and round up their respective cadets for some fun afternoons of touch football. But not in more than three months. Now Frank was obsessed with punishing pranksters, never realizing that his compulsion only made things worse.

Completing the circuit in record time, Ace had ample opportunity on the drive back to think about the offer he'd made Captain St. James. She boggled his mind. Made him forget a lesson he'd learned from a colonel he knew and respected back in the days he hadn't respected much of anything. He could almost hear the man's voice. "Son, decisions made in haste are sure to be repented at leisure." Ace smiled. He'd heard that so many times it should be automatic, yet here he was, jumping in with both feet, knowing he'd be hip deep in alligators. St. James could be trouble for him, in more ways than one.

He guided the Firebird around the corner by their office and saw her lining up cadets, most of them taller than her by far. Her cap was tucked beneath her belt, and sunlight danced through her short curls. She had the posture of a well-toned dancer and the grace, too. What in hell did that have to do with anything? he asked himself angrily.

Ace scowled as he shut off the engine and eyed her narrow waist and trim ankles. He'd grown used to women officers complaining about how unattractive and unflattering their uniforms were. He was shocked to feel sexual stirrings on viewing the captain in hers.

He was stirred, all right, and he wasn't pleased. Something else his colonel friend had extolled—look outside the army for lady friends and wives. Ace always had. For his lady friends, anyway. He hadn't considered himself a good gamble as a husband.

Why was he in such a panic now? After all, he'd only proposed car shopping and pizza, not marriage. Yet, as he climbed from his car, the feeling didn't readily leave him. Perhaps he'd be wise to skip the pizza part. He didn't mind helping her find a car; that much he'd do for any fellow officer, male or female. But sharing a meal with a woman was intimate, and intimacy was something Ace tended to avoid.

Meredith had just aligned the last cadet when she glanced up and saw the major walking toward her with the same loose roll of his hips she'd found so intriguing the night before. She didn't notice his glower until it was obvious he'd caught her ogling him. Suddenly her ears burned, and Meredith knew her face must match. Fair skin was a Marshall trait, as was the tendency to blush. She could only hope the cadets, who'd created a diversion when they came to attention, were too concerned about saving their skins to care about hers.

As she pulled out her cap and settled it on her head, she wondered what she'd done to make him frown.

"At ease," Ace barked in his best military voice. Immediately, he started through the lines.

Meredith's thoughts lingered on his displeasure. Why would she automatically assume he was annoyed with her? After all the time and money she'd spent in therapy to shed such feelings, here she was falling into the same old trap. If that was what being around him did, Meredith wished she hadn't agreed to an entire evening in his company. Her vow not to let anyone make her feel inadequate was still new. He might well turn out to be as dictatorial as her father.

All business now, Ace paused beside a brown-haired cadet in the last row. "Corporal Wellington," he said, "wouldn't you imagine that air-force dress blues are expensive?"

"Yes, sir," the young man said without hesitation.

Ace backed up until he reached a sturdy woman with mischievous blue eyes and untamed red hair. "Corporal Larson."

"Yes, sir," she returned, meeting his gaze squarely.

"Seems to me it would take some fancy acrobatics to get air-force scarecrows nailed halfway up telephone poles."

"Yes, sir," she said again, only this time the mischief was banked. Ace didn't linger beside her. He continued down the second row and stopped near a gangly boy with chocolate-colored skin and eyes like brown velvet. "Sergeant Jefferson, I thought those balloon faces bore a remarkable likeness to Captain Caldwell, didn't you?"

"No, sir." The brown eyes followed the major's progress as he turned.

But then Ace whipped around. "No? Who do you think they resembled, Sergeant?"

Meredith felt sorry for the young man who knew immediately that his honesty had been his undoing.

"They looked like Colonel Loudermilk, sir," the youth said miserably.

"Ah." Ace circled around to row one. "Cadet Captain Granelli, do you agree with me or with Jefferson?"

At first Meredith didn't think the broad-shouldered handsome boy was going to answer. She knew it ran through his mind. But the moment he met the major's steely gaze, the youth wisely fessed up. "I agree with Sergeant Jefferson. Sir," he added belatedly.

Ace was already moseying toward Meredith. "Captain St. James is a new instructor," he informed the cadets. "I could let her first duty be to set your punishment."

All eyes shifted at once. Meredith sputtered until she saw his lazy wink.

"Guess I won't do that. She doesn't know your individual talents like I do. I always wanted artistic talent myself. Maybe that's why it disappoints me to see it wasted."

Meredith saw a ripple of apprehension pass through the lines.

Ace took a sheet of paper out of his shirt pocket and unfolded it layer by layer. "It so happens there's an organization in town that's begging for talent this weekend." He read the letter outlining the project. "Now," he said, "I need some volunteers to help out these nice folks. Sergeant Sutton has a clipboard for sign-up with space for six crews, five to a crew. I think we can fill six crews, don't you?'' Ace smiled. "Oh, one other thing. Those dress blues had better not show up in army trash.'' After scanning each face a moment, he thundered, ''Dismissed!''

Meredith watched the cadets scramble to sign up. She turned to Ace and raised a hand to shade her eyes. ''Six crews at five each? That's your entire cadre. Sneaky, Major.''

He shrugged and dropped his sunglasses over his eyes. ''All's fair...''

''...in love and war,'' she murmured. Then, as she felt his unwavering gaze, she flushed and tried to get out of the hole she'd dug. ''Uh, it's just that your situation didn't seem to fit either category of that old adage. Oh, for pity's sake,'' she said when it was obvious he wasn't planning to comment. ''I'm going in to finish putting my desk in order. Coming, Major?''

''No. I'm going over to play mind games with the air force. To let Frank think I doled out across-the-board punishment. If that doesn't satisfy him, if he wants payment, I'll have to figure out how to tell Colonel O'Dell.''

''Well, good luck,'' she said. ''Oh, does this mean you'll be too busy to look at cars tonight?''

Ace stuck his hands in his pockets and jingled his loose change. She'd just handed him an out. Why didn't he take it? Maybe he wasn't the only one having second thoughts. But why would she? She didn't think it was more than a favor, did she?

''We're still on, Captain, unless *you've* changed your mind.'' She'd have to spell it out if she wanted to cancel. He didn't renege on promises.

Meredith knew she should decline. She never fraternized with officers. But as she opened her mouth to tell him thanks but no thanks, she said, instead, "Eighteen hundred hours. I'll be ready."

Ace nodded and immediately left. He couldn't say why he felt so relieved. Clearly something drastic had to be done about his social life if all it took was haggling over car prices to put a spring in his step.

The Firebird's clock was straight up 1800 when Ace turned onto the captain's street. Of course, he'd been circling the post for the past five minutes—because his watch and the clock in the dash weren't synchronized. When he'd flipped on the radio, he discovered his watch was wrong. If he'd known, he could have done a better job cleaning his kitchen.

Then again, this was probably for the best. This way he hadn't had time to analyze the garbage he'd carted off. He'd simply brought in a large plastic bag from the garage and scooted everything into it that didn't move. Or maybe some of it did. He definitely needed to quit being such a slob.

Ace spotted her immediately standing outside the converted barracks. Why had he assumed she'd be wearing jeans? She'd surprised him again with her simple sleeveless blue dress. Nothing dramatic and not too sexy. It looked soft and comfortable, and fell below her knees. Long sleeves would have given the dress a 1940s look. Or perhaps he only thought that because of the matching floppy-brimmed hat.

She had the hat clipped up in front with a colorful flower, the way an arty renegade like Georgia O'Keefe might have worn it. Except that it made Meredith St. James look younger, sweeter...sexier and left his mouth dry.

As the Firebird rumbled to a stop, Ace just knew he'd punch out the first car salesman who asked if she was his

daughter. Then he reconsidered. Ace knew salesmen—
they'd joke about the dude with the hot car and the
young babe, and there'd be nothing he could do about
it. Maybe the time had come for him to get something
less flashy in the way of wheels. Ace removed his sunglasses and started to get out.

"Hi," she said, opening the passenger door and poking her head inside. "You're punctual. I like that."

His seat belt partially unclipped, all Ace could do was
smile. Wasn't that normally the man's line?

"Keep your seat," she said quickly, climbing in.
"Since this is business, there's no reason to do anything
that'll feed gossip." She waved a hand toward the structure. "Two women I've never met asked about my
'date.' That's one of the reasons I'd never stay in the
BOQ. Zero privacy."

"I didn't think about gossip." Narrowing his eyes,
Ace glanced across the street at the unit where Captain
Holmes lived. Oh, well, it was a little late to worry now.
The Firebird was rather distinctive.

Meredith buckled up. As he pulled away from the curb
she said, "If I'd been thinking faster, I'd have asked
those two lieutenants what made them so sure I was going on a date."

Ace laughed a bit self-consciously. "That's easy. It's
the way you're dressed."

She clutched at the folds of her skirt. "Is there something wrong with my dress?"

He shook his head. "Nothing at all." Ace turned and
ran an assessing eye over her now that she was closer. He
hauled in a deep breath and was smacked in the face by
some lightly provocative scent. "Great dress and nice
perfume," he said when his voice returned. "You be-

long in a Mercedes or a BMW going somewhere more interesting than car lots."

Meredith nervously fingered an Egyptian Coptic cross that hung from a necklace of antique silver beads. "The dress is cotton. Nothing new. So, what's in fashion here, Major?"

Ace tugged at his right ear. "Don't ask me. Do I look like Calvin Klein?"

Her lips curved in a smile. "No. You have broader shoulders, and he drives a foreign sports car."

This time Ace's laugh was spontaneous. "Enough," he said. "Why don't you tell me what you'd like in a car?"

"I'd like a fuel injection, V-6 engine with front-wheel drive," she said. "Oh, and an automatic transmission. But you already know that. Since this is my first visit to Texas, I plan to check out some of the countryside on weekends. Some sort of all-weather tires with good tread would be nice." She wrinkled her brow. "I could replace the tires, I suppose, if the rest of the car is serviceable."

When she didn't lead off naming a color, as most women he knew would, Ace began to wonder if the other women he knew were shallow. "Sure you don't want dual carbs and overhead minicams?" he asked dryly.

She looked startled, then sheepish.

He lifted his sunglasses and slid her a suspicious glance. "Are you sure you need my help?"

"I read consumer magazines and know what's good, Major. I just wouldn't know how to recognize it if it jumped out and bit me."

Ace stared at her a moment longer. She was honest and that, too, was refreshing. "Since we're both out of uniform, shouldn't you call me Ace?"

Her gaze drifted over his shirt, which was blue cham-bray. Both sleeves were rolled up to his elbows, and it was open at the throat, where just a tuft of dark hair peeked out. He'd paired the shirt with well-washed blue jeans, a wide leather belt and some sort of low-heeled boots. Suddenly she wished he were in uniform. It was definitely much less threatening to call him Major. "I suppose that would be all right," she said grudgingly. "But I don't have a nickname. You'll have to call me Meredith."

Ace tipped back his head and laughed. "The only Meredith I've ever met is a man. Six-three, two hundred pounds. A heavyweight boxer who's had his nose bro-ken so many times most of the cartilage is gone. I've tried comparing you two, but frankly there's not much resemblance."

She chuckled, the low throaty sound that made his toes curl.

"You're crazy," she murmured.

Ace had never thought so. At least not until now. "Here," he said to divert her attention. "Our first car lot. If you see something you like, ask the salesman particulars and jot them down. Try not to seem too en-thusiastic in case we decide to come back and deal."

"I do know how to shop for bargains, Major."

"Ace."

The dusky eyes searching out hers in the shadowed interior of the car reminded Meredith of sand-washed gray silk. His tone, however, was firm and not at all se-ductive. She lowered her lashes to block the sensual pull she felt. "I understand—Ace."

He experienced a sudden shortness of breath, as if he'd run too far, too fast. Many women had spoken his name. A few in the throes of passion. None made it sound so...so sexy. It must be her accent. Either that or he *was* crazy. While he still could, Ace crawled out of the Firebird and hurried around to open her door.

Things got off to a bad start with the salesman. As in the town house, the guy started by assuming they were husband and wife. Ace straightened him out, but even then he ignored Meredith and talked only to Ace.

"Whoa!" Ace held up a palm. "You're dealing with the lady. It's her money."

From then on the man treated them both coolly.

"Could we go someplace else?" Meredith asked in an undertone.

"The lady doesn't see anything she wants," Ace said flatly, and turned with her toward the Firebird.

"Doesn't surprise me," the salesman snapped, closing his book. "Women never know what they want when it comes to cars."

"Jerk," Meredith fumed. "He was insulting. Did you see him show me the 'cute little mirror' hidden in the passenger's sun visor? Who did he think would be driving the car while I used that?"

"Well, this isn't Baltimore."

"What does that mean?"

"Hey, don't take it out on me. It means in Texas a number of men still look at *all* women as the weaker sex, especially in circumstances pertaining to business on cars."

"Even after a female governor? Where have they been since we won the right to vote?"

Ace could tell her, but he didn't think this was a productive conversation—and he wasn't the social worker here. "The guy did bring up something we haven't discussed—and tell me if it's none of my business. But do you have credit references for when you fill out the finance papers?''

"References?"

"Well, yes. You're new in town. Businesses are a little more lenient with military personnel, or let me rephrase that—some are. Some consider us fly-by-night transients.''

"I've counseled families who've run into problems like that. You'd think store owners would be nicer to the people who defend our country. But to answer your question, yes, my checking and savings accounts are both in Baltimore.'' When he didn't say anything, she shrugged. "I suppose my bank could wire money for a cashier's check until I get my accounts transferred.''

Ace pulled into another lot, but before she climbed out, he caught her arm. "These are late-model cars you're looking at.''

"Yes. Isn't low mileage better?'' She tugged loose and opened the door.

"Expensive, if you're planning to pay cash.''

"The money isn't a problem,'' she said, hopping out. "I trust you to know if I'm getting good value for my dollar.'' Almost at once she disappeared into the row of gleaming cars.

Spoiled. He should have figured. Generally Ace made it a point to keep his distance from women with money. He'd been eight the day he'd heard his mother crying harder than usual. When he'd asked her about it, she said his old man had married the daughter of a rich rancher—for the money, she said, producing a letter from a velvet box that smelled of violets. Ace often wished he'd told her not to cry, because the cowboy probably fleeced the woman and lit out. He hadn't said it, though, and his mother had cried for weeks. Within a month she was dead, and he'd gone to live with an aunt who'd had enough on her plate without him.

From then on, Ace made sure he steered clear of rich women, and he couldn't stomach violets. No sense breaking old habits now. He followed Meredith, but stayed well back until she motioned him over.

"What do you think of this one?" she asked, pointing to a clean little silver compact. "Would you test-drive it?"

"That's why I'm here, Your Highness."

She looked hurt, but Ace didn't care. If she'd asked why he was being sarcastic, he'd tell her he didn't much like jumping whenever she snapped her fingers.

Now who was being petty? he thought with a stab of guilt. It was, after all, the reason he *was* here. "Are you riding along?" he inquired with a shade more civility when the salesman brought the key.

"Do you mind?"

He sighed. "I don't mind. You should drive it on the way back."

She nodded and climbed in. He glanced at her as he backed carefully out of the lot. "Smooth start and easy shift—if you're taking notes."

"Oh, yes, I am. Sorry, I forgot." She dipped her head and dug in her purse.

Meredith was glad when they got back to the dealership. "It's nice," she said before the salesman could pressure. "I'll let you know. I've just started looking."

Meredith sensed that Ace's mood had changed. She assumed it was something she'd said or done, but if he didn't choose to be more specific, she certainly wasn't going to guess. Or was he always this moody?

They tried six more cars before they all began to look the same. It was getting dark and she was hungry. "I think I've seen enough for now," she said, following Ace to his car. "I've about walked your feet off. How about if I feed you next? I'll spring for something more substantial than pizza if you'd like."

He stopped dead and turned, letting her smack into him. "I invited you. You should have said pizza was beneath you. I'd have stopped at the bank machine before picking you up." He threw the words at her and stalked off the moment they were delivered.

Meredith blinked in surprise and hurried to catch up. "I love pizza. It's just...at home they're sometimes noisier than other restaurants. I didn't mean to insult you. You're going out of your way to help me, and I wanted to show my appreciation."

Ace felt like a fool—and a jerk. "Forget it. It's just that I've had a splitting headache all day," he lied smoothly.

If she'd known him better, Meredith might have remarked on the source of his headache. But she really didn't know him at all. "Pizza it is, then," she said stiffly. "While you order, I'll organize my notes, if that's all right."

The pizza parlor wasn't far. Soon their brief rift was forgotten. They discussed cars as they dived into a large, thick-crust pizza.

Meredith poured soft drinks into glasses from the pitcher Ace brought to the table. "You didn't have to have Coke, you know. I'm sure you'd rather have beer."

Ace shook his head. "I guess I can't blame you for thinking that. You saw me at my worst— I don't normally drink all that much. The Sarge wasn't kidding when he said it was out of character for me. Now, are we going to talk about my bad habits or your car?"

Meredith pulled another wedge from the pizza before she answered. "You tell me which car is soundest before I say which one I like best."

"Okay. The silver one, hands down."

She smiled around a full mouth. After she swallowed, she murmured, "Aren't I lucky? That was my favorite. I'll go back tomorrow and dicker."

Ace raised an eyebrow. "I could've sworn you wanted the jade one with the full back fin." They'd seen it at the second-last dealership they'd visited.

"Nope," Meredith said, wiping her hands on a napkin and putting away her notes. She had, of course, wanted the jade car, but she'd known by the way he frowned and listened so closely to the engine that it wasn't the best choice. Everyone developed a way of dealing with disappointment. Her method was to bury it deep and pretend it didn't exist.

Ace wasn't fooled for long. He'd grown up with disappointment. If not his own, then his mother's. "Liar," he said softly, reaching across the table to lift her chin gently with two fingers.

Startled by the suddenness of it, Meredith let their gazes lock and struggled to maintain her indifference. Ultimately, however, she lost the battle. She gave up and stared past his shoulder, instead. "The jade car had problems. Why would I buy trouble?"

"You wouldn't. But their dealership south of town has the jade in a new model. If money's no object, why buy used?"

"I'll think about it. It might not be worth it if I'm only here for a couple of years."

"How could you lose? Resale would be better. And why would your assignment be only two years? ROTC rotation is generally four."

She didn't want to tell him her father could keep her here forever or ship her to never-never land tomorrow if he chose. "Really? Four, huh?"

"What do your orders say? Colonel O'Dell's faxed copy was pretty sketchy."

She shrugged. "Just that I'm to assist with ROTC training." She watched him closely. He really didn't seem to know anything about her—or her father. Could he be lying? Her mother said the general had selected this post because he was so impressed with Major Bannister's record. Surely they'd talked.

Ace wadded his napkin. "It's funny. I've never known the army to be so vague on orders. Did you know Colonel O'Dell before?"

Meredith shook her head. She wanted to get off a subject that might lead to more questions about her father. "Is the colonel nice?"

Ace grinned. "Tough old war-horse. He's not exactly thrilled to be waiting out his retirement behind a desk. So he doesn't spend much time in ROTC. Mostly you'll find him swapping stories about the *real* war with his cronies out at the fort or playing golf. But, yeah, to answer your question, he's okay."

"*Okay,* because with him out of the picture, you can run things to suit yourself?" Meredith refilled their glasses.

He picked his up and studied her over the rim. "Is this polite conversation we're having, or are you leading up to something?"

"Are you always this touchy, Major?"

"Ah, it's Major again. What's your beef, Baltimore? Is it me personally, or the fact that I'm working the cadets on a weekend? Or did I leave them standing in the sun longer than Emily Post considers socially correct?"

Meredith separated another slice of pizza before she answered. "At the risk of having this go to your head, Major, I was impressed with the way you handled the telephone-pole caper." This time when their eyes met, hers were warm. "How did your meeting with the air-force colonel go?"

Ace smiled thinly. "So-so. But then, Frank and I go way back. We sat out the tail end of Grenada in some little hellhole."

She leaned forward. "Did you and the LC finally work things out?"

"Frank's on a crusade to end goofing off in ROTC. If you ask me, he expects miracles. Say—maybe he needs a social worker in his camp. How do you feel about going out on loan?"

"I don't think so, Ace." She forgot to be self-conscious about using his name. "According to Sergeant Sutton, Colonel Loudermilk inflicts inhumane punishment to make a point. What I believe is that the military can no longer turn out officers like that. Peace will come when people connect with each other, when they act with tolerance and compassion. It's a new frontier of challenge, and the army has to meet it head-on."

"Camel dung!" A muscle in Ace's jaw twitched as he threw his crumpled napkin on the table. Picking up the check, he dug into his jeans pocket for money to pay the bill.

Meredith reached across the table and snatched it out of his hand. She had the cash ready when she stood. "Honestly, you're so narrowly focused you can't see beyond your nose. I don't know why I thought you'd be different from the robots they crank out of the Point."

Plunking the limp hat back on her head, she marched up to the cashier.

Ace battled conflicting emotions. Who was she kidding? *She* came out of the Point. He wasn't a warmonger, but neither was he soft on legitimate enemies. And yet, when she clapped that damnable floppy hat on those impossibly short curls, Ace had the funniest feeling that, for her, he'd lie down and let an enemy rip his heart out.

He'd just caught up with her when the outer door opened and in walked Captain Ron Holmes with some of his Wednesday-night bowling crowd.

Ron's gaze swept over Ace and skipped to Meredith, who was returning her change to her wallet. "I'll say this much, St. James—you don't waste any time sucking up."

Ace didn't think he'd ever felt more like breaking a subordinate's teeth.

She returned her wallet to her purse and said sweetly, "Major Bannister was nice enough to take me car shopping. I don't know how you repay such thoughtfulness in Texas, but where I come from, dinner is acceptable."

Ron Holmes nudged a short muscular man standing near him. "Shall I tell her to call us next time? We'd skip dinner and get right to dessert." Both men guffawed, looking her over as if she were a juicy bone and they were half-starved Dobermans.

Ace had heard enough. He took Meredith's elbow and deftly moved her past Ron. "Too many desserts must be why you're putting a strain on your shirt buttons lately, buddy." Fuming, Ace didn't stop to see if his barb had struck home.

Maybe she was big on changing the army, but it had already changed too much to suit Ace. Not long ago, remarks like the ones Ron had just delivered—made in *or* out of uniform—would have been considered conduct unbecoming an officer. Now it was harder to make such charges stick, especially if the parties were out of uniform and off the post.

"Nice guy," Meredith muttered as they made their way to the car. "And you wanted me to ride to work with him. I'd sooner take my chances with street gangs."

Ace unlocked the passenger door for her. "Ron was jilted when he was in the Gulf. That display is part of the backlash."

"Really?" she said as he got in and started the car. "Sounds like he needs counseling."

"Is that your answer for everything? Typical of a social worker. You think you can single-handedly save the world." He drove out of the parking lot and came up to speed fast.

Meredith turned toward him. "Now that sounds like the voice of experience. Are you a casualty of love gone bad, too, Major?"

Ace snorted. "And that's typical of a woman. Whenever a man acts cynical, women automatically take credit for making him that way. You think I'm jaded and need the love of a good woman to change my attitude?"

She laughed, although she noticed how neatly he'd evaded her question. "You don't strike me as being particularly lovable, Major. What I think is that this conversation has disintegrated. Just as well we've reached the fort."

"So we have. Well, I'll say this—it hasn't been a dull evening." He navigated the Firebird to a smooth stop outside the building where he'd picked her up, yanked on the emergency brake and started to get out.

She touched his arm. "No need for you to escort me to the door. And thanks—I appreciate your advice on the cars." Withdrawing her hand, she slid out. "I'm sorry if my buying dinner ended up causing you problems with your friends. I guess paying's a macho thing around here." Before Ace had a chance to digest her words, she'd closed the door. His fingers curled around the steering wheel so tight they hurt. Damned nice of her to excuse a man's faults.

Would she still do that, he wondered, if he'd acted on his first impulse—to grab her and kiss her?

Wasn't it fortunate, he thought as she dashed up the walkway, that her instincts were better than his? He sat there watching until he saw a light go on upstairs.

Driving home, Ace repeatedly told himself how lucky it was he hadn't done anything rash, like kissing her. Especially since she'd already lumped him into the same category as that insensitive oaf, Holmes.

Long after the Firebird had left the curb, Meredith stood at her bedroom window, her heart beating much too fast. She reasoned it was the result of running up two flights of stairs.

She fanned her face. Major Bannister was certainly a complex man. Good with cadets. Decisive. Lousy at hiding his feelings. Why had he been so quick to avoid talking about his love life? she wondered. A man his age, and as good-looking, must have had his share of love affairs.

Well, that didn't concern her. She had no intention of getting involved with anyone in the military, she reminded herself. "None whatsoever," she said aloud as she stalked off to shower. An unsuccessful attempt, it turned out, to rid herself of the scent of his after-shave.

CHAPTER FOUR

THE NEXT MORNING, Ace entered his office via the back door. Through Holmes and Caldwell's office.

He'd no sooner gotten home after leaving Meredith the night before, than Colonel O'Dell had stopped by to request a study National Headquarters wanted. A comparison of grade points for ROTC graduates with those of general university students over the past five years. Males and females separated. It took Ace about two seconds to choose Ron Holmes as the person to complete it. He thought it a more fitting punishment than reprimanding Ron for the previous night's behavior. Holmes hated computers *and* paperwork.

"Why don't you give this to St. James?" Ron whined once Ace had outlined the task. "Officers coming out of the Point have ten times more computer experience than we do. Oh, I get it. You didn't like what I said to her at the pizza parlor."

"You got it, Captain. This time you were lucky. Next time the lady might not let it slide," Ace said pointedly, passing through to the workroom where he poured himself a cup of coffee. He could hear Ron swearing and grinned. At least he did until he took a sip of coffee and found it thick enough to carve his initials in.

"Sutton," he bellowed, stepping into his office. But the sergeant wasn't at his desk. Captain St. James was alone in the room and standing on tiptoe on a chair, hammering a nail into the wall above her desk.

At the sound of his voice, she glanced over her shoulder. "Major! The sergeant said you'd be late today." She sort of wavered to attention.

Ace swallowed what he'd been about to say to his clerk about the sorry state of the coffee. He also forgot his standard lecture on safety as his gaze traveled from the captain's shoeless feet up her shapely legs. And past—to a neatly curved bottom that did unbelievable things for a government-issue skirt. His stare turned into a scowl and reached her narrow waist, then stopped. A waist he imagined spanning with his hands.

"Major?" she questioned when he failed to set her at ease. "Would you like me to get down and do this right? Standing at attention, I mean."

"Ah...at ease, Captain. Carry on." Ace slammed his cup down on his desk. "Where's Sutton, anyway? Oh, and out of curiosity, what in hell are you hanging? Unlike the academic side of the house, we don't frame and display our credentials, if that's what you're doing."

"It's not." She drove in a second nail some three inches from the first, then climbed awkwardly down to pick up a large frame that Ace hadn't noticed leaning against her desk. It was bigger than a diploma—about twenty-by-thirty inches, he'd guess.

"Sergeant Sutton went to get the mail," she said, her attention riveted on the item she held. "He said you were stopping for a haircut." She looked up. "Oh, you did." She smiled. "Looks great, although I'll have to admit I expected it to be shorter than mine."

Ace watched her climb back up on the chair. She tottered and he jumped to her aid. She righted herself on her own, so he settled back against his desk and said,

"Lily Roberts has a barbershop in her home. I'll give you her number if you'd like. Whatever you do, don't go to the butcher on post or you'll come out looking like— Who's that bald female singer?"

Meredith hesitated. "I know who you mean. You really go to a hairstylist who's a woman? Cool. I wondered what I'd do here. At home I have this friend who owns a salon. He goes in for bizarre effects, though. It was a challenge every time I went in to make sure I didn't come out with stars and stripes or weird colors like shocking purple. He liked to experiment."

"Why on earth did you go there?"

"In the beginning, to defy my father." She caught her lower lip between her teeth, shrugged offhandedly and reached again for the frame. Her chair rocked wildly, and she flailed her arms to keep her balance.

Ace leapt to steady her. "Here, dammit, let me hand you that thing before you kill yourself." He eyed it from several angles before he passed it to her.

"What is this?"

She took the frame, eased her body around and lined the wire hanger up with the nails. Then she hopped down and stood back to view her handiwork. "Ah. Perfect. Great, isn't it?"

"At the risk of repeating myself, *what* is it?" Ace tilted his head from one side to the other. The picture, if that was what it could be called, had four brilliant bands of background color intersected with millions of squiggly black lines. "Don't tell me. Let me guess. It's someone's inkblot test you've enlarged and magnified. No, I know, it's a schematic belonging to your mad hairdresser." He flashed her a teasing grin before reaching over her head to straighten the print. "Didn't help," he said, his expression deadpan.

"Don't tell me you haven't seen three-D art before, Major. Where've you been?"

"Three-D art? I don't see one-D art."

"This one's my favorite. Sun shining down through a lush green forest. Wild animals among the trees. In the sky, an eagle in full flight."

Ace massaged his jaw and stared at her through slitted lids. "Now which of us has been on the sauce, Captain?"

Meredith ignored him and pawed through a large box that sat on the floor beside her desk. She pulled out a diamond-shaped paperweight filled with gold and silver beads and placed it on her desk. Next, a large piece of amethyst quartz for the bookcase.

Amused, Ace asked, "Has the army instituted some beautification program? The only junk taking up extra space around here serves a purpose, in case you haven't noticed."

"I noticed. Your office is boring, Major."

"Boring." Ace loomed over her. "This is the army, St. James. Uncle Sam does not give medals for pretty."

She crossed her arms and glared at him.

"Personally, Captain," he went on, "the sergeant and I like boring. Will you kindly refrain from doing any more decorating?"

Meredith's temper flared for a moment. He was so close she could smell the subtle fragrance of his aftershave. It set her pulse hammering and made her toes curl into the cool tile floor. With some difficulty she controlled her temper; she sat primly in her chair and folded her hands on her desk. "Yes, sir," she said, taking a deep calming breath.

Ace couldn't seem to take his eyes off the pulse that suddenly beat irregularly below her jaw. This was the first time he'd noticed a tiny gold stud nestled in her earlobe. Had she worn earrings yesterday? He couldn't recall. But at this moment, he had the damnedest urge to touch the bit of gold with his tongue. To nip the lobe with his teeth and maybe even trail a row of kisses all the way to her mouth. A sassy mouth that looked just right for kissing a man back....

Fortunately, before Ace could act on an impulse that would probably get his face slapped, in bustled the old master sergeant, his arms loaded with fat envelopes and smaller pieces of mail.

"Major, sir," Sutton said, dropping the lot on Ace's desk. "Looks like we finally got the new forms Washington's been threatening to send for the past month. No more triplicate." For Meredith's benefit, he explained, "Thanks to modern technology we've progressed to quadruplicate."

She smiled and slid back into her pumps. "Protest, Sergeant. Each time you ship a form back, type at the top, 'Save a tree.'"

"Good idea. Hey!" Sergeant Sutton stopped. "You have the three-dimensional eagle, Captain. Beautiful. My grandson bought the space picture with his Christmas money. Looks exactly the way I imagine it does on the moon. Do you know the one I mean?"

Meredith was relieved to have the strange spell broken—or whatever it was she'd been feeling just before Sergeant Sutton had walked in. She nodded. "I know the one you mean. Done in shades of blue. It's nice. So is the one with the Nighthawk aircraft. It'd look good over your desk."

Ace passed an unsteady hand through his freshly cut hair. He stood less than two feet from Sutton, yet he'd be damned if he could see anything in that picture but a mess of lines.

He stared at it for so long the sergeant commented. "Don't you see it, sir? Stand back and just let yourself sort of flow into it."

"To see the inner picture," Meredith said, "you have to relax. Are you tense again, Major?" she asked sweetly.

"Tense? I'm never tense," he snapped. "The whole concept is stupid, if you ask me. Whoever heard of a picture you have to work so hard to see?" He snatched up his coffee cup and took a healthy swig, then grimaced and slapped the cup back down. "I have a class on weapons at 0930, Sergeant. I'd appreciate it very much if by the time I return you'll have had Captain St. James instruct you in brewing decent coffee." Hefting his briefcase, he stalked out.

Meredith ran to the door. "Major, wait. I planned to go with you to that weapons class. I'll give everyone a lesson in coffee making when we return." She shut the door and skipped down the steps.

"No. Absolutely not." Not only did Ace not want her in his weapons class, but after what had happened between them before Sutton arrived...well, he needed to put some distance between them. She'd made his blood sing. Somehow, he didn't think the two-part harmony he'd dreamed up as an encore was something either of them wanted to pursue. Nothing they *should* pursue, at any rate.

"You're not working with secret weapons, are you? I mean, I've seen all of them before, haven't I?" She sounded annoyed.

"Actually we don't use real weapons. We have simulated rubber M-16s. This group missed Military Science I. I'm trying to catch them up so they can go to camp challenge. They need toughening up, not hand-holding." He brightened suddenly. "There goes Captain Caldwell. He's teaching a component of military education this morning on human behavior. The perfect class for you to observe." Stepping to the curb, Ace delivered an earsplitting whistle.

Captain Caldwell turned, waved and jogged back.

"You rang?" The captain's jovial blue eyes twinkled.

"I did, Dean. I want St. James to hear a pro talk to our cadets about civilian-military interaction. You have a problem with her tagging along?"

To his credit, Caldwell didn't insinuate that the major was full of bull. All he did was grin and say, "No, sir. Come along, Captain. Time to get your feet wet."

Meredith felt tempted to protest, but she wasn't in a position to do so. What she really wanted to know was why the major seemed almost desperate to pawn her off on someone else. What bunk did he teach in that weapons class? She fell in beside Captain Caldwell, who made small talk about the weather.

When she found an opportunity to glance back, she was surprised to see the major standing where they'd left him. He certainly was acting odd today. Talk about human behavior! His was about as erratic as any she'd seen. Squaring her shoulders, she turned again and matched her steps to the longer ones of Captain Caldwell.

Sending her tripping off down the street with another instructor didn't give Ace the satisfaction he'd expected. On the contrary, it took all his control to keep from calling her back. Which made no sense. Dean Caldwell was as safe as the Easter Bunny. A man devoted to his wife and children. And unlike Ron Holmes, Dean did his job without giving Ace any flak.

But what difference did any of that make? *He* wasn't St. James's keeper. Ace stepped from the curb and saw her glance back. Noting her surprise at seeing him still there, he abruptly chose an alternate route. The long way. According to his watch, he'd have to make a mad dash or be late. He couldn't explain the effect St. James had on him. But it had to stop.

Ace didn't give her another thought until he walked into his office after lunch and was rocked back on his heels by a riot of color. Vases of all sizes spilled over with silk flowers. Bold purples, reds, yellows and hot orange mixed with bright pinks. His clerk was all but hidden behind a giant bouquet of red poppies.

Ace closed his eyes and counted to ten. *"Where is she?"*

The sergeant scrambled to his feet and beamed. "Isn't it wonderful, sir? Captain St. James thinks it'll make our cadets feel more at home."

Ace continued counting to twenty. "I don't want them to feel at home, Sutton," he said patiently. "The object is to toughen up their soft little butts." Before he could expound further, they heard someone banging around in the workroom.

"Sergeant," Dean Caldwell shouted, "what happened? This is good coffee."

"The pot is clean, sir," Sergeant Sutton called. "Captain St. James bought me a measuring scoop. Saves guessing." He needn't have yelled. Dean appeared in the doorway, stopped dead in his tracks and said, "Hot damn!"

Ace sank into his chair. In all the time he'd known Captain Caldwell, he'd never heard the slightest profanity pass the man's lips—until now. "Our new captain's been busy," Ace drawled. "When she's not playing the miracle worker of gourmet coffee, she moonlights with FTD."

Dean glanced at Ace and gestured with his cup. "Are you sure she graduated from the Point? For ten minutes after class she lectured me about societal awareness, intermilitary rapport and the danger of not homogenizing male-female communications."

Ace groaned, grabbed his telephone and tapped out a series of numbers. "Staff Sergeant Weller, this is Major Bannister. Is Colonel O'Dell in?" Ace closed his eyes, then cradled the receiver between his shoulder and his chin, using both hands to rub his temples. "Playing golf? Do I want him to stop by?" Ace's eyes flew open and lit on the largest floral display. "No," he said quickly. "It's nothing urgent, Weller. I'll catch the colonel later."

"You know," Dean mused aloud as Ace slammed down the phone. "This coffee may even beat my wife's. Well, I've gotta split. I've reserved a racquetball court for five o'clock. Let me know if you want me to rework my lesson plans."

Ace was still staring after Caldwell when the front door opened and in walked three of his best students. "Cool," they said in unison.

"Neat picture!" said one. "Great eagle!" exclaimed another.

Ace straightened his tie with a nervous twist of his fingers. He stared hard at the tangled lines, ultimately choosing to ignore the remarks. "Do you have something specific you want to see me about?"

Maureen Porter, known as Mouse and the one female in the trio, spoke. "Sir, we wondered if you'd chaperon a picnic-volleyball game at the lake facility Saturday night.''

He opened his mouth to remind them of the community-service commitment, but the tallest of the two males beat him to the punch.

"We booked it for after our volunteer work, Major. If you already have a date, sir, you could bring her. ROTC hardly ever gets to use the lake property, and Saturday night was open.''

Ace knew that was true. Normally they had to fight for space to hold extracurricular activities. Saturday was expected to be hot, and he knew from having volunteered last year that the renovation project was hard physical work. Cooling off at the lake sounded like a great way to end the day. "You're positive it's free?'' he asked.

The last cadet to step forward was the corps' best organizer. He spread four sheets of paper in front of Ace and handed him a pen. "Sign by the X on each page, sir. We're preapproved—all we need is for you to be the second chaperon. The vice president's secretary is holding the time open for us.''

"That's thinking ahead, Cadet. It's what the army likes. Good job." Ace scribbled his name, rank and title on each page, Mouse gathering them as he went. When Ace was done, they all thanked him profusely and raced for the door.

"Don't forget to bring the permit and the key back to me. And pass the word that there'd better not be any alcohol. One sniff and the party's over.''

"Yes, sir,'' they chorused.

"Say, who's the other chaperon?''

"Captain St. James," Mouse said. "We asked her after Captain Caldwell's class. She's neat, sir. We don't have a woman professional instructor, other than the nurses." She blushed. "Not that you aren't okay, Major. It's just, well, the air force has women PI's, and we didn't."

Ace was stalled back on the vision of himself and Captain St. James together at a beach party. He let Mouse ramble on. It wasn't until she mumbled, "I hope it was okay to ask her, sir," that Ace realized he'd been woolgathering.

He cleared his throat. "Ordinarily I should approve chaperons *before* you ask them, Cadet Porter. But this time I'll let it go."

"Yes, sir. Sorry, sir." She dashed off a salute and ran after her friends. Almost as quickly, she popped back. "Here comes Colonel O'Dell, sir," she whispered. "I thought you'd like to know."

"Hellfire," Ace said, leaping up as the door banged closed. "Here we are looking like a greenhouse or a damn funeral parlor. We've gotta ditch these blooms."

"Where, sir?" The sergeant glanced around at the cramped office and gave a helpless shrug.

By then it was too late. Colonel O'Dell strode through the door with his usual air of command, and the major and his clerk could do little but come to attention.

"At ease," the colonel said. "Well, where is she, Bannister? I came to meet this West Point harridan who's driving my best officer to drink."

Ace groaned. Little escaped the colonel's underground network. "I haven't seen St. James since she went to Captain Caldwell's class, sir. Dean is back and gone again already."

Sergeant Sutton fidgeted. "Cadet Larson took the captain downtown to pick up her car, sir. Her bank called. She asked if I thought you'd mind."

Ace waved away his concern. "I told her yesterday to take whatever time she needed to get settled."

The colonel opened his mouth to speak, but was interrupted when the front door flew open and in breezed the woman under discussion. "I bought the silver car. It drives like a dream . . . Oops!" She snatched off her cap and arched to attention. "Colonel, sir. I didn't see you, sir."

Colonel O'Dell placed his hands behind his back, narrowed his eyes and studied her.

Ace slumped in his chair. He could almost read the colonel's mind. *This curly-haired sprite, this big-eyed waif, is Ace Bannister's harridan?* Ace dragged his eyelids down with his forefingers and cursed inwardly. Why hadn't he taken the time to correct the colonel's erroneous impression?

"At ease, Captain." Colonel O'Dell put out a large hand. "Welcome, St. James. How are you getting along so far?" He shot Ace a stern glance.

Meredith tracked the crosscurrent. "Fine," she said coolly, unable to read what passed between the men. "I'm getting a feel for the campus, as well as for the methods used in instruction."

Brother, Ace thought. *Here it comes. Trot out Daddy's name and get your social reform incorporated into my program.*

The colonel waited as if for expansion, but when she said nothing more, he coughed. "Your transfer was rather sudden. I assume there's money to create an opening, but until we get clarification, carry on as you are." He glanced around as if realizing something was different.

Ace winced, waiting for the explosion that was sure to follow.

"Might be a little crowded in here, m'boy," the colonel said, stroking his chin. "Just keep the exits clear. We don't want grief from the fire marshal." He nodded at Meredith. "Magnificent eagle in your three-D picture. Is it new?"

"You like it, Colonel?" Meredith stepped forward and cast a subtle smile at Ace. "I think it adds a nice touch."

"Indeed it does. Well, if there's nothing else, Major, I think I'll mosey on out to the fort." The colonel studied Meredith a moment longer before turning to Ace and shaking his head. "The captain's nothing like I'd pictured. You may be due for some R and R, m'boy."

Ace barely found the wherewithal to salute. He thought seriously about following the colonel out and defending himself. True, she was easy on the eyes, but her radical ideas were driving him nuts. And that damned picture. He sneaked another peek. Where was the blasted eagle everyone claimed was so glorious?

She caught him eying her picture and smiled. "Relax, Major. Focus on your own reflection."

Ace sat, yanked open a drawer and got to work filling out some long-overdue forms. The next time he looked up, the sergeant was closing down his computer and Captain St. James had her purse in her hand.

She paused at his desk. "Betsy and Maureen invited me to help out at the project tomorrow."

"I heard. And to chaperon their party later."

Sergeant Sutton announced that he was shutting off the coffee machine. He came out, said good-night at large, then left.

Ace wished she'd go, too.

"Is there a problem with my saying I'd help?" she asked pointedly.

He leaned back in his chair and toyed with a pencil. "No, of course not. What possible problem could there be? Meet us here at 0800 hours for check-in, then we'll be on our way."

"What should I wear?"

That got his attention. A sudden vision of what she'd look like wearing a bikini flashed before his eyes. He shook his head to clear away the image. "It's your basic grunt work, St. James. Wear jeans or cammies. Probably boots and gloves."

She appeared thoughtful. Distracted. He softened his tone. "Look, if this isn't up your alley, say so. I'll make some excuse to the kids. These are old houses, and you might run into snakes or spiders or both. You could meet us at the lake. Casual attire there." He studied the ceiling to avoid thinking about a casual St. James.

"I'm capable of making informed choices, Major, and I've dealt with my share of snakes." She treated him to an icy stare. "So 0800 hours it is."

The door slammed, and Ace felt his breath escape in a hiss. Damn. He had a feeling tomorrow was going to be a long, hot, irritating day.

NORMALLY ACE RAN every morning at dawn. Except on weekends. Then he was more apt to wait until evening, because most Friday nights he had a date and slept late on Saturdays. Today, though, he was out watching the sun break over the eastern horizon at the end of a punishing run. Last night, of all things, he'd stayed home and done laundry.

Laundry. He wiped the sweat from his eyes and stepped up his rhythm. Maybe Colonel O'Dell was right. Maybe he did need rest and recreation.

ROZ DENNY FOX 75

All last evening he'd been planning to call and ask someone over to watch a late movie. Maybe Ruby Tindall. But midnight came and he was still alone—which was Captain St. James's fault. He couldn't seem to get her or that damned picture of hers out of his mind. He'd stared at the blasted thing for a good half hour after she left the office. No eagle. No trees. Nothing.

All he saw was big golden eyes, great legs and skin that begged to be touched.

Breathing hard, Ace crossed his yard, tripped over the sprinkler he'd forgotten to put away and all but fell against his front door. "Good going, old son. Kill yourself. Now *that* would make St. James's day."

Following a bracing shower, he donned close-fitting navy blue shorts, a cotton T-shirt and a worn pair of Nikes. Navy sweatbands around his head and both wrists left him looking more like a man headed out to play tennis than someone who'd be spending the day doing grunt work.

Last year he'd worn jeans to the location. By noon he'd ripped off the legs, he'd been so hot.

Once he'd found his leather gloves and sprinted toward the Firebird, Ace suffered a twinge of guilt about the information he'd given St. James about clothing.

His guilt increased when she showed up for check-in wearing combat boots, heavy canvas cammies and a fatigue shirt with long sleeves. Granted, a few of the women cadets wore jeans or knee-length walking shorts, but in general most had on shorts and tank tops.

To make matters worse, she couldn't have been more cheerful. If St. James wanted to strangle him, Ace didn't see any outward sign of it. She went around with a clipboard, checking off names as if everything was dandy.

Ace handed out the address of the project site. "Okay, you guys," he said, when the last cadet was checked in, "coffee break at 1000. The host is providing doughnuts. Lunch is on me at the nearest hamburger joint, and there's an afternoon break at 1430. I have an ice chest filled with soft drinks for that. Any questions?"

There were none. Ace was pretty proud of them. They might pull a few pranks, but they knew when to knuckle down. Most would make excellent soldiers.

Once the cadets were loaded and on their way, only Ace and Meredith remained. "I'd offer to let you ride in my new car," she said with a saucy tilt of her head, "but the ice chest wouldn't fit in my trunk."

"Stop it, Meredith. Let me have it with both barrels and get it over with."

She hugged the clipboard to her chest and stared at him.

"I know you're sore," he said. "I don't blame you. I'm sorry, okay? Go home and change. I'll cover all the bases until you get back."

Meredith looked down at what she had on—the standard army working uniform minus rifle and steel helmet. "Do I have a rip somewhere?" She strained to look at all her seams. "I don't see anything."

Ace stepped close and grasped her arms. "Look at me, dammit. What's the difference between us?"

Meredith ran a tongue over her dry lips. He looked like a Greek god with the sun gilding his already tanned skin. Her breath stuck in her throat.

His kiss came out of nowhere. One minute he was waiting for her to ream him out, to call him every kind of a louse, and the next minute she was molded to his body and he was kissing her like there was no tomorrow.

Meredith didn't notice the clipboard slipping from her fingers—until it hit the ground, and the sharp sound drove them apart.

Her breath came in short gasps. Slightly unfocused, she didn't quite know what had happened. She only knew his eyes glowed like silver moonbeams and his hands moved restlessly along her upper arms. Giddy and breathless, she felt only one absurd regret—that her arms weren't bare. He had such beautiful hands. It was a shame not to feel their texture against her skin.

Ace released her like a shot. If she didn't stop staring, he'd do something really crazy. Like kiss her again. And if he did *that,* he might not stop. Stepping back to create distance, he bent and retrieved her board. The papers had been knocked loose. As he collected them, Ace noticed how unsteady his fingers were.

Why didn't she say something? Why didn't she slap him or slug him or something?

Rising, he found her still looking dazed. "Are you all right?" He thrust the board and loose papers into her hands. This time he made sure she took them.

"Fine," she whispered. "I'm fine." Roses suddenly bloomed in her cheeks and at once she began edging backward in the direction of her car.

Ace figured when the shock wore off she'd be mad as hell. He couldn't let her leave without explaining. But what should he say? Not that kissing her had been on his mind since yesterday. And not that one kiss had lessened the need to kiss her again, because it hadn't. What, then? Bewildered, he extended a hand.

She turned and bolted for her car.

He followed and saw that her fingers were shaking so hard she couldn't get her key in the lock. "Here," he said gruffly, "let me. Look, something...alien came over me, all right? I can't explain, but it won't happen again." He finally had the door open, and after she'd climbed in, he passed her the keys.

She jabbed at the ignition until she hit it. Her voice was chilly. "I don't mix my personal life with my career, Major. *Not ever.*"

"That must be damned difficult," he snarled, his tone matching hers. "So much for your fine theories of merging a soldier's brain and heart. Or is it a case of do as I say, not as I do?" Turning, he stomped off.

He'd been right in the first place, he figured. She believed in the West Point attitude of class versus mass. Well, he hadn't lied—it *wouldn't* happen again. He'd as soon kiss a buffalo as touch her now.

Meredith heard the roar of his Firebird. She didn't start her car until the sound of his faded, not to make a point but because her heart still pounded so unsteadily. Lord, how had she let such a thing happen? One minute she was standing there, the next minute, wham! But the big problem was that she'd liked his kiss. Far too much.

The instant Meredith was able to breathe, she backed out. What she hated most was finding any military officer attractive. Had she made her objections clear enough?

Throughout the day it remained patently obvious that he was irked. He looked through, not at her whenever their paths crossed. Which, thanks to his maneuvering, was as little as possible.

Of course, the students noticed. Meredith overheard them talking. Well, she couldn't help that; she'd been talked about before. Having a general for a father guaranteed it, especially at a place as rank conscious as West Point.

ACE DID HIS BEST to stay clear of Captain St. James. He was moderately successful throughout the morning. By lunchtime, though, she looked so weary his gaze was drawn to her against his will.

At the restaurant, he slid into the booth across from her and handed her the hamburger she'd unenthusiastically ordered.

She stiffened.

He passed her a tall cup of water, as well as her soft drink, to ward off dehydration. "Tearing out that old rotten fence is a rough job," he murmured. "Why don't I spell you when we go back? You're not used to working in this heat. Anyway, I need a break from riding herd on the kids."

Meredith relaxed a bit and picked up her burger. "If I thought you were patronizing me, Major—"

"I'm not," he said swiftly. "You must feel like a baked clam in that heavy camouflage gear. I have a spare T-shirt in the trunk of my car if you're interested." The West Pointers he'd run afoul of were so by-the-book, Ace really didn't expect her to accept the loan.

"Yes," she said. "I'd be grateful. And thanks for the water. I feel cooler already. Frankly I wonder if I'll ever get used to this heat."

Once again she'd surprised him. "You will," he said. "It takes a while, that's all. I'd probably freeze if they shipped me to Baltimore."

Meredith heard the teasing quality in his voice and her heart tumbled. Then her smile disappeared; her reserve against military men slipped back into place.

Ace felt the shift and knew when to retreat. "I'll go get the shirt," he said. "You may want to use the ladies' room here to change. Then we need to round up our crews."

She changed quickly. Welcomed the opportunity. Except that his shirt was so large it hung to her knees. And wearing material she knew had touched his skin, material still carrying his scent, annoyed her. Bay rum—clean and quietly masculine. Without a doubt, it would drive her crazy all afternoon.

From the moment Ace saw her walk out of the ladies' room and climb into her car, he wished he'd kept his offer of the darned shirt to himself. The sleeves were huge on her and the neck drooped to expose the sharp points of her collarbones. It made her look vulnerable—and incredibly attractive.

By midafternoon break, sweat made the soft fabric cling to her breasts. Breasts, he noticed, that would fit nicely in a man's palms. At break, he passed her soft drink through three sets of hands, rather than risk taking it to her himself. She wasn't the only one who wanted to maintain a distance.

When she approached with an offer to trade jobs again, he snapped at her for no reason. "Do what you're doing. I'm fine."

But he wasn't. Every time she crossed his line of vision, Ace fantasized about how she'd look at the beach party. He imagined she'd "clean up good," as Southerners sometimes put it. He envisioned her in shorts. Skimpy shorts. Then he nailed boards like a demon. By day's end, he was drenched in sweat and his muscles felt like jelly.

Staying only long enough to congratulate the students on a job well-done, Ace arranged to meet them at the gate to the lake property in a couple of hours and left without talking to Meredith. He hadn't, however, missed the excitement in her eyes as she chatted with Betsy Larson about the evening that lay ahead.

Driving home, Ace knew what he had to do to keep his sanity. The instant he stepped inside his house, before he stripped and showered, he yanked up the telephone and invited Ruby Tindall and her kids to go to the lake. It was only after she agreed that he felt the tension leave his body.

CHAPTER FIVE

THE LAKE CAME into view about ten minutes before Ace reached the lane leading to the rec center. He'd chaperoned groups out here twice before. Each time he wondered why he'd bought a house in town.

There was something seductive about the way the water lapped the shore, stirred only by a few fishing boats waiting to load at the ramp. Ace thought he could handle being a weekend fisherman.

"I wish I had a boat," Blake Tindall, Ruby's twelve-year-old son, declared loudly from the back seat. "I'd just float around out there all day and never go to school."

"Blake," his mother scolded.

"That's a stupid statement," said his sister, who, since she'd climbed into the Firebird, had tried to act a mature fourteen to her brother's twelve. "Mom, if he's going to say dumb things around the college kids, I don't even want to go to this picnic. Tell him to wise up, will you?"

"Both of you, back off," Ruby instructed, turning in her seat. "Don't say I didn't warn you," she grumbled to Ace as she faced front again. "I said you'd be sorry for inviting them."

Ace glanced over his shoulder and smiled. It'd been a while since he'd seen Ruby's kids. He had to say the change in both of them surprised him. Lacy wore too much makeup. Dark reds that made her look older. And Blake, who still sounded like a kid, seemed to be trying to copy the high schoolers. He wore his hair long, and a gold earring dangled from one ear. Still, it was rough losing their dad, Ace guessed, no matter what the reason.

"All kids bicker," he said, trying to reassure Ruby. "I thought they'd enjoy the outing. You leave them alone a lot."

She whirled on him, her eyes angry. "What is this? Suddenly everyone's a critic. I may have to listen to my ex yelling at me for two hours about being a rotten mother, but I don't have to take it from you. A lot you know about parenting, Mr. Swinging Bachelor."

Ace darted another look at the kids, who were now burrowed into opposite corners looking sullen. "Hey, lighten up, Ruby. I obviously hit a nerve, and I'm sorry." After all, this had nothing to do with him.

Suddenly he recalled Meredith's saying Ron Holmes needed counseling, and the notion just sprang from nowhere that maybe Ruby did, as well. "Have you ever seen a counselor?"

Ruby tugged at her shorts and bent to find her purse as Ace pulled up next to the fence. She didn't answer. Possibly because four ROTC students rushed over to the car, asking for the key to the gate.

Ace retrieved it from his pocket and absently scanned the cars for Meredith's silver compact. At once he was appalled, both by the turn his conversation with Ruby had taken and the way his mind had automatically veered toward Captain St. James. Yanking his keys out of the ignition, he tossed them to Blake. "There's an ice chest and chips and stuff in the trunk. Why don't you two kids help my cadets haul it down to the tables?"

It was as if the boy and his sister couldn't escape fast
enough. They pushed the seats forward, squeezed out
and opened the trunk.

Ruby pulled out her lipstick. She twisted the Firebird's rearview mirror toward her and began applying
bright red gloss in short angry strokes.

Somehow, that also reminded Ace of Meredith. Or
rather of how indignant she'd become at the salesman
who thought she'd buy a car based on a mirror con-
cealed behind the passenger's visor. He must have
looked strange, because Ruby glanced up and snapped,
"Now what's wrong? Don't you like red-hot red?"

He shrugged and turned away.

"Is something bothering you, Ace? You aren't acting
like yourself. We've been going out off and on for six
months. You never said I needed a shrink before. Why
now?"

"A counselor isn't the same as a psychiatrist, Ruby."

"Yeah, like Roy would give me money for either. I
have to fight to get child support." She dumped her lipstick back into her purse.

"Forget I said anything. It's none of my business."
Thinking she was finished, Ace straightened his rearview mirror and opened the driver's door.

"Wait. Now you're mad. Why'd you even bring it
up?" Suddenly her face crumpled and she started to cry.
"I just don't know what to do anymore. Lacy hears Roy
rip me apart and now she's beginning to talk terrible to
me. Blake runs with boys I don't like. I wish you *would*
make it your business, Ace. The kids respect you." She
stared at him through teary eyes. "Does a girl have to
come right out and ask you to park your shoes under her
bed?"

"Ruby." Ace choked on an intake of air. When a woman talked like that, he always remembered the footloose cowboy whose genes he shared, and tried to change the subject. "I'm not mad . . . exactly."

She fumbled for a tissue, buried her face and sobbed harder.

Ace chewed the inside of his mouth. Few things made him more uncomfortable than a woman's tears. One of the reasons he tended to tune out Ruby's troubles was that neither his mother nor his aunt could ever cope with life's problems. Between them, those two had cried buckets of tears. Even now, Ace began to experience the hot painful flow of acid to his gut that had always seemed to accompany their weeping. As a kid, he hadn't been able to cope with feeling helpless. Hell, if the tight knot in his stomach was any indication, maturity hadn't made much of an improvement.

"Come on, Ruby. This is supposed to be a fun outing. The kids'll wonder why I'm not helping set up volleyball nets. I probably brought up counseling because we just got a social worker in the ROTC program who's been driving me up a wall with all her mumbo jumbo. Dry your eyes, okay?" He handed her a clean handkerchief from his back pocket.

She took it and nodded. "All right. But you go on ahead. I gotta stay and fix my face. Crying makes a mess of my mascara." She blotted her eyes, smearing his handkerchief with black streaks.

He studied her, and thought of Captain St. James with her smooth skin and expressive eyes. Both free of cosmetics.

"Why do you wear all that gunk, Ruby?" Ace asked, thinking it odd he hadn't noticed before. When her tears started again, he wished he'd kept his mouth shut. "I didn't mean you don't look nice, Ruby. I meant—"

"Just go, Ace Bannister. And don't say another word. Every time you open your mouth, you stick your foot in it." She grasped the mirror and twisted it again.

She didn't have to tell him twice. Ace leapt out, glad of an opportunity to escape the waves of emotion that tore at him. Emotion he thought he had well under control. Yet, as he made his way to the picnic area, he agonized over how he might have handled things better. It was obvious Ruby felt more for him than he did for her.

Damn, he hated hurting her. Hesitating, he glanced back. Women were so complicated. What could he say to make things right if he went back? He'd said he was sorry, and he'd meant it. Beyond that...well, it was clear now that he shouldn't have called her.

The cadets had begun to arrive and some had brought guests they wanted Ace to meet. It would have been embarrassing for Ruby if they'd seen her crying.

He was relieved when at last she climbed from the car. And equally relieved when she stopped to chat with someone. They'd have to talk soon, but this wasn't the place. Convinced she was okay, at least for now, Ace set about cleaning and lighting a barbecue.

Later, as he dispatched a crew to string volleyball nets, his thoughts turned again to his missing chaperon. Ace found himself keeping an eye out for her, but only, he told himself, because the rules for using the lake facility were clear about having two staff people available at all times.

Ruby sashayed down the slope toward him, getting sidetracked by three cadets trying to cover a picnic table with a paper tablecloth. Ace heard Mouse tell Ruby the wind blowing off the lake had already ruined one.

Joining them, he suggested using condiment bottles to hold the paper in place.

A car pulled in. Ace checked to see if it was Meredith. It wasn't, so he went back to unloading mustard and catsup bottles.

After the third such interruption, Ruby followed his gaze. "Who *are* you looking for, Ace?"

"Uh, no one," he muttered, perturbed she'd noticed. "I think we're finished here, Ruby. Do you mind asking that lanky kid with the Frisbee to get the horseshoes out of the big closet in the rec center? I see one of our cadets brought a couple of two-man rubber boats. I need to head them off at the dock and set some rules."

"Is this the way it's going to be all night?" she asked. "All I ever see are kids. I expected a little adult companionship tonight."

"I told you when I called what we'd be doing." Ace might have said more, but his eye caught the flash of a silver car. He fell silent and craned his neck to see if it was Meredith.

"Yes, but—" Ruby started to argue, then stopped when it became obvious his attention had wandered. "Who's that?" When he didn't answer, she shaded her eyes and squinted into the sun. "Whoever it is, she's crazy. Nobody wears a white dress to a beach picnic. Gimme a break."

Had Ace been able to get a word past his suddenly parched lips, he wouldn't have said aloud what effect that white dress had on certain parts of his anatomy. And Ruby was absolutely right. The dress was foolish. Try as he might, though, he couldn't keep from tracking Meredith's progress.

The closer she came, the more anxious he grew. Unless his eyes deceived him, the white dress was shot full

of tiny holes. Ace turned away. There was a name for
that type of material, but for the life of him, he couldn't
think what it was. All he knew was that it was hypnotic
watching sun rays wink in and out of the calf-grazing
skirt swirling around Meredith's shapely legs.

Turning back, he held his breath until she drew near
enough so he could see whether she wore a slip or something underneath the dress. Then he felt ridiculous. But
his knees lacked the will to move. It was just as well that
two cadets ran up to help her with the large bakery box
she carried.

Feeling Ruby's eyes on him, Ace let his breath escape
in a rush.

"I thought you had business down at the lake," she
said petulantly.

"In a minute."

Meredith thanked the students and had them take the
box to a picnic table. "Whew, sorry I'm late." She shed
a thin white cardigan and dropped it on a bench. "Betsy
and Mouse ordered a cake. I offered to pick it up. Mur-
phy's Law. It wasn't ready." She shaded her eyes and let
her gaze roam the area. "It's beautiful here. All this
greenery in the middle of desert. How often do we get to
use this facility?"

"Not often enough. Isn't this kind of scenery old hat
to you?"

"Never, Major. I love grass and trees." Her laughter
brought a corresponding chuckle from Ace.

Ruby stepped up suddenly and hooked a proprietary
arm through his.

He blinked, as if startled she was even there.

"I'm Ruby Tindall," she said, taking the lead with
introductions. "You must be the *no one* Ace has been
waiting for." She slanted him a sly smile. "I'm his date."

Ace saw the flicker of surprise in Meredith's eyes, and at first he was furious with Ruby. Then, almost as quickly, his anger subsided. After all, that was exactly why he'd invited her.

He wasn't a proficient enough actor, though, that he could trust himself to be convincing. "Excuse my lapse in manners," he said stiffly. "Ruby, this is Captain Meredith St. James, a new instructor. Ruby is a... friend," he offered Meredith by way of explanation.

She heard the slight hesitation before the word *friend* and drew her own conclusions. It would have been difficult to miss seeing Ruby move closer to Ace and increase the pressure of her hand on his arm.

As a result, Meredith dredged up one of her polished St. James smiles. "Nice meeting you, Ruby. Only I'd say he went beyond a lapse. He should have introduced us at the O-club the night I got into town."

Ruby's mouth fell open. "That was you?"

Lacy Tindall flounced up and barged in. "Mom," she wailed, stamping a foot and pouting, "make Blake quit hanging around me. He's such a dork."

Ruby rolled her eyes. "Lacy, don't call your brother names. What'd he do now?"

"Just everything. Larry Robertson asked me to go on a boat ride, and Blake told him I can't swim."

"Well, you can't."

"What difference does that make?" The girl's pout turned ugly. "You probably paid Blake to spy on me. The way you had someone spy on Dad. I hate you." Spinning on her bare feet, she ran down the slope at breakneck speed.

Ruby's fingers dug into Ace's arm. "I told you Roy was filling her head with lies. I didn't have him spied on."

Ace disengaged his arm from Ruby's hold. He hated scenes. "I need to find out why those guys are offering boat rides at all. You see to Lacy." He was loping toward the lake before the last syllable left his lips.

Meredith sensed Ruby's distress. Dropping her purse onto her sweater, she said casually, "Teenage girls are erratic even if they don't have red hair. You've been twice blessed." She offered an encouraging smile.

Ruby glanced up. "You have a teenager?"

Meredith shook her head. "No. I'm not married. But I've worked with quite a few. I'm a social worker."

"Oh. I see. It's your mumbo jumbo Ace says is driving him nuts."

Meredith's brow furrowed. "I beg your pardon?"

Ruby's hand flew to cover her mouth. "I probably shouldn't have said anything. I gotta go. Ace asked me to have someone set up horseshoes."

Meredith watched her hurry off. The woman's words shouldn't have stung so. After all, Ace Bannister didn't make any secret about what he thought of her ideas. Mumbo jumbo was tame compared to what he might have said.

Still, she felt a little betrayed, considering his kiss earlier. Silly of her to think something so trivial meant his attitude was softening in any way. Not that she *wanted* the kiss to mean anything. Certainly nothing more than the "alien" response he'd claimed. She didn't expect much from male officers, but it did hurt to think he'd joke with his girlfriend at her expense.

When two cadets eyed her warily, Meredith gave herself a shake. Everyone but her seemed to be busy. Since no one had told her what was expected, she decided to find Betsy or Mouse and ask.

"Hi, Betsy." Meredith wandered up behind a group who were counting salads. "I picked up the cake. Where would you like it?"

Betsy glanced up and smiled. "Did they do a good job decorating?"

"I'm sorry, I didn't look. You just said to pick it up."

"Let's go see." Betsy excused herself to follow Meredith. "We asked the bakery to decorate it like a big playing card. An ace of diamonds for Major Bannister's birthday," she explained. "You didn't show it to him, did you? It's a surprise."

"No. He didn't see it. Is today his birthday?"

"Yes. Sergeant Sutton told us. The major's only been with the ROTC program about a year. According to the sergeant, a friend of Major Bannister's swears the major doesn't remember his own birthday."

Meredith sought Ace's broad shoulders in the crowd. "Really?"

Betsy checked to see where he was, too, before peeling back the tape and lifting the lid. "Ooh, looks yummy. You don't think he'll be embarrassed, do you?" Tiny frown lines fanned her brow.

"I don't have the vaguest idea," Meredith said. On the one hand, she didn't want to dampen Betsy's enthusiasm. On the other, she tended to think a person who ignored birthdays must have some good reason for doing so.

A young male cadet paused to look at the cake. "You and the major don't like each other much, do you, Captain St. James?" he asked bluntly.

The remark caught Meredith off guard. Otherwise she might have come up with a plausible joke. As it was, she simply let him walk away. Because Betsy still seemed worried, though, Meredith returned to her original question. "You say Sergeant Sutton gave you the information about the major's birthday?"

The girl nodded.

"Well," Meredith said, "I don't think he'd suggest something that would upset his boss, do you?"

A sunny smile blossomed on Betsy's freckled face. "Oh, I hope not." Happily she smoothed the tape back in place. "Look. They have the volleyball nets up. You can change clothes in the rec center, Captain."

"Change?"

"Didn't you bring jeans?" Betsy sounded surprised. "It's always the men against the women, and we women need all the extra hands we can get."

Meredith just kept shaking her head. "No one told me chaperons participated. I'll either have to play in my dress or watch."

"I'm sorry I didn't mention the game," Betsy said. "Maybe you can referee. Keep those guys honest. They make up rules as they go."

"Thanks heaps." Meredith laughed.

Just then Ace walked over to the nets and blew a whistle. He motioned the students in from the dock, too. "Okay," he said when everyone had gathered, "we've strung two nets. Think you can scrounge up four teams?"

It was obvious to Meredith as she watched them divide up that this was a definite grudge match. With the addition of Ace's girlfriend and her daughter, the women still lacked one person to fill a second team. The girls seemed so disappointed Meredith decided to play.

Ace threw a ball to one set of teams, then ambled toward Meredith. His gaze took in new details. Her soft-soled shoes. The scooped neck of a dress that skimmed her body in a way too . . . feminine for outdoor games.

"Have you ever played volleyball in a dress?" he demanded, resenting the feelings it evoked.

She thought about it. "Once, when I was much younger. Why?"

Ace found himself trying to visualize a younger Meredith St. James. Faintly freckled face. Pigtails? He didn't realize he was scowling until one of the cadets asked why he was glaring at the captain, and everyone snickered.

"I'm not. It seems to me a long skirt would be restrictive, and safety for this outing is my responsibility."

Meredith's cheeks grew warm. It was typical ridicule from male officers. She lifted her chin. "Are you ordering me not to play, Major?"

"No. I was only thinking of you. I'd hate for you to get hurt."

Concern—real or not—wasn't what Meredith had expected. And as most of the students were watching their little byplay, she could do nothing but nod crisply.

Ace wasn't blind to the way the cadets' heads swiveled from Meredith to himself and back. Such things prompted talk, and talk soon became rumors. "Play ball," he said abruptly, tossing the volleyball to one of the team captains. The moment it left his hand, he sauntered off.

In his army uniform, Meredith thought his walk was sinful. In denim cutoffs, she decided there should be a law against anyone getting from point A to point B in the manner Ace Bannister employed. An opponent's first serve landed at her feet, and Meredith didn't so much as move a muscle. Good-natured ribbing from the team jerked her back from gawking at Ace. She faced the net, determined to pay attention to the game.

Ace felt a need to cool off. The captain had stoked a fire in him he didn't want stoked. He thought the horse-shoe pits were far enough away to do the trick, but even when he stood there, horseshoe in hand, his eyes kept straying to the courts.

Finally he leaned a hip against a picnic table and un-abashedly watched her play. She certainly didn't let a little thing like a dress keep her from throwing her all into the game. Her cheeks were pink, and perspiration glistened on skin made rosier by the stark white of her dress.

He saw her jump to block someone at the net. She was so short it was futile, and Ace laughed. But as her dress floated up around her thighs, his laughter stuck in his throat.

He didn't see Ruby's approach until she touched his cheek with a cold can of cream soda and he jumped a foot. "Jeez, Ruby. Don't sneak up on a man like that."

She giggled. "I didn't sneak. You looked lonely down here all by yourself."

"Well, I'm not. Did you get things square with Lacy?"

Ruby plopped down on the bench. "Are you kid-ding? She wouldn't even play on the same team with me. Don't worry. She'll come around when she needs money. Do you want this or not?"

Ace shook his head. "It's too near dinner. I was thinking about starting a batch of hot dogs. Where's Blake?"

Shrugging, Ruby tore the tab off the soda. "Said he was bored. One of the boys brought a boom box for the dance. He let Blake take it inside the rec center."

Ace pushed himself away from the table. "You should make him get out. Do him good to exercise and soak up a little sunshine," he said, walking off.

"You sound like Roy again." Ruby stood, dusted off the seat of her shorts and trailed after him.

From the corner of his eye, Ace saw Meredith step up to serve. She threw the ball in the air, arched her back and hit it with a powerhouse clout that dropped it into her opponents' back row. Her team cheered. Twice more she did the same thing with seeming ease. Ace was impressed.

"Have you heard a word I've said?" Ruby demanded, jabbing him in the ribs.

He hadn't, of course. "Sorry, Ruby. You rag on Roy so much it gets old. He's a louse. You divorced him. Why can't you let it go?"

"As long as he pays child support, the judge says he has a say in the kids' lives. Roy takes that to mean he can gripe about every dime."

They'd reached the barbecue Ace had lit earlier. Instead of responding, he removed the grill and checked the briquettes. They glowed nicely. Perfect timing. Judging from the noise, both volleyball games had ended.

Ace took five packs of hot dogs out of an ice chest, handed them to Ruby to open, then placed the wieners in neat rows over the grill. That was when he noticed her long, perfectly painted nails. "What do you do with yourself all day, Ruby?" It just occurred to Ace that her fingernails always looked flawless.

She blinked. "Do? What do you mean, do?"

"I just wondered why you don't get a job. Make your own money, so Roy doesn't have all the control."

"Why should I? Roy wanted a wife to stay home and raise his kids. He got me pregnant when he was home on leave—before I finished high school. I had one miscarriage and a stillborn. I didn't want to try again, but he insisted. Now he can damn well pay the bills until they turn eighteen."

Ace winced at her tone. He didn't think he'd heard any of this before. But who was he to dispute her logic? After all, he still resented his biological father for not owning up to his responsibilities.

Meredith appeared behind them in time to hear Ruby's outburst. Embarrassed, she tried to sneak away.

Ace saw her and smiled. Actually he looked relieved. "I take it your team won?"

Ruby whirled to see who he was talking to and glared at the intruder.

"I didn't mean to interrupt," Meredith said quietly, "but I came to offer my assistance. We have a lot of hungry mouths to feed. And yes, we won by three points." Her pleasure wouldn't be contained.

Ace felt a little skip in his heartbeat. "Your serves did it."

Meredith hadn't supposed he'd seen. She didn't know why such a small thing made her feel so good. But it did. "Let's say my few points didn't hurt," she said self-consciously. "Now, tell me how I can help."

Ace handed her a package of buns. "Line these up. Keep it simple. Put a bun on each plate, pass it to me for a dog, and we'll get this show on the road." He blew two short blasts on his whistle. All activity stopped and was followed by whoops of glee and a race for plates.

Meredith laughed. It was obvious the crowd converging on them had been through the routine enough times to have it down pat. She only had a second to catch her breath before two lines formed, and she was kept busy opening packages of buns so Ace could slap in the wieners. She looked up once and saw Ruby standing off to one side, glowering at her over a cigarette.

Ace sniffed the air. Turning, he spotted the cause. "Put that out, Ruby. There's no smoking allowed at this facility." In a gentler tone he added, "Why don't you check to see that every table has chips and salads."

She crushed out the cigarette beneath her heel, blew the remaining smoke into the air, then waltzed over and nudged Meredith aside. "I'll do this. Let her take care of the tables."

Ace opened his mouth to protest, but Meredith spoke first. "Fine by me, as long as you save me a couple of hot dogs. I'm starved."

Noting the speculating looks on the faces of the cadets who'd been near enough to witness the incident, Ace bit back what he'd been about to say. He admired the way Meredith had handled herself. Another woman might have made an issue. He wondered if her generosity was a result of the way she'd been raised, or whether it had come from her schooling. Whichever, he'd have to thank her.

When the students had all been served, Ace placed another full batch of wieners on the grill. "Now it's our turn," he told Ruby. "Give Meredith a holler and round up your kids."

Ruby glanced around the park. "Here comes Blake, but I don't see Lacy. Does that woman have to eat with us?" she grumbled. "We could take our plates down by the lake."

"I can't go off and leave Meredith alone. She and I are co-chaperons, Ruby."

"Why did you invite me?" she asked around a pout.

Ace wondered now, too. Nevertheless, he *had* invited her, and he owed her his allegiance. That didn't mean he wasn't glad to see Blake show up. Ace smiled at the boy. "I thought the smell of food would penetrate that haze of rock music sooner or later. How many of these do you want?"

"Four," the boy said without hesitation.

"Have you seen your sister?" Ace asked as he stabbed the last of Blake's wieners and dropped it into a bun. He motioned for Meredith, who'd just walked up, to bring her plate.

Blake jerked a thumb toward the row of parked cars. "Last I saw her she was climbing into that green Chevy with Larry Robertson. They're probably makin' out in the back seat." Tossing back a lank fall of hair, the boy carried his load of food to an empty table and sat down.

Once again Meredith had overheard something that didn't concern her. She thought the flare of anger that lit Ace's eyes justified, however. "Uh ... I'll see the hot dogs don't burn if you want to go check it out," she offered.

Ace looked to Ruby. "Did you hear Blake?"

"Sure. I told you Lacy's a caution. If I went up there she'd throw a fit and scream at me to mind my own business—or worse."

This was a new side of Ruby. And one Ace didn't like. But since she and the children were his guests, it was up to him to handle it. "*I'm* making this my business, Ruby. Larry Robertson isn't one of my cadets, but he must be at least eighteen. That makes him trouble in my book."

Ruby shrugged. "Lacy'll be mad as hell. Even if you go, she'll blame me. But at least she might wait till we get home to throw her tantrum."

Ace shook his head. He really couldn't believe what he was hearing. "You ladies go ahead and eat. I'll be right back with Lacy."

Meredith found it painful to witness how little regard Ruby seemed to show for her daughter. She'd dealt with worse, of course, and in her position tried never to judge. That didn't mean it was easy to hold her tongue.

Ruby filled her plate and selected a table some distance from her son. Meredith followed, thinking she might offer some professional advice.

"I don't suppose it's occurred to you that Ace and I want to eat in privacy," Ruby said.

Meredith looked up from smearing mustard on her bun. Frankly it hadn't. She knew her face must be red. "I, uh . . . I'll just go sit with Blake." She rose and gathered her plate. She'd be darned, however, if she'd apologize. After all, what did she care if Ace chose to flaunt his girlfriend in front of the students?

Ruby spoke again. "You see how Ace feels about my kids. His own life wasn't exactly a clambake, or so I hear. He'll be a wonderful stepfather."

Meredith thought she was beyond shocking, but Ruby's announcement gave her a jolt. The memory of the kiss she and Ace had shared earlier was too vivid for her not to blurt without thinking, "You two are getting married?"

"It's only a matter of time." Ruby said.

Speechless, Meredith turned toward Blake's table. Before she'd taken two steps, she ran smack into Ace. Lacy Tindall was not with him.

"Where are you going?" He glanced at her nearly full plate. "I hope that's not all you're going to eat. For someone who claimed to be starved, you're not making much of a dent."

"I, uh..." She didn't want him to know he'd been the topic of their discussion. "I left my sweater somewhere. Now that the sun's dropped, I'm getting chilly."

"You go back and eat," he said. "I remember where you left it. I'll go grab it."

She nipped in her bottom lip. Then, because she didn't see any way to avoid doing so, she returned to the table where Ruby sat calmly eating.

True to his word, Ace was back in a jiffy with her sweater. He even draped it around her shoulders, and when his hands seemed to linger a bit too long, Meredith could sense Ruby's displeasure. "Thanks," Meredith murmured, discreetly trying to slide out from under his touch.

"So where's Lacy?" Ruby asked offhandedly.

"Cooling her heels in the Firebird."

"I told you she's a brat." Ruby sighed. "Is she real mad?"

Ace narrowed his eyes. "You might say that. She's also fine, if it matters. I've asked Granelli to take you and the kids home after we eat."

"I don't want to leave," Ruby said, shooting Meredith a poisonous look.

"Ruby, you need to talk with Lacy tonight." Ace picked up his Coke and took a long drink. "Wasn't just chitchat going on in that back seat."

Ruby wadded up her napkin and threw it on her plate. "I happen to know you're no saint, Ace Bannister."

Ace's jaw tensed. "I'm not fourteen, either."

"And when you were?" Ruby's eyes glittered.

Meredith cleared her throat. "Look, I'll leave you two to your discussion," she said. However, just as she rose, Betsy Larson climbed up on an empty table, clapped her hands and called for everyone's attention.

"Save your plates and forks," she shouted. "We have a surprise." Suddenly out of a dark huddle of girls off to Betsy's right, two young women emerged carrying a sheet cake ablaze with candles.

Meredith sat back down.

"Okay," Betsy yelled. "A little bird told us this is Major Bannister's thirty-fifth birthday. Let's all sing 'Happy Birthday'!"

In the artificial light cast by the rec center's flood lamps, Meredith observed shock settle over his sharply etched features. Before the entourage reached his table and set the cake in front of him, Meredith watched his shock change to embarrassment, then shift again to helpless vulnerability.

"Me?" he exclaimed, glancing around when the singing ended. "You're kidding? You guys did this for me?" His voice fell to one of wonder. "No one's ever given me a birthday cake," he said softly, reaching out to touch a candle as if fearing it would evaporate before his eyes. "Not in my whole life."

At first Meredith thought she must have heard wrong. One look at his eyes and she knew she hadn't. Her heart sat like a big lump in her chest. For all her father's military rule, she couldn't think of a single year in all of her twenty-seven that she'd missed having some kind of birthday celebration. Not even when she'd been at the Point.

She glanced at Ruby now and frowned. Why was the woman acting as if his birthday was news to her? Something Meredith was sure of—if Ruby Tindall didn't know or care enough about Ace Bannister to surprise him on his special day, the woman did not deserve to marry him. To heck with all that rot about his being a great stepfather. He was a man first. A human being.

Then Meredith smiled. Because at this very moment, the battle-toughened major looked more like an excited boy.

CHAPTER SIX

SUNDAY, FOLLOWING the lake outing, Ace sat at his kitchen table nursing a cup of coffee and staring off into space, instead of reading the newspaper. He still couldn't get over those kids buying him a birthday cake. The card they'd all signed occupied a prominent place on his counter. Funny, he'd never expected to care about all the hoopla he'd missed growing up. Or rather, he thought he'd gotten over caring. Once, it had hurt like hell.

Something he knew today though, that he hadn't known before last night—when he had kids they were going to celebrate every single occasion that could be celebrated. He was going to personally buy them cards and gifts and decorated cakes. He caught himself smiling.

"Whoa, Bannister. First things first. To get kids, you need a wife." The words of caution rang out in a silent room. Ace sat straighter and looked around, feeling slightly embarrassed. Considering the unreliability of his genes, what woman would want to take a chance on him?

Captain St. James wormed her way into his mind, and seeing her so clearly irritated him. Good Lord, he had an entire address book full of candidates to alter his bachelor status. More likely candidates than St. James and her high-toned, mile-long pedigree.

But somehow Ace knew she'd come to mind because, of everyone at the lake last night, she alone seemed attuned to what he was feeling. It was written all over her face when he glanced up from trying his damnedest to blow out all those trick candles and accidentally connected with her eyes. Everyone laughed but her. They found it hysterical that he honestly didn't know why those stupid candles stayed lit.

Yet there wasn't a shred of pity in her eyes. He would have hated it if she'd felt sorry for him—as she seemed to know. Instead, her eyes reflected his joy in experiencing something brand-new, no matter how silly it made him look. It was almost as if she'd taken each step with him. And for the briefest of moments, he'd imagined what it would be like making love with her.

Ace reached for his coffee. No sense letting his thoughts dwell on an unlikely situation. Fat chance he'd ever invite her into his bed. She probably placed lovemaking in the same category as combat. And he'd heard her views on that subject.

Getting back to the cake episode...Ace realized that, in contrast, Ruby, who'd known him far longer than Meredith, had appeared oblivious to his longings.

He took a swig of cold coffee and grimaced. Perhaps he was judging Ruby too harshly. She had a lot on her plate with those two kids. It was pretty plain she needed a man who didn't tune out her problems. She needed someone interested in going beyond casual dating. Ruby needed someone to lean on.

He, on the other hand, needed someone who could stand alone. Someone who didn't require one scrap of emotional support.

Rising, Ace dumped the dregs of his coffee into the sink. God, he'd never liked being alone with his feelings. Mostly because it always ended the same way—with thoughts that didn't paint a very nice picture of Major A. C. Bannister.

Sundays were the worst for self-castigation. On Sunday, time dragged. He looked around and felt the walls closing in. What he needed was something to do. And someone to do it with.

Snapping up the phone, Ace called Joe Poston, a single guy like himself, to see if he wanted to hit a few buckets of balls on the driving range. Joe didn't answer, which probably meant he'd spent the night with Alexis, a woman he was beginning to get downright serious about.

Ace found that faintly disturbing, too. Poston had only recently hit thirty. Here Ace was at thirty-five, still unsettled.

He stood with a hand on the phone. There weren't many activities available on Sunday mornings. Bobby Wells would be at the track running his stock car. Ace guessed he could go hang out there and breathe in a lot of noxious fumes. Somehow that didn't appeal today.

Alvin Beckett was probably getting ready to go skeet shooting. Ace quickly dialed him and woke Al's roommate, who said Al had left already.

Suddenly Ace remembered Meredith saying she wanted to see some of the countryside. He thought about places she might enjoy, places they could drive to and from in one day. Like Fredericksburg, a historic German town. Few shops were open, but she might be interested in the Admiral Nimitz Museum. Or they could visit the Caverns at Sonora.

Excited at the prospect of showing off part of his state, Ace called Information for her phone number and dialed before he got cold feet. "Meredith, this is Ace. I didn't get you out of bed, did I?...No? Good." Why, then, did her greeting sound a bit thin?

"I was sitting here drinking my morning coffee and I remembered how you said you wanted to see some of the territory." Taking a deep breath, he plunged ahead. "I wondered how you'd feel about having me as a guide for the day."

Her silence didn't bode well. And when she said she was just on her way out, a hole opened in the pit of his stomach. "Ah...I see. Well, it was just a thought. Maybe another time."

Damn, he didn't want her to hear his disappointment. Then, instead of hanging up, she began to explain.

"You made a reservation to go on the Vanishing River Cruise?" he repeated. "No, I've never been. Uh, yes, I know about where that is— Do you need directions?" After a moment of awkward silence, she invited him to go with her.

"I shouldn't impose, but, hey, if you're asking, I'll tag along." He tugged his wallet out of his back pocket and fanned through the cash to see if he had enough to offer dinner, since she said she was picking him up. "Sounds great," he said after giving her directions to his house. "Third single-story on the block, remember. I'll hang around out front."

Ten minutes, she'd said. About time enough to brush his teeth. As Ace dashed down the hall, he had to admit the day was looking up.

She was prompt. He saw her car seconds before she turned the corner. It wasn't like him, but he felt nervous. Should he volunteer to drive or would she prefer to do it herself? And what would she be wearing? Were his jeans too casual? Lordy, for someone who taught a load of kids how to stay cool in the face of enemy fire, he was doing a piss-poor job of it himself.

All at once it was too late to wonder. She pulled up next to the curb. Her tires threw gravel on his toes. She gave a little wave and smiled as if she was really glad to see him. His heart skipped a beat. Suddenly the old Ace Bannister was back in control.

He opened the passenger door. "Hi. Looks like it's going to be a great day for sight-seeing."

"I think I got too much sun yesterday." She drew his attention to her nose, which was a sort of cherry red.

"Ouch." He shuddered. "I meant to tell you about aloe. I have a tube, if you want to wait half a second. It really takes the fire out."

"I'd be grateful. Do you mind driving? I'll put it on my face and arms now."

"No problem. Be back in a flash."

And he was, with a Texas map and the promised gel.

Meredith barely had time to switch seats and wonder for about the hundredth time why he'd called her—since he was practically engaged to Ruby Tindall. "You must be really organized," she murmured as he handed her the tube. "If that was me, I'd still be digging through my medicine cabinet."

He laughed as he slid under the wheel, buckled his seat belt and started the car. "I bought it on the way home last night. My neck was pretty well-done."

She cast him a glance. "You look tanned to me. I just burn," she lamented as she smoothed the gel over her bare arms.

He couldn't watch. "So, this is some kind of boat ride? Won't you burn to a crisp?"

"They said it was a sixty-foot covered tour boat. And the man on the phone mentioned the wind gets cool."

"Yes, you'll learn about our Texas wind if you stay here long. Some places it'll blow a man off his horse."

She looked amused. "I've already learned how Texans exaggerate. Truthfully, though, I wasn't prepared for it to be so hot this early in the day. Is this weather unusual?"

"In Texas *nothing* is unusual."

She angled a hand behind her neck and rubbed the gel beneath the collar of her dress.

Ace's gaze, hidden behind dark glasses, followed its progress. He fought a desire to pull off the road and help her. When he swung his gaze ahead again, he discovered he was coming up fast on the tail of a loaded horse trailer and was forced to brake more sharply than he would have liked.

Meredith was thrown forward. She dropped the cap to the tube. Glancing out at the lazily whipping tails of two horses, she laughed and bent to retrieve the fallen cap. "What's the matter, Bannister? My new car got too much horsepower for you?"

That broke the tension. He made a face at her. "In your dreams, St. James. Those two hay-burners up ahead could outrun this compact any day of the week. If you don't object, maybe I'll kick it into passing gear and burn out some carbon for you."

"Fine, but you blow the engine and you pay to replace it."

He backed off on the gas and rolled up his window. Motioning her to do the same, he flipped on the air. "Can't say essence of barnyard is my favorite fragrance, but this is a shakedown cruise for your bucket of bolts. With luck, we'll lose our friend Flicka at one of the ranch roads coming up."

"Flicka? Don't you mean Thunderhead? They look albino to me."

"Where'd you learn so much about horses, Baltimore?" He cast her a quick admiring glance, then paused to check out the loose weave of her floral-print dress. "I had you pegged as the dolls-and-tea-party type."

With a finger, she outlined one of the flowers in her multicolored skirt. "By the dolls-and-tea-party stage, my father had pretty much given up on the idea of producing a son to follow in his footsteps. In his inimitable way, the general ordered me to start a crash reading course in military history, beginning with the Revolutionary War. War stories gave me nightmares. Mother graciously allowed a book of my own choice before bedtime. I loved stories about wild horses. They seemed so...so free." Discovering she'd balled her hands in her lap, Meredith gave herself a shake. "I'm sure you don't want to hear about my boring childhood."

Ace had just made up his mind to pass the pickup and horse trailer when she made that curious statement. She was partially right. Ordinarily he didn't like conversations about childhood. But amazingly, he found he wanted to know everything about this woman. He especially wanted to know how she'd ended up an army captain if war stories gave her nightmares. He would have asked, too, if not for the guarded expression that crept into her eyes.

After pulling safely around the other vehicle, Ace changed the subject. "Tell me about this Vanishing River Cruise, why don't you?"

Her eyes brightened. "I don't know much. According to an ad in today's paper, it's a guided nature tour up the Colorado River. The thing that interested me is the possibility of seeing bald eagles. The man I spoke with on the phone said they'd spotted a pair yesterday."

"Eagles, huh? That's something worth seeing."

"Look." She pointed out the side window. "That's the second sign I've seen for the Bluebonnet Trail. What exactly is that?"

"In another month this whole area will be blanketed with them—the Texas state flower," he clarified. "People come from all over to take pictures."

"And to pick bouquets?"

He smiled. "I can see your brain working overtime. More flowers for the office, right? Well, forget it, St. James. Bluebonnets are protected by law. Picking them will get you a hefty fine."

"I had no idea. It does make sense, if as many visitors as you say take this trail. There'd be none left."

"During wildflower season the Native Plant Society sets up a display at Buchanan Dam—if you'd like to learn more about Texas wildflowers."

"I would. My movers are due tomorrow. Once I get settled, I'll start listing special events on my calendar."

"If you need help moving I could probably have Ron take my afternoon classes."

"Thanks, but the movers will unload. I don't think it would work to have other people put my junk away. I'd never find anything."

Ace couldn't imagine why he felt disappointed at being told no to hauling heavy boxes up two flights of stairs, but he did. "Well, the offer's open if you change your mind. Why don't you take the day off work?"

"Take the day off from what work, Major? Have you assigned me a class at last?"

Ace cleared his throat. "Uh . . . I've been waiting until Colonel O'Dell says we're funded. Something you *can* do, though—I need all the shoulder braid and tassels collected from the cadets and bagged for the cleaners. Brass from Fort Benning are due in next week. ROTC was asked to march in a big parade during festivities at Fort Freeman."

"I'll collect the rope, but it won't exactly fill my week."

"No, it won't. Are you, by any chance, well versed in army traditions and customs? Captain Caldwell teaches two classes a week and might like some input. I know you grew up in a military family. I'd imagine that after living on bases all over the world, you'd have personal insights to pass along."

"Actually, no. The general thought soldiers should be free to soldier, unencumbered by the personal baggage of a family. So we stayed in Baltimore whenever he was assigned anywhere."

"Wasn't that hard on you and your mother?"

"My mother's father was army, too. And her grandfather. My mother is the perfect army wife. She follows the general's orders to the letter." Meredith folded her hands and watched the passing scenery.

Ace thought he detected a hint of sadness. If he was smart he'd drop the subject. But, if he didn't ask he'd never resolve some of the baffling contradictions about her. "You've said some things in the past few days that make me wonder why you went into the military. Lord knows there are easier places to get a degree than West Point."

Her lips turned up in a wry smile. "I have yet to meet any man, woman or child who says no to my father. If you'd ever met General Harding Addison St. James, you'd understand."

Ace did a double take. "Harding Addison..." He pushed his sunglasses into his hair and gaped at her before turning his gaze back to the road.

She seemed to melt into the corner. "You know him?"

"Uh...there was a commander in the Gulf...at field headquarters." Ace felt his way. To create a delay, he reached over and cranked up the air.

"My father was in the Gulf. Don't keep me in suspense, Major. Tell me what you were about to say."

"I, uh, it's the name. Harding Addison. Troops in the field called him...Hard Ass." He flushed. "Somehow, I thought Addison was his last name. But yes, we met on occasion."

"Hard Ass is a nickname he earned at the Point, so don't be embarrassed to use it. A disagreeable upperclassman I had the misfortune to meet there made the connection between the general and me. He made my life miserable. He'd wait until he gathered an audience, find a way to bring my father's name into the conversation, then point out our differences. On top of that, he got his friends to call me Marshmallow, or M and M after the candy...." She made a sour face. "I survived. I'm much tougher than I look, Major."

"Ace, remember? Out of uniform, I'm just plain Ace." His lips curved in a smile. "Let's forget the army today and have fun, shall we?"

She took a deep breath, wondering why she'd shared something so painful with him. "All right...Ace," she said. Really, it surprised Meredith that he'd abandoned a chance to discuss the general. Pleased her, actually. Most officers she met saw her as some sort of stepping stone to a man they thought could influence their careers.

Ace watched a sunny smile drive the shadows from her eyes. Lord, if anyone could empathize with the pain that came from being harassed about one's old man—or, in his case, the lack thereof—Ace could. The difference was that he'd fought back. With words, fists or whatever it took. Not something you could do at the Point, he supposed.

No matter. He released the breath he'd been holding and whistled an aimless tune.

"You want me to turn on the radio?" she asked. "Sorry I don't have any cassettes yet. I will when my things arrive."

"Is my whistling that bad?" he asked.

"No." She hesitated, her hand on the knob.

"Go ahead and try it," he said. "Reception here is lousy, but maybe you'll get lucky."

"I won't do it if it's going to hurt your feelings."

He reached for the sunglasses nested in his hair and settled them back on the bridge of his nose. "Texans don't have feelings, Baltimore," he said almost too lightly. "Haven't you heard? We're men of steel."

"Yeah, right." She snorted. "All men talk big."

"Hey, no social psychology, either. Okay?" He leaned over and yanked one of her wispy curls. "Today we'll declare a moratorium on all subjects where we can't agree."

She pretended to think about it for a minute. "All right, but I predict a very silent, boring trip."

His laughter filled the car. "Come on. We're not that bad."

Meredith recalled the way his eyes had sliced her to ribbons the night they met. And how he'd gone from begging for a transfer to a kiss that had knocked her socks off. "Well," she murmured, "there's not much middle ground with us."

For some reason Ace didn't want to agree. Or to argue. When Buchanan Dam came into view, he jumped at the chance to introduce a new subject. "Look on your right—the dam." He slowed, giving her a chance to sightsee. "We'll stop later."

"I'd like that. Do you think we'll have time to poke around any of the craft and antique stores we passed?" she asked wistfully.

"It's Sunday. I doubt they'll be open," he said.

"Why not?" She turned to look at him, but he continued to shake his head.

"You'll have to go on a Saturday. In west Texas, Sunday's reserved for family."

"I guess I've been in the city too long. Nothing stops. It goes twenty-four hours a day. This might be a nice change," she murmured.

"You like your own company, then?"

She looked surprised. "Mostly. Yes, I guess I do. Although I've never thought of it in those terms. I have a lot of hobbies. What do you do in your spare time, Ace?"

He rubbed a hand slowly over his chin. "I'm not good with spare time."

"What's not to be good with?" She laughed. "You mean you spend all your extra time on your house—like mowing the yard and stuff? Or do you mean that you don't relax well?"

He scowled. "I thought we agreed. No social psychology."

"I didn't mean to pry. Sorry." She bit her lip. Was he this touchy on all personal issues?

Ace nudged her. "Hey, is that a sign for the cruise?" He slowed the car. "Yes." He made a sharp left turn. "Take a gander at the map and see how far it is from here. This road looks like it runs into nowhere."

"It is desolate. I'm glad I didn't come alone. I'd never have found my way from the directions they gave." She studied the map. "This looks right."

He followed the single-lane road for several miles without talking. About the time he began to seriously question whether this was the right way, they came to a small but well-kept motel.

"We're close now," Meredith said. "That's one of the landmarks they gave. Oh, wait, we should have parked there." She pointed. "He said not to drive all the way to the river."

Ace didn't slow at all.

"What are you doing?" She frowned.

"That's somebody's cow pasture. Besides, you can't just say turn here and expect me to whip around on a dime."

"Well, excuse me. I hope you can back up this hill. The man said there's no room to turn around below."

"Why? If it's a big boat, there must be a big landing."

"Didn't you see those three tourist buses in your so-called pasture?"

He hadn't. And by now, he was wishing he'd listened to her. Her car faced a huge cypress tree that had the biggest trunk Ace had ever seen.

He gauged the distance between Meredith's side of the car and a white picket fence. Beyond, it seemed the road petered out. If he'd been driving the Firebird he wouldn't have made it. But with her car, he thought he just might—if he was careful.

"Go ahead, say it," he growled as he jockeyed the small car through the minuscule space and rocked it back and forth in short spurts to get around the tree. "I'm glad no other fool decided to follow me. We'd be in a pickle."

Meredith couldn't see any reason to comment on something so obvious. "Pretty country, but I don't know that I could live in the boonies."

"Amen to that," Ace murmured. "Oh, and thanks for not crowing. Would you like to be let out here? I'll park above and walk down."

"No. The walk'll do me good. We've been sitting for a while, and the boat ride takes about two and a half hours."

"That long?"

"You didn't have to come."

"No arguing, remember?" Ace couldn't very well tell her that he'd have gone to a pig feed today if that was where she'd been headed.

The hike back did take some of the kinks out. He had to admit it felt good. *Being with her* felt good.

She slipped on a rock and he grabbed her arm to keep her from falling.

"These shoes aren't very practical," she admitted. "I didn't realize I'd need all-weather tread."

He joined her laughter as he looked her over from her woven sandals to her gently flowing dress to her shining crown of curls. A band tightened around his chest. None of the women he'd dated had ever been this petite. Oh, there was a lady he'd met once in France, someone he'd thought he might get serious about. She'd been soft and feminine—but she'd also turned out to be helpless and clinging. It hadn't taken Ace long to decide he was just lonesome and too far from home. Meredith, now, had an underlying strength, yet she was feminine through and through.

As Ace breathed in her subtle perfume, he was reluctant to loosen his grip on the soft skin of her inside arm. He was forced to eventually, though, so he could go purchase tickets.

"My treat," Meredith said, stepping briskly up to the window.

"No way," Ace objected. "It was your car and your gas." They both blinked in surprise when the woman behind the counter said she didn't care who paid, as long as they didn't hold up the line.

"Dutch treat," they proclaimed together, then shared a chuckle.

Boarding the riverboat, Ace guided her to seats on the lower deck. As it pulled away from the dock, Ace figured it was going to be a dull trip. Before long, though, Meredith's enthusiasm roped him into helping spot the egrets, ospreys and turkey buzzards their guide mentioned.

When they came to a sheer granite wall and she jumped up to locate a family of mountain goats said to be on a ledge, Ace moved to the rail and craned his neck, too.

"I wish we'd thought to bring binoculars," she said, forced to be content with only a glimpse of white.

"Me, too. Wow, look at that waterfall." They'd come to a break in the cliffs where the river widened. Water thundered over a wide falls.

"Wait! What's he saying about petroglyphs?" Meredith clutched Ace's arm.

He took her hand, lacing their fingers, and smiled; he cared nothing about ancient drawings, only about the sparkle in her eyes. "We'll see them on the return trip," he promised. Although he thought he'd like to continue riding like this forever.

Rounding a bend, they faced a long section of jagged cliffs bleached white by the sun. Thousands of small birds flew overhead. The captain cut the boat's engine and they could hear the muffled beating of the birds' wings. Meredith tightened her grasp on his hand. "They build nests in every crypt. It looks so steep. You don't think the babies fall out, do you?"

Ace released her hand and slid his arm around her shoulders, drawing her to his side. "I'm sure they don't," he murmured.

It might have been then that he relaxed and began to fully enjoy the outing. Or it could have begun when they spotted a bald eagle's nest and clung together silently, watching as one of the magnificent birds swooped down not fifty feet away and plucked a silver fish out of the water with powerful talons. Or maybe it was during the return trip, as he enjoyed the pull of the lazy current—and the feel of Meredith's silken hair brushing his chin—as they strained to see the ancient petroglyphs. But regardless of when it had occurred, by the time they docked, Ace was about as mellow as he'd ever been. "That was the fastest two and a half hours I've ever spent," he grumbled, handing Meredith from the boat to the dock.

"Wasn't it glorious? I wish I'd brought a camera. I would have loved a picture of that eagle. Did you ever see anything so beautiful?"

Ace stared down at her upturned face—her eyes shimmering like crystallized amber—and for a moment he thought his legs hadn't made the transition from sea to land.

If Meredith hadn't suddenly spied a little souvenir shop and said she wanted to buy postcards, Ace was certain he would have kissed her. And recalling how she'd reacted the last time, it was a good thing the shop was there.

"I guess you don't do postcards, huh?" she asked, showing him her packet.

"I don't have anyone to send them to."

She paused on the steps leading back to the road. "No family at all? No aunts, uncles, cousins? No one?" she exclaimed in disbelief as he shook his head.

He shrugged and took her arm. "Don't look so horrified. I wasn't found under a rock."

"I didn't suppose you were. Are your parents both dead, then?"

Ace felt the old tension return. "I could have a whole raft of pedigreed half brothers and sisters," he said gruffly, urging her forward. "My old man skated off and married somebody who had money. My mother was dirt-poor. I guess that makes me a mongrel. End of conversation, okay?"

Before she put voice to the pity he saw forming in her eyes, he hurriedly asked, "Are you hungry? Out on the main road there's a place that serves the best darned barbecued ribs I've ever tasted. You haven't experienced Texas until you've gorged yourself on brisket or ribs. My treat."

Meredith watched him unlock the car doors. She could tell he'd thought she was going to say how sorry she was for him. Little did he know how many times in her life she'd fantasized about being an orphan. It wasn't that she'd been neglected, and certainly not abused. *Ruled* was more like it. In every thought, word and deed. But maybe that didn't compare to being dirt-poor and abandoned by your father. Deciding against any comment, she held out her hand for the keys. "I'll drive, if you navigate. You know, I *am* famished. And we'll split the bill."

A short time later, Meredith groaned and added one last bare rib to the pile on her plate. The food was everything Ace had promised.

He laughed at her. "You were hungry. Should I tell you that you have sauce from ear to ear?"

"I'm sure. I probably have it up to my elbows and in my eyebrows. But what's the use of eating barbecue if you can't enjoy it?"

"No use." He picked up his iced tea. "Thing is, I'd rather have a nap than make the long drive home."

"Well, since I'm driving, you can sleep."

"And end up in Mexico? I don't think so."

"I'm very good with directions, I'll have you know."

"Okay, then. Are we still stopping at the dam?"

She stood. "We have time, right?"

"Yep. You need to use the facilities before we go?"

"Unless you don't mind being seen with this sticky face. Come to think of it, I don't remember seeing a rest stop along the way."

"They're few and far between. Texas is so big."

"What do pregnant women do, I wonder? Well, anyway, I'll be right back."

Ace watched her walk away. He didn't seem to have control over a mind determined to visualize her pregnant with his child. He smiled, thinking what it would be like to go home every night to an impish miniature of Meredith. Pushing his chair back so quickly it almost tipped over, he elected to wait for her outside. Maybe notions like that wouldn't sneak up on him if he paced for a bit.

She was prompt coming out. They headed for the dam and had plenty of time for a leisurely walk around its well-kept grounds. On the drive home, Ace hadn't planned to doze, but he did.

Meredith saw and laughed softly. She had enjoyed the day in his company much more than she'd anticipated.

Ace awakened with a start to find it was dusk. He yawned and caught her doing the same. "Hey, no sleeping on the job. There's danger of hitting a deer out here. Do you want me to spell you?"

"Would you mind? I am sleepy." Once they'd traded places, she seemed wide-awake again and they talked nonstop for the next twenty minutes.

Ace was disappointed to see the exit for his street loom out of the darkness. They'd nearly reached his house when he glanced at her and said without warning, "Are you busy next Saturday? I'd like to show you Fredericksburg. They have more craft stores than you can shake a stick at."

Meredith ran her tongue nervously over her lips as he pulled up to the curb. "I don't know, Ace." As the lights of town had come into view, she'd begun to feel guilty. Eyes averted, she asked bluntly, "What about Ruby?" And what about her own determination to avoid military men?

He had just set the emergency brake and was leaning over to deliver the kiss that had been building between them all day. "Pardon?" The thumb stroking her lower lip hesitated. "What *about* Ruby?"

She edged away and licked her lip where he'd left it tingling. "Ruby said..." All at once, Meredith couldn't see any point in this conversation. He was in the army for the count. End of relationship.

Fumbling behind her, she opened the passenger door and scrambled out. Although her knees weren't steady, she was able to walk around the car and stand beside his door, waiting for him to get out.

Confused and tense, Ace unfolded his length from her car. When she would have scooted in without a word, he caught her arm. "What did Ruby say?"

She shook her head and slipped into the seat that still bore his imprint. Closing the door, she rolled the window down a few inches.

Ace had wanted to block the door with his body, but light from a streetlamp revealed the distress in her eyes and he drew back.

He looked so frustrated that Meredith decided it wasn't fair to leave him hanging. "Ruby told me you two were getting married."

"What?" Ace roared. Then, because she flinched, he calmed down and ran a hand through his hair. "It's not true. I swear."

Meredith gazed at him unhappily. "Why would she say so if you hadn't given her some reason to think it? Still, I can't regret today. It would be best, though, if we confined our relationship to the office from now on. Don't you agree, Major?" She put the car in gear.

"Meredith, wait!" Ace curled his fingers over the edge of her window.

She pulled away slowly, forcing him to step back.

"Dammit!" Her taillights faded, and Ace swore again. He'd never discussed marriage with Ruby, and he couldn't imagine why she would say he had. Given his family history, he hadn't discussed marriage with any woman.

Tonight, though, when he walked into his empty house with memories fresh from a special day spent with Meredith St. James, thoughts of marriage not only crossed Ace Bannister's mind, they lingered well after he went to bed.

CHAPTER SEVEN

SHORTLY AFTER DAWN, Ace decided he'd go into the office early, take Meredith out for coffee and make her understand that he wasn't tied to any woman. Later he'd stop at Ruby's and set her straight, too.

As he drove the familiar route to work, he puzzled over a sudden preoccupation with marriage that had kept him awake half the night.

Or was it so sudden? Last year he'd admitted to being lonely and had let one of his friends fix him up. Alvin Beckett had introduced him to an artist friend of his girlfriend's. Two dates was all it took. She'd wanted Ace to pose for her—nude. Major Centerfold. Wouldn't that have pleased the army?

He grimaced and cut his speed to drive through campus. Meredith had beaten him in again. Good. But Ace couldn't help hoping she'd lost sleep, too. Angling in next to her silver compact, he climbed out and felt a wave of heat from the hood of her car. He grinned. She hadn't beaten him by much. Still, he wasn't prepared to walk in and smack her with the door.

Why in blazes was she standing there?

Meredith heard the door seconds before it hit her. She threw a frightened glance over her shoulder. When she discovered Ace behind her, she did her best to come to attention.

"It's just me," he said inanely, snatching off his hat. "At ease, St. James. Why in thunder aren't you at your desk? Oh, don't tell me—you're figuring where to stuff another bouquet."

She opened her mouth, but could only wave a hand helplessly toward her corner. "Is this your idea of a joke, Major?" she managed to squeak. "It must have taken you half the night to move things around."

Ace glanced beyond her. "Move what around?" Then he saw. Everything on her side of the room faced the wall. Her desk, bookcases, file cabinets, the picture everyone raved over. At a glance he'd say Sergeant Sutton's area had received the same treatment.

Ace closed his eyes and dragged a hand down the hollows of his cheeks. "You think I'd pull a dumb trick like this?" he exploded. "I must have made a hell of an impression on you, Captain."

Meredith's hands balled at her sides. "Excuse me, but I don't see that anything of yours has been touched. I'd say the evidence speaks for itself."

Setting her roughly aside, Ace strode over to his desk and jerked up the phone. He cradled it with his shoulder as he whipped through his Rolodex. Once he found the card he was looking for, he punched out a number with his free hand. "Cadet Captain Granelli," he roared without prelude, "I want a squad at my office on the double. I'll be very disappointed if the following cadets don't show." He rattled off six names before he slammed the receiver down. "Don't touch a thing," he ordered Meredith when she moved her chair and stood on tiptoe to reach her picture. "I want our mischief-makers to enjoy putting every stick of this back to rights."

"Our cadets did this? But why?" Her eyes rounded.

"It's just a hunch, but probably to cause friction between us. You recall how at the lake a few wise guys seemed pretty interested in our verbal . . . skirmishes?"

She wrinkled her brow. "Vaguely. I remember heads swiveling back and forth. However, I doubt I'd know any of those kids if I saw them again."

"If you're going to work in ROTC, you need to develop a sixth sense. The little weasels pounce on the slightest weakness." He chuckled. "It's part and parcel of the system. To get back at the brass."

The front door opened and Sergeant Sutton strolled in, followed by Colonel Loudermilk. The sergeant stopped midstride. "Holy cow! What happened, sir?" He gaped at Ace.

Before Ace could answer, Frank Loudermilk puffed out his chest and bellowed, "It's those damned kids. Maybe now you won't be so namby-pamby about helping me crack down on the little bastards, Bannister," he said, advancing on Ace.

"Now, Colonel," Ace returned smoothly, "it seems a harmless enough stunt. Matter of fact, I have a volunteer cleanup crew on the way."

"How you choose to handle it is your business, of course," the air-force colonel said stiffly. "But someone needs to teach these kids respect for military property. Maybe this will open your eyes." He slapped a paper on Ace's desk.

"What is it?" Ace ambled over and picked it up.

"A bill for six sets of ruined uniforms," Frank snapped. "I'm calling it willful destruction of U.S. military property. If it was me, I'd flunk the lot. Let 'em lose scholarships. Drop a few smart alecks out of school. I guarantee the others will shape up."

Meredith stepped forward. "Isn't that a little harsh, Colonel? Without scholarships most ROTC students would never finish college."

The colonel's eyes narrowed, ultimately coming to rest on her captain's bars. "I'm not in the habit of explaining myself to subordinates, Captain. I suppose you're a graduate of the program? And if I may say, a good example of the lackadaisical attitude that prevails."

Ace darted Meredith a warning glance. "Colonel, I don't believe you've met Captain St. James—a graduate of West Point." It crossed Ace's mind to mention her father's position at the Pentagon, but on seeing sparks building in her eyes, he decided the wise thing to do would be to get Frank out of there.

Ace threw the bill on his desk as the front door flew open again. This time, in trooped a row of uniformed cadets. As if on cue, each one saluted smartly.

"At ease," Ace growled. For Frank's benefit, he mustered the gruffest voice possible. "I'm on my way out for coffee—er—a conference with Colonel Loudermilk. Captain St. James is about to go meet her movers."

Ace sauntered slowly down the line of cadets, looking for outward signs of guilt. When they were sufficiently nervous, he barked, "You jokers have twenty minutes to put every last stick of furniture back to rights. In addition," he thundered, "not one second after 0900 tomorrow morning, I want a five-page paper from each of you. That paper will spell out in great detail why you, personally, should be allowed to attend the military ball on Saturday night. Any questions?"

The last cadet in line tucked in his chin and asked in a small voice, "Single- or double-spaced on that paper, sir?"

Ace appeared to give it thought as he edged Frank toward the door. "Double will be fine. But those papers had better be convincing. Supremely convincing. Is that clear?"

"Yes, sir," they mouthed in unison as he strode out the door and slammed it behind him.

"What kind of punishment do you call that, Bannister?" Loudermilk blustered the moment they were alone. "Half of them probably have girlfriends who'll write the damn papers for them."

Ace grinned. "*All* of them have girlfriends. I happen to know each of those ladies has spent a fortune on a dress for that ball."

"Then you do intend to prevent them from attending," the colonel said, rubbing his hands together gleefully.

"Frank, Frank, Frank," Ace chided, "don't you think sweating it out is punishment enough? I'll collect their papers tomorrow, but I'll delay making a final decision until late Friday. I predict they'll all be quite humble by the time I say they can go."

"Hmph. I'd confine the lot to quarters and let everyone else know—the way we did in the old days when the military stood for something."

Ace bristled as he drew a cup of coffee from the machine in the cafeteria. "I guess that's the difference between my idea of discipline and yours, Frank." Ace didn't add that he thought his way was more humane, because it struck him that this was the same argument he'd had with Captain St. James, only in reverse—which gave him a zinger.

Talk between the men turned to other matters. When they'd drained their refills and started back across campus, Frank reminded Ace that he expected prompt restitution for those uniforms. As they parted company at the crossroads, Ace promised to discuss it with Colonel O'Dell later in the day.

Continuing on by himself, Ace wondered what O'Dell would say to taking up a collection from every army ROTC student. Maybe Frank had a point. Maybe they did need to be confronted with the cost of their pranks.

It troubled him to think that there was this lack of concern for taxpayers' property. But on the other hand, when he was their age he hadn't respected anything. In the end, he'd gotten his priorities straight. But threat of hard time was pretty drastic. Under the circumstances, depriving these kids of a much-anticipated social event was drastic, too. They were just having fun.

Ace was still deep in thought when he turned down the walkway toward the office and met Meredith rushing out. He'd assumed she'd be long gone. "I hope you didn't think I meant for you to oversee those turkeys."

She shook her head. "The moving company called to say they'd be an hour late. I took the opportunity to pick up the rope and tassels you said needed cleaning. Sergeant Sutton explained about the drop point. They'll be cleaned and delivered back here tomorrow. Now I'm off to meet the movers."

"Will you be in tomorrow morning? We have some unfinished business."

She was afraid he meant last night and chose to misunderstand. "You mean you need help reading all those essays?"

"No." Ace shifted from one foot to the other and cleared his throat. "If you like, we can meet for coffee in the cafeteria. This concerns how we left things yesterday. I'm also planning to see Ruby today—to ask why she lied to you."

Meredith pretended interest in a group of boisterous students hurrying past the building. "*If* Ruby lied to me," she said after they'd passed, "I'm sure it's because she cares deeply for you. Apparently you date regularly. Frequency is telling, Major. Not to mention how you dealt with her children."

His voice rose. "*Someone* had to stop what was going on in the back seat of that Chevy."

"You won't get an argument from me. I agree. Lacy and Blake will benefit from having you for a stepfather."

Ace's jaw jutted. "Dammit, will you stop twisting my words and listen? I am not—I repeat, *not*—getting married. Is that clear?"

Unexpectedly Ron Holmes stepped around the corner of the building, a cigarette dangling from his smirking lips. "Need help, Major? Is Captain St. James trying to coerce you into marriage?"

For a moment both Ace and Meredith looked stunned. Ace recovered first. "I'm squelching scuttlebutt passed along to Captain St. James, Ron. And the colonel will be most unhappy if it gets any farther," he said firmly.

Meredith set her cap at a jaunty angle atop her flaxen curls and fixed Captain Holmes with a cool stare. "Should I ever solicit matrimony, Captain Holmes, I assure you that it won't be with a man who's career military." She stepped back, saluted Ace smartly, spun around and had nearly reached her car by the time he returned her salute.

Ace couldn't put a finger on exactly why her declaration annoyed him so much. All he knew was that it took a colossal effort not to lash out at Holmes, who seemed to find her announcement quite amusing.

"How are the stats coming, Ron?" Ace tried but failed to keep his tone level. "Colonel O'Dell needs them Friday. I trust that won't be a problem."

Ron all but snarled, "No...sir," before he tossed his cigarette to the sidewalk and shredded it beneath his shoe. Whirling, he headed back around the building. "This is a nonsmoking area," Ace called. "I'll expect this tobacco mess cleaned up before I go to class." Even as he said it and stormed inside, Ace knew he'd dug his hole deeper with Ron Holmes. Communication between them had been strained enough since Ron was passed over for promotion—about the time Ace came into the ROTC program. Not that he'd had anything to do with the decision, but Ace doubted anyone would ever convince Ron of that. Still, things hadn't been so openly hostile before Captain St. James's arrival. Had Holmes taken a fancy to her, too?

Too? Wait just a darn minute, Bannister! Ace stopped dead beside his desk and stared at her blasted picture. St. James couldn't have made her feelings for him much plainer out there—not if she'd tossed him a hate letter tied to a grenade.

Yesterday he'd have sworn she felt differently.

"Is something wrong?" Sergeant Sutton rose and came to stand by Ace, his gaze following the major's. "Did the lads miss something? They tried so hard to get every detail right."

"Hmm?" Ace murmured absently as he made a frame of his hands and peered at Meredith's print. "Have you ever taken the Vanishing River Cruise, Sergeant?"

"Yes, as a matter of fact." The old man's leathery features rearranged themselves into a smile. "Last year I took my grandson. But what has that— Ah, I see. The eagle."

Ace dropped his hands and sighed in disgust. "You wouldn't all be pulling my leg, would you? I mean, that picture isn't some trick the cadets have talked you into helping with, is it?"

Sergeant Sutton laughed and returned to his desk. "I guarantee it's all there. The eagle, the trees, everything. I can't believe you don't see them."

Ace muttered to himself as he stalked across the room and yanked open the door to his closet. "Sergeant, remind me that I need to get these two dress uniforms cleaned. One for Friday's parade, the other for the ball."

"Yes, sir," Sutton said briskly. "I'll make a note. Oh, by the way, Colonel O'Dell's wife called while you were out. She's making up the army's seating chart for the ball and wants to know if you or any of your staff officers are taking guests."

Ace turned from placing his hat on the shelf. If this had come up last week, he probably would have invited Ruby. As things stood, he mulled over other possibilities. Not without reluctance, Ace told the sergeant that he believed he'd go alone. "I'm reasonably certain Captain Caldwell plans to take his wife, but I have no idea about Captain Holmes. Why don't you ask them? Then let me know what they say. I'm meeting Colonel O'Dell this afternoon to find out what he wants done about those air-force uniforms. I'll be glad to pass along the information to his wife."

"Very good, sir. And what about Captain St. James, sir?" Sutton glanced up from his list.

"What about her?" Ace asked, taking a seat at his desk. He loosened his tie and picked up a folder of correspondence.

"How will I find out if she requires seating for a guest? I don't believe the captain plans to be back today, and Mrs. O'Dell needs to know before tomorrow morning."

Ace started to say, "Mark her down as a single," because she was too new in town to have met anyone. But, hell, she was so anti-uniform, for all he knew, she might be inviting one of her movers this very minute. The thought delivered a spurt of acid to Ace's stomach. "Leave hers blank," he said. "I'll go by at lunch and get an answer."

"Fine, sir. I'll check with Captain Caldwell and Captain Holmes."

"Uh, you do that, Sergeant." Ace was rifling through his bottom drawer, looking for the notebook with his master plan of class assignments. He'd decided to work up a tentative class schedule for St. James. There must be a few subjects in which her radical ideas wouldn't carry any impact.

Ace leaned back and rocked gently. Staring into space, he daydreamed about the sparkle that lit her eyes when she launched into one of her lectures. Hell, after what he'd said to Frank, he wasn't certain she didn't have him jumping on her bandwagon himself.

His chair squeaked, ruining his contemplation. Well, he couldn't just leave her in limbo. And he damn sure didn't want her following him to class all the time. The fantasies he wove were altogether too real.

She hadn't seemed very enthusiastic about the prospect of teaching human behavior, but neither had she balked. If he gave her one class in army-personnel management systems and relieved Ron of a military history—she couldn't change history, could she? Ace tapped his lips with his pencil. Surely not.

His proposed schedule would take care of her mornings. Perhaps Colonel O'Dell could send her off to recruit in the afternoon. It wouldn't hurt to ask. She'd probably be good at it. He had to get her out of this tiny office before he started liking those damned flowers of hers.

Grimly he finished the proposal and dropped it on the sergeant's desk for typing. It was time for his class in laws of war, and was he glad St. James was otherwise occupied! Ace had a vivid idea of the havoc she could wreak in that class. He could hear her lambasting the Geneva Convention's law of armed conflict. No one, trained soldier or not, enjoyed rehashing the horrors of war, but some facts were irrefutable. And the cadets needed to know what they might face someday.

His thoughts ranged back to the captain and he wondered how things were going with her move. She was the type to skip lunch, he'd bet. Thin as she was, she couldn't afford to miss meals. Dammit! If she chose not to eat for a week, it wasn't his concern.

But he'd promised to get her answer about the ball, and *he* didn't intend to miss lunch. He supposed he might as well pick up something for her, too.

Ace didn't purposely rush through the morning's lesson, but neither did he assign busywork when class ended early. Halfway to his Firebird, he was stopped by two cadets claiming to have completed their five-page papers.

"You fellows didn't take much time on this," Ace said. "Are you satisfied it's your best effort?"

"Yes, sir," they chimed, although they exchanged uneasy glances.

One of the cadets—Ace would have staked his entire paycheck that he was the instigator of the midnight caper—cleared his throat.

"Something else on your mind, Cadet?"

"Uh, about the ball, sir. My, uh, my mother will be upset if I don't get to participate in such a time-honored tradition, sir."

"Bull," Ace said. "I doubt your mother gives a tinker's damn one way or the other. Don't play me for a fool. I wasn't born yesterday."

Both young men looked downcast. "Pictures, sir," the cadet who wore glasses said as he pushed a pair of marbled frames higher on his sunburned nose. "Our mothers are counting on photographs of us in our dress greens. Mothers like to brag around the neighborhood, you know."

Ace wanted to laugh. These two were inventive, he'd give them that. Wait until he told Meredith. She'd love the story. He frowned. How had that popped into his head? Inventive or not, it was way too soon to let them wiggle off the hook. Ace opened his briefcase and dropped the work inside. "Honesty, men—the army is big on honesty. And so am I. Good try, but no cigar." He barked a dismissal and left them looking crushed.

After a couple of steps he remembered a caper or two from his own boot camp. "I'll try to read these tomorrow. See that you two keep your noses clean until I make a decision."

"Yes, sir," they chorused, a thread of hope creeping in.

Because he already knew the outcome, Ace thrust the business from his mind and worried, instead, about what to get Meredith for lunch. Something nourishing. Unpacking was hard work.

At a grocery-store deli, he selected a variety of salads, sliced meats, cheeses and rolls. As an afterthought, he tossed in a few cans of soda, a quart of milk and cereal for her breakfast. Ace had helped with too many

moves to imagine she'd feel like grocery shopping tonight. Heck, he'd do as much for Dean or Ron. Well,
maybe not Ron. When he reached Meredith's building,
he parked on the shady side, then carried his purchases
around front. The movers weren't finished. Lord, how
much stuff did she have? Somehow, he'd thought she
lived with her family.

Partway up the stairs, Ace ran into four burly men
who blocked his passage with a piano dolly. Above, he
could see Meredith gesturing wildly. Then an errant gust
of wind blew her full skirt up above her knees, and her
cheeks turned as pink as the deep-pocketed dress she
wore. Soon it was obvious her spinet was more important than her respectability, because she gave up on the
skirt.

Watching the drama unfold, Ace fell in love—with the
highly polished upright piano that peeked out from beneath quilted throws.

When he was a child, growing up in a sorry part of
San Antonio, there'd been one bright spot in his life. A
beautiful mahogany piano that had belonged to his
neighbor, Mrs. Rodriguez. A wizened woman of sev-
enty, she supplemented her meager income by giving piano lessons to neighborhood children whose parents
could afford a few dollars a week. Which his mother
could not.

Ace remembered being too proud to let anyone in the
development know they couldn't afford the small fee
Mrs. Rodriguez charged. To maintain an image, he se-
cretly ran errands—in exchange for the privilege of sitting on her porch at night and listening to her play.

Then one day the old lady couldn't pay her rent, and
the landlord locked her out. The bastard sold her piano
for what he claimed she owed in back rent. She had to go

down the street to live with her son. Mrs. Rodriguez didn't make it through the winter.

By spring, his mother had found out the cowboy had himself a rich wife. While summer heat dried lawns to a crisp, the boy who loved music hustled his first hubcaps during the idle evening hours.

Ace battled a strange catch in his throat as the memories washed over him. He hadn't thought of Mrs. Rodriguez in years. And he wasn't happy about being reminded now. He considered leaving before Meredith St. James of Baltimore discovered him standing there like a ninny, drooling over her piano. Social workers probably had a sixth sense about such things, and Ace didn't want her or any other woman tapping into his secrets.

But before he gathered his wits, she did see him and called out a greeting.

"Major?" Leaning over the wrought-iron balustrade, she smiled and motioned him upstairs.

Lured by her smile, Ace only vaguely heard what she said about the piano being the last piece to come off the truck. He graciously stepped aside for a brawny man who brushed past carrying the piano bench.

"That does it," Meredith announced. "Every box accounted for." Signing the work order, she tore off a copy and handed it to a bronzed, shirtless workman. As he disappeared through the door, she stopped to inspect the sacks Ace carried. "Groceries? What a wonderful housewarming gift—if we can find the kitchen." She laughed.

Her teasing comment broke the tension building in Ace. He laughed, too. "Actually it's lunch, and a little more. I didn't realize they'd still be carting things in. Do your folks know you've cleaned out their house?"

Meredith gave him a strange look as she led the way through a maze of boxes. "You've seen my kitchen," she said. "It's somewhere through there. Give me a minute to finish signing off. I imagine these men would like lunch, too."

A well-muscled, suntanned Adonis sporting a wealth of curly black hair on his head and chest winked at her. "Is that an invitation, doll?" he asked in a sensual drawl.

Ace noticed her face clash with her petal pink dress. He wanted to pick the bastard up bodily and toss him over the decorative railing. Because the inclination was so strong, Ace made his way to the kitchen. It didn't help to hear Meredith explain to the mover that Ace was *sort of* her boss.

Refrigerating the perishables helped cool his flare of jealousy. Finally he heard Meredith usher the movers out. Mood substantially improved, he washed his hands and busied himself placing meat and cheese on paper plates.

"Now . . . to answer your earlier question," she said, walking in, "I don't know what gave you the idea I lived with my parents. I leased a small house from an aunt and uncle. Here, though, where I don't know a soul, I figured an upstairs apartment would be safer." She snitched a piece of cheese from the display and popped it into her mouth.

"You keep coming on to hairy apes who're just passing through town and this place won't be safe, either," Ace growled.

"Hairy ape? Oh—" she waved a hand "—you mean Nicky." A faint flush worked its way up her neck. "He's only doing this to earn money to go back to college. I thought he was kind of sweet."

"Like King Kong was sweet," Ace snorted.

A smile lifted one corner of her mouth. "Why, Major. Do you fancy yourself a champion of my virtue?"

Ace glared at her across the small island. She seemed full of innocence and mischief, all rolled into temptation. He told himself to just ask the question he came to ask and get out. Before he volunteered to help assemble a bed. Did she have no earthly clue how unvirtuous she looked? Probably not.

When Ace failed to make any comeback, smart-mouthed or otherwise, Meredith shrugged. "If it'll put your mind at ease," she said quietly, "I passed self-defense with flying colors. I don't *like* the physical stuff, but I can take care of myself if I have to." She broke apart a roll and began preparing a sandwich.

Ace ran her statement through his overcharged brain. She might look like strawberry parfait, but in truth she was a captain in the United States Army. She didn't need his protection, and he should damn well remember that.

"So do you play that piano?" he asked to fill the silence. "Or do you just polish it and keep it around for show?"

Meredith blinked, not certain she wanted to know why his mind leapt from defending her virtue to an inquiry about her musical talents. Regretfully she thought the change of subject was for the best, since this protective *sexy* man had, only moments ago, given her a look that melted her shoelaces.

Just answer the man's question, Meredith. It wasn't as if she knew *nothing* about flirting. She'd learned a few things from her brief engagement to that smooth-talking, two-timing accountant. Then again, what kind of fool would court a flirtation with a military man? A man like her father, who had run his wife, his home and his family as if they were extensions of his command.

Holding his gaze for the longest moment, Meredith carefully chewed and swallowed a bite of sandwich. "I play piano and also the flute," she admitted. "Both instruments deemed suitable for a young girl." She wrinkled her nose and laughed.

A laugh hollow enough that Ace arched an eyebrow.

She shrugged, deciding to elaborate. "My mother wasted a fortune on music lessons before it dawned on the general that I was his only option to keep the St. James name marching through military history. Dear old Dad promptly exchanged my Mary Janes for a pair of combat boots." Meredith set her sandwich aside. She'd lost her appetite.

Ace thought about what he knew of her father. Mostly foxhole talk, and he didn't know how reliable that was. General St. James had a reputation for being tough—a good characteristic in battle. But what if you were his beautiful daughter who was expected to fill a son's shoes?

"I can't see that it's affected your femininity," he muttered, stumbling a bit on the word. He flushed when it became apparent his honesty had embarrassed her, too. "I meant that as a compliment, St. James. Maybe it has to do with this being jeans country, and you're always in . . . dresses."

She toyed with her discarded sandwich. "I'll have to buy a pair of jeans, I guess. I'm not trying to be different. It's just . . ." She glanced out the window. "I doubt you'll understand."

He reached out and touched the small pearl earring embedded in her left ear. "Try me," he said, his voice gravelly.

She felt as if he'd brushed her soul. Still, she struggled to find the strength to rebuff him. "Don't," she whispered. "Believe me, you're better off with Ruby."

Her eyes looked so bleak that Ace wanted to take her in his arms—to somehow reassure her that everything would be all right. Instead, he let his fingers fall away from her ear, recalling the only other time he'd tried to protect someone. His mother. Ace could never be the man she wanted, either. Toward the end she had called him by that cowboy's name. *Jarrod.* Ace had hated that.

"We were discussing your music," he said suddenly, turning their conversation down safer avenues.

She shed her gloom at once. "Well, I decided since the money spent on lessons was already spent, it shouldn't be a total waste. Music helps me relax. Do you play?"

Ace shook his head. A rueful smile tugged at his lips.

"No, I guess you wouldn't." Her offhand shrug said more—that she had placed him in a pigeonhole. Macho Texan. Army major.

He read the implication and smiled. "Don't be so hasty to judge me, St. James. I used to think I'd someday be the Van Cliburn of the Southwest."

"You? Classical?"

He looked indignant. "Wild and rebellious as I was, I would have sold my soul to be able to play Schubert or Chopin. But then, you'd probably say I did sell my soul. Because when the man finally came to town I couldn't scare up the price of a ticket. So while San Antonio's elite basked in his music, I helped shake down his limo."

"You didn't!"

"I did. Then I felt so damn guilty that I got the name of his booking agency and sent them my portion of the take. Which I suppose should have told me that I wasn't cut out for a life of crime. But when you're poor, lack direction and have fallen through the cracks in the educational system, you get cast in a certain mold and it's hard to break out."

"Breaking out of any mold is difficult," she murmured. "But the limitations that hold people captive aren't always socioeconomic."

Sadness darkened her eyes again. Ace couldn't deal with her pity. He might wish things were different, but there was no changing fact. He was his father's son. And she was her father's daughter.

"Are you finished eating?" he asked abruptly, having hardly touched a bite himself.

She visibly shifted gears, stiffened a bit and nodded.

Ace turned toward the sink to pick up the empty deli sacks.

"I'll clean up," she insisted, rushing over to shoo his hands away. "Goodness, where are my manners? Not only haven't I thanked you for feeding me, my yammering has probably kept you from something important."

Ace glanced at his watch. He was surprised by the lateness of the hour. "Actually, I do need to get going. I have an appointment with Colonel O'Dell. I nearly forgot. His wife needs some information from you."

"From me?" Meredith closed the refrigerator door with a bang. "What about?" The guarded look was back in her eyes.

Ace waved a hand to dispel her concern. "Saturday is the annual all-service ROTC ball in Lubbock. Mrs. O'Dell has to turn our seating list in tomorrow. Do you think you might take a date?"

"I beg your pardon?"

"A date—as in a member of the opposite sex. This is a big deal in ROTC, St. James. A banquet, a formal dance, the whole nine yards."

She bit her lip. "I . . . I don't think I'll even go. Look at this mess. I doubt I'll have dug my way out by Saturday."

"I'm afraid it's a command performance for instructors."

She frowned. "And I guess everyone pairs up."

It was a statement, not a question. If he was any kind of nice guy, he'd volunteer to find her an escort.

Well, he thought sourly, he'd never claimed to be nice. He did always try to be honest, though. "I, uh, I'm not taking a date this year. I'll give you a lift if you'd like."

Relief edged out her slight frown. A smile bloomed, transforming her features into a beauty that made him ache.

"Thank you," she said. "I didn't relish the idea of locating a strange city at night. And don't worry, I promise to disappear into the woodwork the moment we arrive."

When he looked confused, she clarified her statement. "You know, so people won't think we're a couple or anything."

Grabbing his hat, he strode quickly past the piano that had triggered too many turbulent memories. *She* created turbulence in him. He should just thank her for being intuitive. After all, he didn't want to see any rumors start, either. She'd only said thirty different ways that she didn't want to get involved with him. Which was damn fine as far as he was concerned.

If that was true, why, after he'd bidden her a terse goodbye and stepped out into a brilliant afternoon, did it seem to Ace as if a terrible dark cloud had descended on his life?

CHAPTER EIGHT

THURSDAY, ACE STRODE into his office and into chaos. He was in no mood to deal with problems today. Yesterday after he'd left Meredith at her apartment, his day had gone straight to hell. Not only had Colonel O'Dell balked at paying for air-force uniforms, while Ace was there, the old man had gotten a call from Meredith's father that smacked of blackmail. As if that wasn't enough, the visit he'd had later with Ruby ended in a less-than-satisfactory resolution. Hence another sleepless night.

Several cadets were clustered around Captain St. James's desk, each trying to outshout the other. No one realized Ace had come in.

"Attention!" The one word spoken in deadly precision brought silence, except for a mad scramble of bodies trying to find space in which to salute.

"Now," he said softly, "before I place anyone at ease, I want to hear from one person at a time. Cadet Corporal Wellington, suppose you start."

"Well, sir, Captain St. James picked up our shoulder ropes to be cleaned for the parade tomorrow. Today, when we came to get them, we discovered that one full bag of gold braid isn't gold but black."

"Black?"

"Yes, sir. Jet black."

Whatever Ace had expected the problem to be, it wasn't this. "Captain St. James," he said, singling her out, "what do you think happened? I've never had to deal with ropes that magically change color before."

"Major, sir!" Her eyes and her words denied wrong-doing on her part. "I collected a rope from each cadet as you ordered and put them in bags provided by the sergeant. Then I filled out the paperwork and dropped the bundles at the pickup station. Standard procedure, just the way he said."

Ace placed his briefcase on his desk and dropped his hat on top. "All right. At ease, everyone. But that doesn't mean I want to hear you chattering like magpies. Show me the problem." The huddle of cadets parted, and Ace could see the mound of black ropes piled on Meredith's desk.

"Where's Sergeant Sutton?" he asked Meredith as he cut across to her desk and picked up a handful of the ruined braid.

"He had a dental appointment, sir. I signed the receipt for these bags," she said unhappily. "I should have checked them, but I didn't."

"They're stiff," he exclaimed. "Like they've been spray painted."

"That would be my guess, too." She looked unhappier still.

Ace passed a hand over his clean-shaven jaw and frowned as he mentally calculated the cost of replacement. Provided they could *find* replacements. It came to him then. "Those no good..." He snapped his fingers. "We've been had by the air force, guys," he said, turning to the cadets, a wicked grin replacing his frown. "We copped their uniforms, they pilfered our gold rope."

The faces ringing him fell. "But what'll we do, sir?" Cadet Sergeant Jefferson asked. "The parade is tomorrow."

"First, apologize to Captain St. James for the way you badgered her. Then I suggest someone get on the horn and call the supply sergeant at the fort. Ask if they have gold rope in stock."

Ace couldn't wait to see Frank. Couldn't wait to tell the old buzzard that they'd be deducting the price of braid from the bill for the uniforms. Anticipation was sweet, even if Ace was beginning to agree with Frank—these pranks were getting out of hand.

Once apologies were tendered, he suggested the cadets retire to the student office to take care of their calls. "I've got papers to read," he told them. "Let me know if you run into trouble with supply."

Cadet Captain Granelli hung back until the others had gone. "Major, sir," he said, sounding more subdued than Ace had ever seen this brash young man. "About the papers, sir, and the ball..."

"Yes, Cadet?" Ace prompted. "Spit it out. What about the papers and the ball?"

"Will we know today whether or not we get to go?"

Ace felt bad about dragging this out but, dammit, they had to learn. "I'm not promising a thing, Vinnie. Surely you see how the cost of these so-called jokes is mounting. As a rule, you know I'd be the last person to stand in the way of fun. But even I think things have gone too far. If you want a word of advice, Cadet, I'd suggest you police your own ranks a little better. As for my decision, I'll make it sometime tomorrow."

"Yes, sir," Granelli mumbled. He did manage a smart salute at the door.

Ace sighed, sat down and picked up the first paper.

Meredith brought him a cup of coffee.

"Thanks. But you don't have to wait on me."

"I know. You look a little ragged around the edges, though."

He took a bracing swig. "Colonel O'Dell hit the ceiling over those air-force blues," he said. "And it was a mistake to see Ruby. She went to pieces, started bawling and saying she'd do away with herself. Scared the hell out of me, so I didn't break off clean the way I intended. Now I feel like a louse."

Ace elected not to bring up the call from Meredith's father that pressed Colonel O'Dell to involve her in classes where Ace didn't want her meddling. Such as nuclear warfare, tactics and weapons. Wouldn't that be fun? Bombs falling and her instructing everyone to smile and wave at the guys dropping them. Truth be known, Ace was steamed at Meredith. For all her hints about not hitting it off with her old man, if she hadn't bellyached to him, how in hell would Daddy know what she was or wasn't teaching?

Meredith interrupted his musing. "Do you think Ruby is capable of suicide?"

"Suicide? God, Meredith!" Ace lost some of his tan.

"Isn't that what doing away with oneself means, Major? I happen to think it's a subject that can't be ignored or sugarcoated."

He rubbed his neck with a flat hand. "You're right. It's just that I don't have a clue whether she was serious or only being melodramatic. We met when she was still married to Roy. Since the divorce, I've dated her some. But... I'm beginning to think I don't know the woman at all." He glanced up, looking miserable. "What would you suggest, Captain? You're the counselor."

Meredith rose and paced the floor between their desks. "She needs to talk with someone trained to listen for certain signals, trouble signs. I don't know if she'll open up to me, but I could try. Why don't you invite her to the parade tomorrow? I'll try to work in a casual chat."

"I have to ride the bus with the cadets performing in the ceremony."

"That's perfect, then. Tell Ruby I'll pick her up."

He didn't say anything, just rolled up his shirtsleeves and leaned back in his chair to stare up at the ceiling.

"What?" she asked him sharply. "You want to help her, don't you?"

His silvery eyes grew stormy. "Help her, yes. But not foster false expectations. I've dated a lot of women, St. James, Ruby Tindall among them. At no time did the words 'will you marry me' cross my lips."

Meredith flattened her palms on his desk. "Unfortunately when it comes to love, men and women rarely speak the same language, Major."

"What do you mean by that? I don't say things I don't mean to get a woman into my bed, if that's what you're driving at."

No, Meredith thought, taking in his broad shoulders, his thick dark hair and those killer eyes that'd seduce a saint, the major wouldn't need many words to give a woman the wrong impression.

"Look," she said, straightening. "I'm not accusing you of anything. I'm only trying to say that sometimes even honesty can be misconstrued. Some men have a way of looking at a woman that closes out everything and everyone else. That in itself can make a woman feel like she's number one in his life. Or a man might be a toucher. Touching sends strong messages."

She flushed, remembering how Ace tended to place his palm at the small of her back when they walked. She recalled the sensation of heat radiating from his fingertips. And, yesterday, he'd touched her earring with his thumb and forefinger, his eyes strangely soft. The memory sent a shiver up her spine. She trotted briskly back to her desk.

Meredith's words left Ace uncomfortable. He guessed he'd have to say he was guilty on all counts. Perhaps he lacked the sensitivity to be aware of other people's reactions, especially women's. The army did its best to stamp out every shred of a man's softness. Apparently in his case they'd done a damn good job. At least until St. James blew in. She provoked memories Ace had thought long dead. Sparked feelings that left him vulnerable. And vulnerable men weren't effective leaders.

"So," she prodded him from across the room, "are you going to ask Ruby to the parade?"

Sighing, he dropped the paper he'd been trying to read. Ineffective leader or not, what kind of man would refuse and take a chance that Ruby might do something foolish?

"I'll ask her," he said. "In the morning you can just show up. Tell her Colonel O'Dell decided at the last minute that I needed to ride the bus with the cadets. Which he did," Ace hastened to add.

"Good plan, Major. That'll give her less opportunity to back out."

"A good plan, provided you watch what you say on my behalf, St. James. Now, if you don't mind, I have a pile of essays and reports to wade through."

She smiled. "I don't mind. Would you like me to take your class at 0930?"

Ace's first inclination was to say no. Then he remembered Colonel O'Dell's parting shot—that General St. James would consider it a personal favor if the major would take Meredith under his wing. Or words to that effect. The implication made him furious. It was ironic that today he needed her help. Taking the class would be a simple matter, though, of handing out tests and monitoring to see that no one cheated.

"Okay, Captain," he said, shocking her. "I'll take you up on the offer." Standing, he handed her the tests and gave her a brief rundown, adding, "Would you stop by the student office after class to see what our cadets found out about the braid? I'm going to surprise Frank with lunch and that bag of black ropes."

"Give him enough rope," she said nimbly, "and if we're lucky, he'll hang himself."

Ace laughed. "Why, Captain, I wouldn't have thought you social workers were the vindictive sort."

She made a face and headed for the door. "If I'm going to be accused of being insubordinate, I might as well live up to the reputation."

Ace sat there smiling even after she'd left. He was still smiling when Sergeant Sutton returned from his trip to the dentist.

"Something tickle your funny bone, sir?" Sutton asked as he took off his cap and sat down at his computer.

Ace leaned forward, wiping the grin from his face. "It's these papers, Sergeant." He bent the truth. "We have some real comedians in our cadre."

"Uh, if you say so, sir. Somehow I doubt Colonel Loudermilk will agree. It's all over campus what the air force did to our ropes."

"Damn," Ace said. "I pity the ones responsible. But I was going to rat on them, anyway. Since Frank's so all-fired hot to charge us for the uniforms, I'm going to demand restitution for our shoulder ropes. This whole thing is mushrooming, Sergeant."

"Yes," the other man agreed, "but rivalry between the blue and the green will be around long after you two retire."

"Maybe. That doesn't mean I want it to get out of hand while I'm in charge."

"You'll have a captive audience tomorrow, going to the parade, sir."

"I suppose." Ace wasn't enthusiastic. "I hate delivering those kick-butt lectures. I always suspect that when an officer throws his weight around, he's asking for more rebellion."

The sergeant pursed his lips. "Captain St. James said something like that earlier. Seems you two think alike on that score, sir."

"Not hardly." Ace scowled. "I'm no commando, but I'm no damn dove, either, Sutton. I'm an officer in the U.S. Army. Tomorrow, those meatheads are going to get hit between the eyes. Bank on it."

A THUNDERSTORM HAD BLOWN in during the night, taking the edge off an unusually hot spring. Ace would have welcomed the respite, except that skies were ominous and there was a threat of tornadoes. The cadets scheduled to march were keyed up. Ace himself was jumpy. Partly because he wanted his cadre to make a good showing for visiting brass and partly because he was worried about how St. James was faring with Ruby.

Ace couldn't help feeling he was somehow guilty of hiding behind the captain's skirts—which in itself probably made him snappier than usual. It was the only excuse for the way he bit off Sergeant Jefferson's head when the kid asked a simple question about whether or not the major had made his decision. "No, I haven't, Sergeant, and if one more of you asks me before I make up my mind, the answer's going to be no across the board on general principle. Those were the sorriest damn bunch of papers I've ever read. Twelve-year-olds heading off to summer camp could have done better. I wasn't expecting Pulitzer-prize material, mind you, but I did think some of you had guts enough to give me truth, not fiction. Furthermore, you may want to spend Saturday setting up a car wash. I'm not budgeted for this extra gold braid." He flicked Corporal Wellington's gleaming new ropes to make his point.

The bus was silent then, except for a sudden crack of lightning outside the window and the faint roll of thunder that was fortunately behind them, not out toward the fort. Ace's lecture wasn't the mild one he'd planned to deliver, but sometimes a man had to get tough.

Even then it was so out of character that by the time the bus pulled through the gates at Fort Freeman, he regretted having taken out his bad mood on his cadets. He climbed out of the bus first and noticed the wind had picked up considerably. It cut a cold swath through the jacket of his dress uniform. Overhead, the flags of country, state and army stretched out at full attention in the brisk gulf wind. On the spur of the moment, he decided to make a substitution in his color guard. The sophomore he'd selected to carry the flag bearing the gold-and-green ROTC leadership shield was a lightweight.

"Cadet Corporal Larson," he called to the young redhead who was exiting the bus. "Let Cadet Corporal

Kwan carry the rifle. You adjust the harness and carry the shield flag."

"Yes, sir!" If her surprised drawl hadn't told him how pleased she was, her ear-to-ear grin would have.

"Keep a firm seat on it," he reminded her, "and make sure it rides below the Stars and Stripes. You've got a good four inches' height on Kwan." A diplomat, Ace said nothing about the few extra pounds.

"Do you think we're really going to have a tornado?" asked a low smoky voice from behind him.

Whirling, Ace stared down into Meredith's guarded eyes. "We're under a watch, not a warning," he said. "Warnings are more severe, but don't discount either one. If you hear sirens, take cover. You've been through hurricanes, haven't you, Baltimore?" he teased, reaching out to push a windblown curl from her forehead. Then, because he remembered what she'd said yesterday about the messages touching could give off, he dropped his hand and curled his fingers into a loose fist.

She didn't seem to notice his reversal. "Hurricanes occasionally whipped in off Chesapeake Bay. But you get more warning with a hurricane. Tornadoes are so... so unpredictable."

Peering behind her, he said, "Speaking of unpredictable, did Ruby decide to stay home or what?"

Meredith shook her head. "No, she's staked out a place in the front row. I didn't tell her I was coming to offer you my help."

"Everything's under control here. How's Ruby?"

"I think she's glad to be out of the house. On the drive I got an unabridged edition of her life story. It's not been easy for her."

"Did you get a reading on her psyche?" he asked anxiously.

"I have a feeling she always uses tears and threats to get her way. Sounds to me like her ex-husband gets the same song and dance. You should know that she expects you to take her home. She made no bones about my riding on the bus in your place. It's okay by me," Meredith said hurriedly. "Since you'll have my car, it'll give you a reason to drop her and run."

"I'd rather not, considering, but..." He shrugged. "I did invite her to the parade. And, Meredith... thanks. It's a relief to get your opinion."

"Yes, well, you're welcome. Let me give you my car keys now. Afterward, I'll head straight for the bus."

"I sat on the cadets pretty hard on the way over here. They'll probably be hyper on the trip back to campus."

"That's okay. I need something to take my mind off tornadoes."

"Toughen up, St. James. Who do you think they call out in times of disaster?"

She made a face at him, turned, then tossed a reply back over her shoulder. "Who, Major? The Boy Scouts?"

Ace was still laughing when he caught up with his cadets. In spite of the storm warnings, his day had brightened considerably.

MEREDITH HUDDLED in the front row beside Ruby, who had selected the spot, then complained about it throughout the parade.

The speeches and presentations were long-winded and self-serving, as Meredith knew they would be. Having cut her teeth on tedious military events, she undoubtedly found it easier to suffer through than Ruby did.

Weather notwithstanding, Meredith took pride in their cadets' presentation of the colors—even if Betsy did

forget to look serious. More than once the girl's freckled face broke out in a wide grin, and Meredith couldn't
help grinning back.

In Meredith's estimation, the entire parade was worth
standing in the cold. Apparently she didn't dislike everything about the army. The best news, however, was
when someone down the line whispered that the tornado watch had ended.

Ruby immediately took off, her mission to locate Ace,
and somehow, as the crowd broke and dispersed, Meredith missed him in passing. She'd intended to congratulate him on a successful showing; she knew he must
have spent long hours drilling the cadets. Well, she'd
catch him back at the office.

Boy, had Ace been right about the noise level. The
cadets were so wound up she didn't have the heart to yell
at them. After all, this was new and exciting stuff to kids
who'd chosen the army as a career. At least, she sin-
cerely doubted it had been forced on any of them—
which might just be the crux of her problem. The army
today stood for freedom of choice. Why couldn't her
father see she'd been denied that?

Sometimes Meredith wished she'd gotten out. She'd
thought the advanced degree would, if nothing else, help
her better understand her feelings. But there was no denying she still carried a lot of emotional baggage.

The question was, did it—as Ace Bannister believed—hinder her ability to teach future soldiers?

Fortunately the bus pulled onto campus and she was
kept from delving too deeply. "Okay, Cadets," Meredith warned as they left the bus, "Major Bannister wants
these colors stored in apple-pie order. I think he'll do an
inspection, so don't give him reason to chew out your
fannies."

"Captain St. James," someone called, "do you know if the major's going to let us go to the ball tomorrow night?"

She shook her head. "And if I were you, I wouldn't bug him." It remained her last comment. Lord, she was beginning to sound like him.

Sergeant Sutton had left her a note. He was out running errands for the colonel's wife. When Ace finally walked in, Meredith was at her desk speculating as to whether Mrs. O'Dell was anything like her own mother. She sprang to attention and took immediate note that something was wrong.

"What happened?" she asked, seconds after he growled, "At ease," and dropped her car keys into her outstretched palm.

Ace ripped off his hat, sailed it across his desk and threw himself into his chair. "Have you ever been really, really wrong about someone?" he muttered, raking a hand through his hair.

"Ruby?" she asked, instead of answering his question.

"Yeah, Ruby. Can you believe it? On the way home, she came right out and admitted she's been sleeping with Ron Holmes for the past six months. She's going to the ball with him, too." Ace spun his chair toward the wall. "All this came out when I suggested, once again, that she look into family counseling."

Meredith was so shocked it didn't register that Ace had recommended counseling. "She was sleeping with both you and Ron?"

He whipped his chair back around, his eyes dark with fury. "I never—we...went to the club, that's all. To dance. Do you think I'd spend the night with someone whose kids are old enough to know what's going on in

Mama's bedroom?'' His anger suddenly seemed to fade into chagrin. "What's hard is that I'm the last to know. You know how rumors usually fly."

The information he'd just delivered loosened the knot in Meredith's stomach. "I'm sorry," she said, surprised to find that she really meant it. "I don't know Captain Holmes well, but I know his type. Frankly, I can't see him marrying her. Sad thing is, her kids will end up the big losers."

"That's called *life*," he said cynically.

"Will it bother you to see them together at the ball?" she asked gently.

He laced his hands behind his head and tilted back in his chair. "No." He snapped forward. "But if I asked you not to disappear on me, would you think I was using you?"

She stared for a moment at the tangle of dark curls drooped appealingly over his brow. "Would you be?"

"Absolutely not."

The knot that had eased tightened again. "All right. I believe you." With some effort, she tore her gaze away from his.

Somehow Ace knew it had cost her to give him that vote of confidence. Admittedly he was on shaky ground himself. He had come very close to snatching back his request. Even if he and Ruby weren't going steady, the rumors now would be embarrassing. He'd better leave before Meredith had time to reconsider and change her mind about being seen with some dumb schmo.

"Hey, great. Can you handle things here? I need to go save the day for a few guys who've been running around campus with faces hanging to their knees. If I don't get back before you leave... shine up your dancing shoes.

Lubbock's quite a distance, so I'll pick you up at 1400 hours. See you tomorrow!''

Meredith could do little more than nod as he grabbed his hat and left, actually whistling a little off-key as he went.

SATURDAY, AS MEREDITH opened boxes and found special places for personal treasures, she contemplated the evening ahead. It had been a while since she'd gone on a date, and longer since she'd looked forward to one this much.

She moved a vase of silk flowers and reminded herself that he hadn't *called* it a date. He'd only asked her not to disappear and leave him on his own. A sigh slipped out. When had he become such a major attraction? Ha! More like major abomination. After a stern mental shake, she got back to the task of unpacking.

Later, when she unearthed her freestanding, full-length mirror, Meredith suddenly wished she weren't stuck wearing a uniform. Men always looked so dashing in theirs. Women looked...utilitarian. They looked practical. She refused to say frumpy, although others did.

Short hair might have seemed chic when she'd first indulged the whim to irritate her father. But now it struck her as another minus in the column of feminine attributes—not that she was counting.

Ace probably preferred long hair. Most men did, or so she'd read once in some women's magazine. But if he'd wanted a leggy statuesque partner who had a plethora of hair, he probably wouldn't have invited her. Would he?

Resigned to her fate, Meredith began her beauty routine by soaking for an hour in a bubble bath generously doused with her favorite gardenia scent.

Men, she thought, sinking in up to her chin. They probably never worried about a date the way women did.

ACE PACED his bedroom, feeling as nervous as a kid contemplating his first date. He'd picked up his uniform from the cleaners and it had reeked of cleaning fluid when he took it out of the plastic. So he'd hung it on his back porch to air while he showered and shaved.

He'd taken too long deciding what flowers to get Meredith, and now he had to rush. Last night, on impulse, he'd gone car hunting. He'd spent precious hours today signing papers. He had, however, become the proud new owner of a ritzy silver-gray Lexus.

Leaving his Firebird at the dealership had been like leaving a piece of his heart. But the Lexus drove like a dream, and it did have a certain class his old car lacked. As for the flowers, they wouldn't have been so much trouble if every cadet in the cadre hadn't been at the florist's picking up corsages. Ace didn't want to be razzed, so he'd driven back and forth outside the shop waiting for the place to empty. Which was just as well. During one of his passes, he happened to see Betsy Larson's boyfriend walk out with a vase of cut flowers. That was when it dawned on him—Meredith couldn't wear a corsage with her uniform.

In the end, after much agonizing, he chose a single salmon pink rosebud and had placed it in a sterling-silver vase. Now, as he looked in the mirror and smoothed an astringent skin bracer over his close shave, Ace wondered if maybe he shouldn't have bought the pale yellow orchids, instead.

He dashed out in his underwear to grab his uniform off the porch. Then, because Meredith noticed such things, he took care to get every medal straight and his tie in a perfect knot.

Lord, would he have been this nervous if he'd gone to the high school prom? No sense wondering. The guys he'd hung out with hadn't exactly been the type to attend school dances.

As he climbed into the Lexus and swallowed a gulp of new-car air, Ace reminded himself that he was thirty-five damn years old. This was no big deal. He'd been to plenty of army shindigs. And most of them had meant a whole lot more to his career than this one.

For pity's sake, he wasn't even sure the lady he was on his way to collect considered this a date. What if she backed out at the last minute?

She didn't. In fact, the way Meredith jerked the door open almost the instant he knocked, Ace guessed she'd been watching at the window.

"A rose," she breathed when he thrust the vase into her hands. "It's beautiful. But you shouldn't have." She stroked the petals lightly.

Ace shrugged—nonchalantly, he hoped, as every nerve in his body had gone on red alert. God, her hair shone like a platinum crown, and her skin gleamed like pearls. A trace of brown enhanced eyes that reminded him of rich butterscotch candy. Tiny diamonds winked at her ears.

A month ago he wouldn't have noticed. Now everything about this woman fascinated him.

"Do we have a minute for me to put this in my bedroom?" she asked, burying her nose in the exquisite bud.

"Lucky rose," he murmured, stepping inside.

"Oh, don't come in," she said, suddenly flustered. "Except for the kitchen and my bedroom, it looks like one of your Texas tornadoes hit here."

"I'll wait right here by the door. Don't be long. We need to get going." Though, he'd prefer not to let her out of his sight.

She wasn't gone a minute, and had her door keys out to lock up when she returned. "Where's your car?" she asked, trailing him down the stairs.

"You're looking at my new wheels." With a flourish he whipped open the passenger door of the Lexus.

She gaped. "You're kidding."

"What? You think you've got the corner on flashy silver cars?"

"Oh, sure. Mine just looks like a poor relation."

"You think the car is me?"

"Well—" her eyes twinkled "—I guess it's more in keeping with your age."

"Yeah, that's what I thought. Although the showroom next door had a sweet red convertible. But *Consumer Guide* says its safety stats stink."

Meredith burrowed into the smooth leather. "This *feels* safe, and it smells heavenly. I love the smell of a new car."

"You smell heavenly," he said unexpectedly. "What is that you're wearing?

"Gardenia," she told him. "It's not overpowering, is it?"

"Gardenia," he murmured softly. "I, ah, couldn't place it. Too bad you can't wear a ball gown tonight. I picture you in champagne lace with a gardenia in your hair."

"Why, Major, I had no idea you were such a romantic."

He arched a brow. "Ace. Tonight you've gotta call me Ace."

She laughed a throaty laugh that spun out into a mellow chuckle. "I'll try to remember. It's something about the uniform, I'm afraid. At home we always called my father by his rank. When I got to be a teen, I wondered if my mother did that in the bedroom, too. I swear I was ten before I knew his name was Harding."

"I promise you, lady, beneath this uniform is an everyday man. Whether this outfit's on or off, I want to be called Ace."

Meredith cast him a sidelong glance. Somehow, imagining the manly flesh residing beneath that uniform set her pulse skyrocketing. She thought it best to let his remark slide and studied the flat fields of cotton, allowing him to concentrate on driving.

Ace didn't find the silence awkward. He liked that she didn't always need to be talking. The drive was surprisingly quick, even without conversation. Mrs. O'Dell's directions led him right to the building on the university campus where the ball was being held, and his elegant new car fit right in with the rented limousines.

Meredith was surprised when she was seated next to him at the banquet table, since neither of them had told the colonel's wife about their change in plans. As second-ranking officer in the ROTC program, Ace sat across from Colonel O'Dell, and Meredith faced his wife. Dean Caldwell and his wife were on their right. Next were two nursing instructors, which placed Ron Holmes and Ruby Tindall too far away for idle chitchat.

The food was good and spicy, the speeches short and sweet. Meredith found Mrs. O'Dell funny and unpretentious. As a result, she was definitely mellower than usual by the time the band began to play.

Ace let two songs go by before he asked her to dance. The first was more or less reserved for senior officers. The second for ranking ROTC students and their dates. Then came a slow dreamy tune out of the seventies. Ace gathered Meredith into his arms, and in spite of a small clash of brass buttons, their steps soon flowed together across the polished floor.

Twice they were bumped rudely from behind, and before either could murmur an "Excuse us," Ron Holmes swished Ruby past, issuing a hostile glare.

"What do you suppose that was all about?" Ace muttered, moving Meredith to the edge of the floor to give the other couple a wide berth.

"One-upmanship?" Meredith ventured.

"You think? Me, I'm just glad Ruby's not suicidal." He sighed and nuzzled his partner's ear and wished the room were a little darker so he could steal a kiss. During a fancy dip, he did manage to sneak one in.

But after three more collisions apparently engineered deliberately by Ron and his date, Ace suggested they sit out a number.

"It's not my preference, understand," he said. "Short of causing a scene, though, I don't know what to do."

"I'm sorry. Maybe if you'd brought someone else…"

"Don't even finish that thought," he warned. "Ron's mad because I pressured him about the colonel's stats." Ace ran a finger over her cheek. "We'll go dancing soon, somewhere in town."

She nodded, thinking that was highly unlikely. "Shall we leave? I'm pretty tired from unpacking."

"We can't leave before the commander. Plus, I want you to see the presentation of arms—all the cadets and their dates walking through the arch."

"I'd like that."

And it was pretty. But by the time the band resumed playing, Meredith was fighting to keep her eyes open.

"That's it," Ace said when he noticed her eyes drifting shut for the umpteenth time. "The O'Dells just left. Let's go."

The night air woke Meredith up a bit. On the drive home, they touched on a wide range of topics, surprised to find they had similar tastes in music, movies and, strangely, even sports.

They'd passed the outskirts of town and talk was winding down when Meredith stretched and said around a yawn, "I read in the paper that the rodeo starts at the end of next week. There's a carnival, a craft show and a dance. I've never been to a rodeo. I suppose it's old hat to you, but if you're planning to go," she finished shyly, "I wouldn't mind tagging along."

Ace gripped the wheel hard. His stomach took a sickening plunge.

When he didn't answer, Meredith glanced at him as he parked in front of her building. "If you already have plans to go with someone else, just say so, Ace. It won't be the end of the world if I have to go alone." For some reason, though, she was very disappointed. He climbed out of the car and walked around to open her door.

"I don't go to rodeos, Meredith. I'll take you anywhere else. But not to a rodeo."

"All right." She didn't understand his vehemence, but she respected his right to say no. It was just that... Didn't he know her well enough by now to explain?

It disturbed her more than she cared to admit. Enough that when he tried to kiss her good-night, she evaded his lips. "Thanks for the lovely flower and for taking me."

She unlocked her door and slipped inside. "See you Monday," she said, withdrawing quickly.

The closed door seemed so final that for a moment Ace wondered where he'd gone wrong. Couldn't she see his feelings about rodeos had nothing to do with her?

Common sense told Ace that in all probability his old man no longer competed. And common sense told him he shouldn't lump all cowboys in one rotten heap. Yet he couldn't stand the thought of Meredith on a dance floor, wrapped in the arms of some slick rodeo cowboy.

CHAPTER NINE

SUNDAY, ACE SLEPT late and awakened when he did only because some ambitious neighbor was out mowing his lawn. That was what he should be doing. Mowing his lawn and pulling weeds. To keep his body moving and his mind off Captain St. James.

Stifling a yawn, he stumbled into a crumpled pair of shorts left on the floor of his closet and went out to the kitchen, where he drank orange juice straight from the carton. He picked up the Sunday paper and gave it a cursory glance. He might have read it more thoroughly had he not come upon a supplement devoted to the rodeo. Disgusted, he threw the whole thing in the trash and stormed outside to rev up his mower.

He was a little more than half-finished when his neighbor motioned him to the fence and handed him a tall glass of iced tea, then plied him with questions about his Lexus. They hung over the fence swapping car stories until the man's wife reminded him there were flowers to plant.

"Thanks for the tea," Ace said. "We'll take a test spin later if you like."

Nodding, the fellow accepted Ace's empty glass and disappeared inside.

Ace's own yard work didn't take as long as he'd figured. Too soon he was at loose ends again.

Back inside, he discovered the sports channel didn't have a decent game on. Not only had he read every book on his shelves, but over the past few weeks he'd lost touch with his single male buddies, too.

If he and Meredith had parted on a more positive note last night, he could pop over there and watch her unpack. Or help. He grimaced. The way things stood, he'd be better off taking in an afternoon movie by himself.

But he didn't want to go alone. Halfheartedly he dialed Sonya Robbins, one of the eligible ladies on his old telephone list. He was trying to remember the last time he'd invited her out. Bowling—several months back. He recalled that she wasn't long on talk. Well, boy howdy, she had no reticence today, Ace grumbled as he hung up. Sonya informed him in no uncertain terms that she hadn't heard from him in five months, and if he thought he could call at the last minute and expect her to jump through hoops, he was mistaken.

Ego stung, Ace wasn't eager to try anyone else. He knew it had been longer than that since he'd dated Lana, a schoolteacher, and Melody, a teller at his bank, was seeing someone steady. Anyway, they'd only met for drinks once after work. Rather than suffer a similar fate at Lana's hands, Ace elected to go to the theater alone.

The movie, a comedy, at least made him laugh. More than once he wished for someone with whom to share the jokes. Someone special. He refused to let Meredith's image creep in.

Afterward, en route home, Ace decided that man wasn't meant to go through life alone. Maybe he needed a dog. Man's best friend and all. Next week he'd stop at the pet store in the mall. Before now, he hadn't lived in one place long enough. But then he decided it might not be such a good idea. After all, in a few weeks he was

scheduled to take an advanced corps of students to the
desert for specialized training. It wouldn't be fair to
board a new pet.

He was less than enthusiastic about the expedition.
Looking on the bright side, though, at least St. James
wouldn't be there to bug him with her gardenia scent and
not-so-innocent earrings.

Damn, what do other single guys do on weekends?

Well, the ones he knew tinkered with cars, drank beer
and watched ball games. Or they sweet-talked their way
into some lady's bed.

Triple damn!

Ace stripped off his shirt, dug out the shorts again and
ran his regular route, plus. He really punished himself
because his mind kept wandering into dangerous territory—namely, toward one Meredith St. James.

Dinner was a peanut-butter-and-jelly sandwich. After washing it down with milk, he meandered next door
to see if his neighbor wanted that test drive. Turned out
they had company. All couples. Weekends were the pits.

In bed by 2100 hours, Ace at last gave in to his fantasies. He lay naked on his bed, arms crossed behind his
head, and tortured himself with thoughts of a certain
lady captain.

The result—another sleepless night.

Monday, for no reason at all, he was late to work.

She sat at her desk polishing her fingernails in a pale,
shell pink color that reminded Ace acutely of the inside
of her ear. "This isn't a damn beauty parlor," he snarled
when she'd capped the bottle and, acting decidedly cool,
slowly got up and came to attention.

Far from cool himself, Ace placed her at ease. Yanking open his closet door, he slammed his hat on the shelf.

"From here on, please take care of your beauty routine at home."

"I made the coffee, dusted all three desks and filed the correspondence left over from Friday," she said, sounding mutinous.

"Why did you do the filing? Where's Sergeant Sutton?"

"His grandson's in town. Don't you remember? He has the next two weeks off. *They're* going to the rodeo."

He'd forgotten, but he'd be damned if he'd touch that loaded statement. Not even with a long bayonet. Ignoring her, he sat at his desk and opened his briefcase.

She drummed her newly polished nails on her desk for several moments. Finally she said, "I wrote down some ideas I have for incorporating a component of compassion into your leadership program, and I made you a copy."

His head popped up over the case.

"Friday's class. The one I took for you," she reminded when he looked blank.

"Compassion?" His eyebrow arched. "The ROTC environment demands that we teach cadets to overcome fear, St. James. We show them how to take charge in any emergency. *Soldiers*—" his tone underscored the term "—are often called upon to perform physical and mental feats beyond normal capabilities. They need guts, St. James. Not compassion."

She fiddled with her bottle of polish and finally dropped it into her center drawer. "I wouldn't expect *you* to change, Major. But I have high hopes that the younger officers can overcome the commando craze."

"St. James, I'm pretty damn sick and tired of your taking potshots at the way I teach. Lord knows," he drawled, "Daddy will pull rank on behalf of his one and only." He snorted. "I'm sure you won't be surprised to hear you now have a class schedule of your own." He snatched the folder from Sutton's desk, thumbed out a page and smacked it down in front of her.

She drew it toward her gingerly. "What did you mean by that nasty crack?"

He waved a hand. "We all have mentors, St. James. Some are more influential than others. By the way, that's your copy. Initial the original and give it back." He slapped it down beside her copy. "When you're finished, please ask Captains Caldwell and Holmes to come in. As they'll be turning over some of their classes, I want everything out in the open."

Meredith remained stuck on his innuendo. Surely he didn't think she'd ask the general for favors! From his curt tone, though, it was obvious that *something* had him ticked off.

Ace returned to his chair. She took her time reading the document. What he'd done was plain. Picked all *safe* classes. Military courtesy, traditions and conduct. She sighed. Maybe the general *had* poked his nose in. He had no use for social workers, either; they'd argued constantly. He believed in rough-and-ready soldiers. Meredith had hoped for more from Ace.

Hiding her disappointment, she scribbled her initials on his stupid original, rose and marched through the workroom to call the others.

As Ace anticipated, Ron Holmes complained.

"Giving St. James all the cushy classes, eh?" Ron sneered. "I think she should get out in the sun and sweat with the rest of us."

Ace quelled him with a glance. "This isn't open for discussion, Captain Holmes. Captain St. James's schedule has been approved by Colonel O'Dell. I'm simply informing you of the changes, effective today.'' He closed the folder, signaling the meeting was at end.

Dean Caldwell had been leaning against a file cabinet. He straightened. "No complaints here. Gives me more time to meet with remedial students. I've thought for a long time that we were short staffed. Welcome to the rat race,'' he said to Meredith, tossing her a casual salute.

It was a start, she supposed. Really, Ace Bannister didn't know how resourceful she could be. There were ways to plant seeds in those cadets' minds, seeds that would sprout and come to life in the form of questions in his classes. Her smile wasn't feigned when she gave Dean a mock bow. "You don't know how glad I am to have something to do besides tag along after you guys.''

Ron muttered something unintelligible and stomped back through the workroom to his own office. He almost ripped the accordion door off its track.

Dean turned to Ace and shrugged. "He'll get over it. Are you ready to take the B-squad out to the fort for rappelling?''

"You bet. Let me give the student office a jingle to see who's available to answer phones. Sutton's on a few days' leave,'' he explained.

"Is rappelling an all-day thing?'' Meredith asked. "I have only one short class this morning, then I'll be free to baby-sit the phones.''

"Will you refrain from redecorating while we're gone?'' Ace demanded, getting to his feet.

She offered a plastic smile. "What? You don't want chintz-covered chairs and lace curtains?'' She gathered the books he'd plunked on her desk, saluted smartly, then sashayed out the front door without a backward glance.

Ace took in the exaggerated sway of her hips. It was a sneaky punch. Below the belt. He dropped into his chair to hide a purely involuntary response.

Dean arched an amused brow. "I'm sure Salome with her seven veils didn't do as much damage to a man's ticker. How's your heart, buddy? In good shape, I hope."

Ace shot him a dark glance. "I thought you were happily married, Caldwell."

"Married doesn't mean brain-dead. What's with you? Suddenly you've become a monk? I can't believe you're immune to St. James."

Ace leaned back and gave a rueful shake of his head. "Would that I were. It has more to do with not mixing business and pleasure." *Her idea, not his.*

"Seemed like you were doing a fair job of it Saturday night. When did this guilty revelation strike?"

"Don't tell me you think it would be politic to pursue a relationship. I'm her superior, Dean—and her daddy hobnobs with *the* commander in chief."

"What difference does that make? She's a woman. You're a man."

"Tell me something I don't know," Ace said dryly.

"So what? You think Daddy-o's going pull out the big guns and say leave my daughter alone? She's not exactly a kid, Ace."

Ace dug his coffee cup out of his drawer and headed into the workroom—a signal that their discussion was over. It would be indiscreet to mention the pressure General St. James had already applied via Colonel O'Dell.

"Let me down a quick cup of coffee, Dean, then I'll change into fatigues and meet you at the bus stop. If you get there first, make sure we have ropes. And check to see those jokers have full packs."

The captain smiled. "Is this your way of telling me to butt out of your love life?"

Ace snorted. "I haven't had a love life in so long the foil packet I stashed probably died of old age."

Dean threw back his head and hooted. "That's serious. Judging by the friction you two generate whenever you're in the same room, my advice, old pal, is to drop by the infirmary and replenish your supply."

"Go on, get outa here. And don't let me hear a word of this coming back to me through your sidekick in there." Ace jerked a thumb toward the room where Ron Holmes had disappeared earlier.

"As if I'd gossip to that dipstick." Caldwell rolled his eyes. Before he left he said softly, "Think on what I've said. I've seen how St. James looks at you. She's plenty interested."

Ace carried his cup into the washroom the two offices shared and mulled over Dean's comments while he changed into battle dress. Captain Caldwell had been on target regarding the friction between him and St. James. From Ace's perspective, it was mostly one-sided. He'd be smart to make tracks before she returned. Her class wasn't but forty minutes long.

He was still stuffing his shirt into his pants when she burst through the front door, shouting that there was a fire in the grassy area between the air-force offices and theirs.

"What?" Ace ran past her, nearly bowling her over.

Meredith righted herself and followed him.

Assessing the low-creeping blaze, Ace saw that it was contained in the field. "Dammit," he muttered as the city fire siren sounded. "Where are those kids with the water balloons when you need 'em? The college prez'll have a fit. You know, a few people could put this out." He turned to Meredith. "We have sprinklers on our perimeter. There's an override valve in the closet. Hit that, while I'll see if Frank has a hose. Wetting the grass might keep the fire from spreading."

She turned at once and ran back inside.

By the time the fire trucks arrived, Ace, Meredith and Colonel Loudermilk were all grimy from smoke and soaked. The field was barely smoldering.

Ace nudged Frank and pointed. "Look there."

In the center of the field, someone had carefully trenched out the words *U.S. Air Force is #1.* It screamed out from the blackened stubble.

Frank was hyperventilating. Ace thought at any moment the man would explode and go into orbit. His eyes bulged and his face turned bright red.

"This has gone too damn far," he bellowed. "I'll find out who's responsible, and when I do I'll kick their tails so hard they'll think they've got a free ride on the lunar lander."

"Maybe the fire was an accident," Ace said, trying to calm the colonel. "Pretty obvious your boys spaded the message, but anyone could have accidentally set it on fire. You don't know they planned it, Frank."

Loudermilk refused to consider the possibility. "They did it. You can bet your boots I'll find the little bastards. Shit!" he exclaimed, his face mottled purple. "Look who's coming. Our favorite VP. Vogle hates ROTC."

"I'm sorry to dump on you, Frank. But I'm late to take a squad rappelling." Ace grabbed Meredith's arm and whisked her away. "If you've never met our esteemed university VP," he hissed, "now is not the time. Vogle is hell on wheels. Frank wasn't kidding. The man hates ROTC."

"Phew, thanks. And you didn't fib. Your bus pulled in already."

"You're wet to the skin, St. James. If you don't have dry things here, feel free to lock up and go home." He turned her toward him, his fingers curved around her upper arm. "I want you to know that was speedy action on your part, Captain. I'm going to make note of this to Colonel O'Dell. You deserve a commendation."

His compliment surprised Meredith. She was used to never quite measuring up. She was also conscious of his nearness. Needing to switch attention from herself, she escaped his hold and made light of his compliment. "Um, I finished unpacking over the weekend. You should stop and take a look on your way home." Then, on the spur of the moment she said, "I could fix dinner. It'd be nice to eat on the balcony. It's not large, but there's room for a small table and two chairs."

Ace fully intended to say no. Except that she sounded so wistful. He said yes, instead.

"Really?" She backed away. "Um, well...do you have any idea what time that might be?"

"Seven at least. Or maybe that's too late?"

"No." She nibbled her lip, wondering if he regretted saying he'd come.

"Seven, then," he said. "I'll bring wine. Red or white?"

She let herself smile. "White, I think. Shouldn't you hurry? The bus might leave without you. Oh, wait—you're wet, too."

"I'll dry hanging out on a cliff," he said, anxious to leave. All the way to the bus he berated himself. If Dean Caldwell ever got wind of this, Ace could count on being heckled unmercifully—especially after all that baloney he'd just fed his friend. But there was no reason for Dean to find out.

Tonight he'd just keep things casual. Ace suddenly realized how arrogant that sounded. As if he thought she had more in mind. He reminded himself that getting moved in and unpacked was a huge accomplishment. Didn't he know what it was like to have a landmark occasion and no one to share it with? Why, she even thought the food he'd brought for lunch was a housewarming gift! It hadn't been, but he could tell stuff like that was important to her. Maybe if he got home early enough, he'd buy her a real gift.

It was pushing seven when Ace got home, tired, sweaty and starved. He would have backed out, but her new phone was unlisted, so he couldn't call to cancel. It took time to clean up and dash out beyond the city limits to a liquor store. Did she know that this town, like many in west Texas, was dry? He'd have to tell her.

Driving back into town, a warm bottle of wine on the seat beside him, Ace debated whether or not he should stop at the mall for a gift.

How long could it take? He was already late.

A plant would be easiest, he supposed, but he sort of knew what he wanted. Sunday, as he'd waited for the movie ahead of his to let out, he'd spent some time window-shopping. A colorful, stained-glass wind chime had caught his eye. She could hang it on her balcony, and he wouldn't have to worry about matching her decor.

Luckily the one he liked was still there, and the clerk was nice enough to wrap it in bright tissue and place it in one of those gift-bag things. Ace thanked her profusely. He hadn't even thought about wrapping.

Dusk had fallen by the time he angled his silver car into a visitors' parking slot. He felt somewhat guilty, because now it might be too dark to eat on the balcony. Taking a deep breath, he stuffed the gift bag inside the sack with the wine, slammed his car door and took the stairs two at a time. Eating inside was just as well, he thought, slicking a nervous hand through his hair. He had a weakness for Texas sunsets. They tended to make him amorous, and amorous wasn't what he wanted to be with St. James.

"Like hell," an interior voice taunted.

Tonight he noticed there was a gap of some minutes between the time he rang the doorbell and when she released the lock, opening the door the length of the chain. "Oh, hi!" She sounded surprised. "I decided you weren't coming."

His "Sorry I'm late" got buried in the rattle as she released the chain and opened the door wide enough for him to enter. Then, for a moment thereafter, Ace was unable to speak. She wore some kind of clinging ivory pants with a matching overdress in lace. It was scoop necked with covered buttons all the way down the front. The top two were casually undone, hinting at cleavage. And at a point below her tiny waist the dress opened to the hem, allowing the form fitting pants to show. Small opals flashed like fire at her ears when she switched on the hall light.

Ace forgot her living room was slightly sunken. He stumbled going in and she put out a hand. "Careful. Honestly, I don't know why architects torture us with sunken living rooms. Lends new meaning to the expression 'Break a leg.' Well," she said, beaming at him. "How do you like it?"

His eyes lingered on her incredibly sexy outfit. "Beautiful," he mumbled, "absolutely bea-utiful." He followed with a soft wolf whistle.

"You're not looking at the room," she accused, with a blush. "Oh, what did I expect? You hated what I did at the office."

Her words sank in and he glanced around the room. Then he wished he hadn't. The warmth and charm hit him right between the eyes. For a minute he felt a rising panic, and some part of him wanted to cut and run. The furnishings were eclectic, and she had another of those screwy prints with all the intersecting lines hanging above her piano. But as a whole, the room touched some long-buried part of Ace. The lonely child he'd once been? Certainly not the tough kid who'd stopped dreaming long ago about coming home every night to something like this.

How could he tell her that in less than a week she'd accomplished the effect he'd been aiming for at his place, but hadn't managed in nearly two years? She'd turned four walls into a home. His heart tripped wildly.

"What is it?" she asked, seeing something like pain flicker in his silvery eyes.

"Uh, nothing," he said, passing an unsteady hand over his jaw. "Looks great. And smells even better," he said, shoving the sack into her hands. "I was afraid you might already have eaten."

She knew there was something bothering him. Casting a glance around, she wondered unhappily what it was. But rather than delve into an area that might make them both uncomfortable, she said, "Actually, you got here by the skin of your teeth." She held up the sack. "Aren't you lucky I allowed time for a glass of wine before dinner? Now, though, you'll have to settle for saving this or have it with the meal."

"It's warm. I was late getting back into town. It's okay by me if you want to chill it and serve it later."

"I have a bottle—Zinfandel—but it's warm, too." She opened the sack and peeked inside. "What's this?" She pulled out the bright gift bag.

"Nothing much. We have mud swallows that nest under the eaves. Like on your balcony. Noise discourages the little beggars."

Meredith pulled out the tissue and unwrapped the wind chime. Holding it aloft, the pieces brushed and tinkled appealingly. "Oh, I love stained glass," she breathed. "Will you help me hang it?"

He took the sack and pulled out the wine. "Stick this in the fridge. I'll hang the chimes."

"Okay, let's trade. Give me the wine. I have a package of plant hooks—I'll bet one of those will work as a hanger. Come to the kitchen. I set up my junk drawer out there."

He chuckled. "In my house every drawer is a junk drawer."

"I doubt that. Oh, this is a local wine." She paused, her hand on the refrigerator door. "Nice. I didn't know this was wine country."

"Texas has everything, Baltimore. And don't you forget it."

She laughed, slid the bottle in to cool, then found the plant hooks. "Don't break your neck out there. I haven't transferred my insurance policy."

As the refrigerator door snicked closed, her perfume wafted up and hit Ace full in the face. It wasn't gardenia this time, but something subtle. Unassuming, but effective. He didn't want to hang the wind chime or talk about insurance. He wanted to kiss her. The desire was so overwhelming he almost ran out the sliding glass doors onto her balcony.

"Light's on your left," she called. "You have five minutes and then, ready or not, I'm bringing dinner."

Ace wished for a cool breeze to douse his sudden passion, but unfortunately the night was warm and a large golden moon was just peeking over the distant trees. It was going to be hard tonight to remind himself that the captain had a powerful mentor. One capable of pulling strings.

"Oh, that's perfect," she said a few moments later when she stepped out and lowered two steaming plates of food onto the prettily set table. "During the day it'll catch the sun, and when I'm out here at night, it'll pick up light from the carriage lamps."

Ace didn't even give the chime a second glance. The carriage lamps also glowed softly against her pale skin and glinted off her short blond curls. The acute pain that slammed into his gut was not caused by hunger. He didn't breathe again until she went inside to get another dish.

When she promptly stuck her head back out to ask if he thought chilled glasses would work to cool the wine, he said yes, because he felt in bad need of alcohol-induced courage. But after he pulled the cork, filled their glasses and took a seat across from her—as that first swallow warmed a trail to his stomach—Ace thought perhaps he'd made a mistake. He didn't need the added jolt of wine. Wondering what it would be like to undo the rest of those darned buttons had suddenly become an almost irresistible temptation.

"So tell me about Texas," she prompted once they'd both eaten a few bites. "Have you ever been to the Alamo?"

Ace had grown up in San Antonio, but for the life of him he couldn't remember one pertinent fact about the Alamo.

She cocked her head and ventured a smile. He hadn't said two words since she'd served the food. Goodness, did he hate herbed chicken or glazed carrots? Or was it her? Trying not to let her smile falter, Meredith picked up the bottle and refilled both glasses. "This is good wine," she murmured.

"Yes, it is," he agreed, practically draining his glass in one gulp. "It's warm out here," he muttered, popping the top button of his short-sleeved shirt.

She picked up her wineglass and settled back in her chair. "Sitting out in the evening like this is a treat for me. But we could go inside if you'd like. I'm sorry you don't like your meal." Her sentences tripped over one another, not from nervousness but because when he opened his shirt and exposed tufts of dark hair, Meredith found her thoughts straying to other hungers. Hungers of the type that had been running amok since he'd walked in wearing gray slacks that matched his eyes and a blue knit shirt that showed off his beautifully tanned biceps.

Ace blanched. "Forgive my bad manners. The food's great. Better than great. Truth is, you have me at a loss for words, Meredith." He poured them each more wine.

"Seeing you like this—" he waved a hand expansively "—your home, your gourmet cooking, the way you're dressed . . . I have a hard time remembering you've been through West Point."

She pulled in a deep breath and turned to study the moon. "Is it so important that you remember?" she asked softly. Just for tonight she didn't want to be military. And she didn't want him to be, either.

He ate two more bites of the tender chicken before he picked up his wineglass, touched it to hers and grinned. "It's important, but how about if for tonight we forget *why*."

Meredith was slow to respond. At last she grasped the slender stem of her glass and clinked it lightly with his.

"Welcome to west Texas," he murmured.

A mischievous smile curved her lips. "Remember the Alamo!" They both laughed then and polished off everything in sight. She offered him apple pie for dessert, but he declined, saying he was too full.

Ace helped carry the dishes inside. She insisted he leave them in the sink. "I'll do them later. Hey, how about some more wine? Why don't you open the Zinfandel, and we'll take it into the living room where it's more comfortable."

"Will you play the piano?" he asked, half-afraid she'd say no, yet not altogether certain he wanted her to say yes.

"You really want me to bore you?"

When he nodded, she placed the wine bottle and their glasses on a tray and let him take it while she led the way into the living room. She settled on the piano bench.

She played from memory, mostly soft romantic tunes, the ones she knew he liked.

Ace was enthralled. Each time she stopped to take a sip of her wine, he topped up their glasses and begged her to play more. Finally she insisted he come and sit beside her.

Soon her cheeks were pink from the wine and the effort of playing.

Entranced by the music and her beauty, Ace leaned over and laid an impulsive trail of kisses down her neck and along her jaw.

Her fingers stumbled over the keys. When she glanced up, intending to scold him, their eyes locked and she was powerless to escape the more ardent kiss he pressed against her lips. Neither noticed when the music faded, and her hands sneaked around his waist and slid up his back.

Ace deepened the kiss and found the bench too narrow. Too restrictive. One by one he parted the buttons down the front of her lacy dress until he reached the warm naked skin beneath. The shock of finding her pale breasts unconfined brought a sharp hiss of air through his lips.

She shivered, closed her eyes and dropped her head back to give him better access.

When his hands touched her again, her eyes opened lazily. What he read in them clutched at his heart and sent a shaft of heat spiraling to his groin. His kisses grew more desperate, and so did hers.

Almost without knowing how they got there, Ace found himself in the middle of a bed, Meredith cradled against his bare chest. They were lying hip to hip on a ruffled rose bedspread. The scent of her was intoxicating. Her fingers made light forays across his chest, and it was as if he was once again engulfed in her music.

He peeled off her white leggings as he'd envisioned doing from that first moment on. Starting at her toes, Ace kissed his way up to the softer skin inside her thighs, until they both broke out in a fine sweat.

She divested him of his gray slacks and in satisfaction watched them slither to a heap on the floor. He was beautiful to look at even in the dim light. She didn't take time to wonder if he found her the same as she sought his lips again.

Ace groaned. He was almost beyond making rational decisions when he thought to protect her and paused to pull his billfold out of the back pocket of his slacks. With shaking fingers, he hunted for the foil packet he'd carried for so long he forgot which compartment it was in. When at last he found it and hauled it out, the package all but fell apart in his palm. Reality had him breaking out in a cold sweat. He really hadn't expected things to go so far. The conversation he'd had earlier with Captain Caldwell screamed inside his head. Damn, he'd been joking with Dean. The truth hit him now. He couldn't trust this one to do its job.

Meredith sensed something was wrong. Her head reeled, whether from his lovemaking or the wine, she wasn't sure. She did know—without knowing why—that he'd withdrawn. Her spine tingled as she caught a glimpse of his chilly eyes. No longer like liquid smoke, they more closely resembled an impending storm. *Déjà vu!*

CHAPTER TEN

SHE SHOULD HAVE KNOWN from experience that she wasn't cut out for a sexual relationship. That her training at the Point threatened a man's masculinity. There was another man, an accountant in Baltimore, who'd gladly attest to that.

Meredith snapped on the bedside lamp and covered herself with a corner of the ruffled spread.

Ace blinked to ward off the bright light as he battled disappointment. Some part of his sluggish mind registered Meredith's retreat. And why not? She probably thought he was the most inept lover who'd ever lived.

"I'm sorry," he muttered. The least he owed her was an apology.

Feeling awkward, she yanked the spread higher. She wanted it up to her chin, but his weight held it fast.

He shot her a glance. All the humiliation she'd suffered as a result of his poor planning was there in her amber eyes.

"Don't. Don't say another word," she commanded. "Frankly, Ace, I'm not up to platitudes."

He reached for her. "What in the hell are you talking about? You think I'm saying that I'm sorry we ended up in bed?" He shook his head. "Meredith, I'm apologizing for not having the sense to replace that condom. I've carried the damn thing around since before the Gulf War."

Ace was almost embarrassed to admit how long it had been since he'd been in bed with a woman. What would she think? That there was something wrong with him? "I haven't needed protection in a while," he mumbled. Lord, he could feel her eyes on him. Golden eyes, all-seeing of his faults. When she still didn't stir or make a peep, he decided to give easing the tension one last shot. "Meredith, please quit looking at me like that and come here. It's not the end of the world."

Her head ached. She just wished he'd leave.

He rolled onto his elbow and tossed the useless packet into her lap. "I don't suppose you have any of these on hand?"

Feeling as frustrated as he sounded, Meredith shook her head.

"No—" he smiled ruefully "—I didn't suppose you would. Can't say I'm sorry about that."

She touched the condom poking through one of the many splits in the foil. "You really haven't? I mean . . . you've been home from the Gulf for a long time."

"Yeah." He gave a self-conscious shrug. "Couldn't you tell?"

When she continued to stare at him, he ran a finger-tip experimentally around one of her opal earrings. A kaleidoscope of colors danced in the lamplight. "Naw, maybe you couldn't," he murmured, thinking no woman ever looked less worldly than she did at this mo-ment. "What's wrong with those guys at the Point, anyway?" he asked, slipping his hand around her neck to pull her steadily toward his waiting lips.

"Ace," she gasped the moment he stopped to breathe. "I don't think this is a good idea." She was trembling. Then, as his hands swept the bedspread away and returned to cup her breasts, she shuddered and fell silent in the wake of a spiral of heat.

"Shh." He nipped his way across her lower lip, then back to caress it with his tongue. As she tried to protest, he moved on to suck gently at the soft flesh of her ear, and she forgot why she should be protesting at all.

Groaning, he murmured, "We've got other options, sweetheart. Will you trust me?"

Trust? If there were reasons she shouldn't, they were lost under the magic he was eliciting with his hands. "Nothing kinky. I'm pretty old-fashioned," she whispered.

"Me, too," he growled in her ear. "So be careful where you touch."

"Yes, sir," she murmured, chasing his lips as their legs tangled.

"Meredith," he warned raggedly when her fingers roamed down his chest and tickled his stomach near the snug band of his jockey shorts. Immediately she abandoned the forbidden forage and let her hands wander up his back.

He shuddered when she walked them down his vertebrae one at a time. Cursing himself for thinking a man who'd been without a woman as long as he had could think this was safe, Ace began kissing her at her neck and didn't pause until he reached her toes. By then she was begging him both to stop—and never to stop. She opened for him, all liquid heat and fire, and abandoned herself to trust.

Ace brought about her release as tenderly as he knew how, and it was as if the earth moved for him, too. Spellbound, he watched the changing expressions on her face until at last she chanted his name like a litany and flew apart under his ministrations.

Humbled beyond belief, Ace gathered her close until the trembling in both of them receded. As he smoothed a hand through her short damp curls, he realized the experience held both privilege and pleasure.

As a rule Ace considered himself a caring lover—one who looked after his partner's needs. Yet he'd always gone into sex with all cards on the table. Mutual pleasure. No pretty words and no ties. For the first time in his life, Ace Bannister found himself searching for words to describe what he felt at simply satisfying a woman, this woman, without regard to his own needs.

But mere words sounded banal to him just now. For that reason, and no other, he held her as tightly as he could and said nothing.

Meredith's fingers flexed in the crisp hair on his chest. What she'd just undergone seemed incredible—to one whose first and only sexual venture had ended in harsh words and a broken engagement. Her former fiancé had claimed he couldn't get past her uniform; he'd said she was trained to kill, not to love. Her, trained to kill. What a laugh.

And now she wasn't sure what was expected, either. How were these brief modern sexual encounters handled? No matter what, she refused to call it a one-night stand. Lord—was that all it had been to him?

As he continued to stroke her back without comment, a kind of mortifying lethargy set in. She wasn't so green that she hadn't realized everything had been one-sided. And she had really, really tried not to fall for him. He knew that, as well. *This* time, though, she'd be darned if she would bear all the guilt. Pushing away, she sat up.

She was an adult. She could handle this. Without a word she scrambled from the bed.

"Don't tell me you're cold?" he teased in a lazy be-mused tone as she opened her closet door, grabbed a bathrobe and quickly belted it around her waist.

She ran a hand nervously through her hair, then let it flutter to cup her throat. She was having difficulty get-ting words out past the lump that had formed there. "I, ah, it's getting late."

Ace straightened at that. The dim light didn't quite reach to where she stood, but he heard something in her voice that sent a bolt of fear to his stomach. "Mere-dith? What's the matter?"

She stepped back until she stood flat against the closet. "Nothing."

He reached for his slacks and slid into them. "It sounds like something to me. Did I hurt you?" The thought left his hands shaking so hard he had difficulty zipping his pants. "Will you turn on the damn light? I can't see you over there in the dark."

"No. No light—please."

Ace found his shirt, shrugged into it, then picked up his billfold from where it had fallen and buttoned it into his back pocket. "We will have some light. Dammit, if I hurt you, Meredith, I'll never forgive myself." He stalked around the bed and reached for the lamp switch.

"No, don't!" she exclaimed. "You didn't hurt me." But she *was* in pain. What hurt so badly was knowing she'd begun to care too much for a man whose first love, whose *real* love, would always be the army.

"It's my head," she lied. "The wine, I think. I'm not much of a drinker."

Ace smiled at her admission and felt the relief clear to his toes. "We did sort of overcelebrate. Wine has a sneaky habit of coming back to haunt you in the morn-ing, too. I'll take your first class. That way you can sleep late," he said. A generous offer, he thought, considering how impatient he'd be to see her.

"And give Ron Holmes more reason to accuse you of playing favorites? Not on your life, Major. Or was this about having me in your debt?" Her voice rose more sharply than she'd intended. But somehow, lashing out at him helped lessen her feelings of need. Of guilt.

He wasn't quite sure how they'd gone from one of the sweetest interludes he'd ever known to absolute drivel, but Ace didn't like it one bit. He closed the distance between them in two strides. Gripping her shoulders, he pulled her against his chest. When they were nose to nose and she was forced to look at him, he poured every drop of frustration into a kiss destined to right whatever had suddenly gone wrong between them.

The kiss started out ruthless, but the minute he felt a slight tremor rush through her slender body, he eased back, enfolded her in his arms and tucked her silken hair under his chin, loosing a long ragged sigh. "I know this session of lovemaking sort of blew up like wildfire and raced out of control," he said. "I know it was a letdown. I'll take full responsibility for not being prepared, but hang it all, Meredith, it had nothing to do with my title compared to yours or the uniforms we wear. Not one damned thing."

She leaned on him because if she didn't her legs would give way. More than anything in the world, Meredith wanted to believe him. Except she knew better. "You're wrong," she said. "I wish you weren't, but you are. Titles and uniforms are who we are. You can't separate the person from those things, like milk from cream."

Drawing away, she turned and walked over to the room's one window—where she had yet to close the ruffled curtains. Moonlight spilled in, casting shadows on the wall. For a moment she stared at the large golden moon, and although she wasn't a woman prone to tears, one trickled down her cheek.

Gilded as she was in moonbeams, Ace had difficulty remembering what either of them did for a living. Until he stared long enough at the West Point arch of her spine and the rigid set of her shoulders. Clearly *she* remembered their differences and thought he should, too.

Ace had never forced himself on a woman in his life, and he wasn't about to start now. Meredith was the first woman in a long while who sparked something inside him that a cynical Ace Bannister feared had been left out of his makeup—a capacity to love.

It was much too early in their relationship, however, to label the unsettled feelings he battled as that most elusive emotion. But if he could ever love someone the way a man was supposed to love a woman he'd share forever with, Meredith Marshall St. James certainly filled the bill. And he didn't give a tinker's damn how many titles came and went in front of her name, or his. Or... her father's, for that matter.

"I'm leaving," he said quietly. "I just want to tell you that this is a long way from over. Maybe we put the cart before the horse tonight, but I don't believe for a minute it was just the wine." He took a step toward her. "Let's go somewhere this weekend. For fun. No pressure. You already know I'd like to show you Fredericksburg. Or if you'd rather, we could take a run to Austin. What do you say?"

She faced him, her eyes asking why he was doing this to her. Why he was persisting. "I already told you, Ace. I'm going to the rodeo. I've never been to one and I plan to take in every event. Want to go with me?"

He didn't have time to mask the repugnance he always felt when anyone mentioned rodeos. Logically, Ace knew the broncobuster who had fathered him and then discarded him like an unwanted puppy had probably left the rodeo circuit by now. But time hadn't lessened the pain and the anger that went with knowing he'd been of no more consequence to the man than some insignificant whelp. It had festered inside him for too many years. Not even for Meredith could he take such a big step.

"Then that's that," he said stiffly, already backing out of the room. "I happen to think there's better entertainment than watching a bunch of cowboys fall on their butts in the dirt. I'll show myself out."

At the bedroom door, he suffered a moment's contrition. "I'll see you at the office tomorrow," he said gently. "Come on, lock up after me."

With that, he was gone, although he waited on the landing until he heard her turn the lock and slide the chain home. It felt as if she'd locked him out of her life.

As HAD BECOME HABIT, Meredith was first in the office the next day.

When Ace arrived, she was in her seat working on lesson plans, looking so bright and chipper that for a moment he suffered a shiver of anger. He'd spent the night reliving every minute of their time together—cursing himself for everything that had gone wrong and dreaming about how it could have ended. And there she sat, looking as well rested and innocent as Goldilocks.

Obviously she hadn't been as affected by what had happened as he had. Ace ground his teeth when she came to attention so prettily; he really wanted to throw something across the room. Mostly because her perfume—the same one he'd smelled on her pillow last night—rose as she did and settled over him like a cloud. The simple floral scent seized his lungs and made placing her at ease impossible.

Suddenly Ace was struck by the most incredible thing. "My God!" he exclaimed, his entire body tensing. His briefcase slipped from his hand. It struck the floor with a crash that popped the clasp. Papers spewed everywhere. Still he didn't move a muscle.

Meredith had already begun to regard his strange behavior with some curiosity when he dropped the case. As he stiffened and his eyes blanked out, she rushed around her desk. "Ace, what is it?" His set expression so frightened her she forgot to call him sir.

"It's there. Everything you said. Mountains, trees, forest animals...the eagle. I see every last one." He threw his arms around her and danced her around the small space between their desks just as Ron Holmes sauntered in from the workroom.

"I knew it," Ron sneered. "Even when Caldwell tried to convince me there was nothing going on between you two, I knew he was lying. Did I interrupt a quickie on the major's desk?" His tone took a darker turn. "Won't Colonel O'Dell be interested to hear about this?"

The smile died on Ace's lips. "You know nothing, Ron. I'd have hugged her even if the colonel himself had been here. I won't dignify what's running through your filthy mind with an explanation. If you came here for a reason, you can start with a salute and go from there. *Ten-hut!*"

Ace dropped his arm from around Meredith's shoulders, his eyes deadly cold.

Although the curl of derision never left Ron's lips, he came to attention as commanded.

Both men knew it was a show of power that Ace rarely, if ever, exercised. Since he'd been promoted over Ron, he'd gone to great lengths to keep office protocol less stringent. Breaking off the formal salute now, Ace was furious that he'd let Ron force his back to the wall like this.

"Speak your piece," Ace snapped. "I have a class at 0900."

Ron assumed an aggressive stance. "I don't know why I thought you'd be interested to know that Ruby's kid is in jail." For a moment the hatred left his eyes and uneasiness crept in. "She's hysterical." He ran a hand over his old-fashioned crew cut. "She called before sunup. Got me out of bed. Claims Roy'll kill her. Hell if I know what she wants me to do. It's none of my business. I've only seen the kid once."

Ace had bent to scoop all the papers back into his briefcase. The news brought him to his feet. "Lacy, you mean? What's the charge?"

Ron shook his head. "It's Blake. They caught him dealing dope."

"Buying?" Ace asked sharply. He barely registered Meredith's gasp.

"Selling," Ron said, stuffing his hands in his pockets.

Ace slapped his briefcase onto his desk. "Selling. To whom? Blake's just a kid."

Meredith placed a restraining hand on Ace's arm. "Trafficking is reaching clear down into our elementary schools. Does Ruby still have military privileges? Access to legal services? A family counselor?"

Ace looked to Ron, who only mumbled, "Yeah. I think Roy still carries the kids as dependents. But he wouldn't lift a finger to help her."

Glancing at his watch, Ace sighed heavily. "I'm going to be late for class. I'm tied up for the next hour."

"So am I," Meredith said. "I have the class on customs and traditions, if you recall. After that, I'd be happy to make some inquiries through Family Services, if someone can get me Blake's ID number."

"Ron?" Ace deferred to the captain.

"I suppose I could," he said, still sounding resentful.

Meredith arched an eyebrow. "How committed are you to Ruby?" she asked Ron.

"What kind of a question is that?" he tossed back belligerently. "And what damn business is it of yours?"

"None. But I thought I'd tell you that kids, even young ones, don't get off easy anymore. The court may decide Blake doesn't belong with his mother—unless she can provide a more stable home. If that's the case, they'll look to the father. If he has a good attorney... Well, I've seen cases where they've overturned custody for other children in the family, as well."

Ron threw up his hands. "Look, I'm sorry I ever got hooked up with the dame, okay? We go to a tavern a few times a month to drink and dance, and more often than not hit a no-tell motel on the way home. And that's all." Ron began edging away. "Leave me out of it. She and I are history as of now." He bolted, all but running back through the workroom.

"Butthead," Meredith exclaimed, hands on her hips.

Ace did a double take at her comment, then checked his watch again. "Hey, time we locked up and got moving or we'll have classrooms filled with mischief makers." Closing his briefcase, he motioned for her to precede him. "Circumstances being what they are, I'd just as soon not see Ruby—" he was going to say "alone," but Meredith interrupted.

"Oh, so you're ratting out on the poor woman, too. Here I thought you were better than Ron. You're two of a kind. She was fine when you guys wanted a good-time girl, but let her need help, and you both blow her off without a second thought."

Ace stopped in his mad flight toward the door. "Don't judge me, Meredith. Ruby and I had nothing more than a superficial alliance to begin with, and she wasn't exactly honest with me at that. The way I see it, she doesn't win any awards for mother of the year, either. Maybe Blake'd be better off without her." His eyes blazed and his jaw was set inflexibly.

Meredith followed him outside, turned the lock and shut the door. She didn't see any sense in antagonizing him further. "So, what about his father?"

"Lieutenant Tindall is an abusive alcoholic. One more incident and he's headed for a court-martial. Not all kids have fine upstanding parents like yours, Captain."

Meredith would have shouted at him, except that they'd reached the walkway and a group of students were coming toward them. "You don't want to be judged, Major. The same goes for me. Fine upstanding parents don't guarantee a happy childhood," she imparted in a stiff whisper. "Anyway, it's not for us to decide. In my field we don't lay blame. We offer suggestions that we hope will give people alternative choices to make family life better."

Ace thought of his mother. She could have benefited from someone like Meredith. Instead, there'd only been his aunt, who was equally unstable. They fed off one another's weaknesses. As it turned out, *his* alternative had been the army. Brow furrowed, he said, "I'd hate to see Blake get lost in the system. How about if after class we both go visit Ruby? I'll try to keep an open mind."

They'd reached the crossroads, and were poised to go in opposite directions.

Meredith offered a quick nod, but found herself smiling as she crossed the street. Ace wasn't anything like Ron Holmes. When they met again, she'd apologize for jumping down his throat. It was pretty evident his childhood had been bad. Funny how convinced he was that hers had been perfect. They were quite a pair, weren't they?

She sucked in a deep breath. All the more reason not to get involved in a personal relationship with him. They both had scars. If only he'd quit confusing her. Just when she thought she had him firmly at arm's length, he showed her another facet of Major A. C. Bannister. A sensitive side. A quality Meredith had been convinced all male military officers lacked.

The two of them met back at the office after class, and Ace made a few phone calls to determine what, if anything, was being done for Blake Tindall. He found out the boy was being held in juvenile detention pending a hearing. The court had appointed him an attorney, but so far Blake had been too stubborn or too scared to talk to anyone in authority.

Meredith called the army's legal officer. He was reluctant to meet them at Ruby's, but said he'd be available if she came to his office. Meredith slammed the phone down. "Red tape. I hate it."

Ace laughed. "Come on. When the unflappable Captain St. James gets flapped, it's time to try another tactic. Let's go."

Meredith picked up her purse and grinned. "Didn't I tell you I have no patience for the system?"

"I detected that," he said with a straight face as he led the way to his new car. They spoke little on the short drive to the Tindall residence.

A much subdued Ruby, compared to the flamboyant woman Meredith had first met, answered the door when they knocked. Her hair wasn't combed. Her eyes weren't made up and they showed the ravages of tears, tears that spilled over again as she unhooked the screen to let them in. "I wouldn't have expected you to come, Ace." She started to sob. "Oh, God, it's so awful."

Ace took her arm and guided her into the living room. "Ron was pretty sketchy. You feel like giving us the story? Meredith thinks there are options available through the military that you may not have explored."

Ruby sniffled. "I doubt I'll have anything available for long. Friday, Roy came to the house, drunk and in a rage. Apparently someone saw me leave the Heavenly Days Motel with Ron Holmes the night before." She picked at her nail polish. "I told Roy I didn't owe him any explanation. I have a right to a life outside of raising the kids. He hit me and threatened to cut my dependent allotment. Blake jumped between us and told his dad we didn't need his money. Said he'd earn enough to take care of me and Lacy. I thought it was all talk. I told Roy to leave or I'd call the MPs. He left."

She jumped up from the couch and wrung her hands. "I didn't know some older guy at the bowling alley where Blake and his friends hang out has been offering the kids money to solicit new customers for...for drugs." She dissolved into another spate of tears. "Blake's just a baby. I didn't dream he knew about stuff like that."

"So did Blake have drugs on him when he was arrested?" Meredith asked.

Ruby nodded glumly. "He hadn't approached anybody, or so he swears. Some kid told on him before he had a chance."

"Then they only have him for possession, right?" Ace said.

Ruby shrugged. "I don't know. No one will tell me anything except that he's refusing to talk to the attorney they assigned him. He's scared spitless, and so am I."

Meredith outlined a few things she thought Ruby could do.

"Thanks," Ruby said, drying her eyes. She acted surprised that Meredith wanted to help. "I'm sorry I was so hateful to you. I've done a lot of dumb things lately. I should have sold the house and moved back to Oregon after my divorce."

"Is that still a possibility?" Meredith asked.

Ruby didn't answer. She grabbed a pack of cigarettes and shook one out. Lighting it, she crossed her arms and stared out the window.

"Have you talked to your family recently?" Ace tried.

Ruby shook her head. "Time was, I hoped you'd..." She let the sentence trail off. "I know Ron's not much better than Roy." She looked sad. "I haven't wanted to face raising two kids alone. They need someone like you, Ace. Someone who's firm. I'm not good with discipline."

Ace didn't want Meredith thinking there'd ever been such a possibility. "Kids want discipline, Ruby," he said. "Even Lacy."

Ruby took another puff from her cigarette, then bent and stubbed it out in an already overflowing ashtray. "Lacy's been a real trooper. When the police called, I got hysterical. She took down all the information, then helped me find my clothes. I think it's made an impression on her. She hugged me this morning before she went to school. I can't tell you how long it's been since we didn't start the day with a fight.''

"Why don't you call legal counsel at the fort right now," Meredith urged. "Since you have Lacy's attention, maybe you should act fast. What about trying to get Blake off on probation? If you tell the judge you can start over in Oregon, he might consider it.''

"You think maybe?" Ruby brightened. "Would you mind going with me?" she asked Meredith shyly. "I wouldn't know what to ask.''

"I'd be happy to. And so would Ace.''

He rose. "I need to get back to campus for a tactics class.''

Ruby excused herself to go write Lacy a note in case the girl came home before they returned. Meredith nodded at her, and frowned at Ace. "Couldn't you cancel this once?''

He shook his head. "Dean and I have pooled classes. We start paper exercises today. My class develops a simulated technical offense and his sets up enemy countermoves.''

"Swell," Meredith said. "I hope you remember to tell the players that each one of those pins you sacrifice represents a human life. No one ever thinks to mention that fact.''

Ace rolled his eyes and walked to the door. "Don't start, Meredith. If they're going to make mistakes, wouldn't you rather it be on paper, where the consequences are insignificant?''

Meredith followed him. "The point is, on paper it's too easy to focus on the high-tech part and forget the blood.''

"They'll get a big dose of reality in a few weeks. New cadets go up north to Basic Camp. Third-year students join the regular army at Fort Riley for Advanced Camp. I'm taking the highest achievers to Arizona for hands-on combat training."

"Ah, reality, huh? Do you plan to march them over land mines? Let them swelter in hundred-degree heat in winter uniforms and withhold MREs until they're so hungry that even scorpions look good? That's the reality of war, isn't it, Major?"

Ace started to debate the issue, but saw that she was too worked up. On some things he and Meredith would simply never agree. He shrugged and resorted to teasing. "I think two weeks of Meals Ready to Eat is plenty of reality. You know, of course, that soldiers in the field refer to them as 'Meals Ready to Excrete.'"

Ruby walked back in as Meredith growled in frustration.

Ace tossed off a two-fingered salute. "I assume Ruby will drive you home." Donning his hat, he left before Meredith could hit him with another of her choice comebacks.

"He's so muleheaded!" Meredith slammed the screen door in his wake.

Ruby put her cigarettes in her purse and dug out her car keys. "You two having a spat?" she asked with interest.

Meredith realized how they must have sounded to a bystander. "Don't mind me. I was just delivering one of my standard soapbox lectures. I survived West Point, but it doesn't mean I buy their crap about army officers being tough unyielding masters of the universe."

"Well, I agree with you there," Ruby said, leading Meredith to her car. Once they were settled inside she took up the conversation as if there'd been no lapse. "I'm surprised to hear Ace talk like that. He never struck me as the 'rah-rah and glory' type. Not like my ex. And Ron." She giggled. "Lacy calls it the Rambo mentality. The guys flex their muscles and carry on like the uniform places them a step above God."

Meredith fastened her seat belt and fell silent. She didn't want to discuss what she perceived as shortcomings in military philosophy with Ruby. Anyway, most women would agree with her—unless, like her mother, they'd allowed themselves to be brainwashed. The sad fact of life was that most men would side with Ace. Hence the stalemate.

"If you feel so strongly," Ruby said as she turned her aging vehicle down the street that led to the fort, "why don't you get out?"

It appeared the subject wasn't going to die, despite Meredith's wishes. Reluctantly she said, "I took the one hiatus a Point graduate is allowed and went on to the University of Baltimore to get my master's. Now I'm in a spot that's like yours in some ways. You don't like your role as a single parent, but you're stuck, so you just keep chipping away at the problems the best you can. I owe them the rest of this year. Then I expect to resign."

Ruby laughed. "I haven't found any way to resign from parenting. Believe me, I keep saying I resign. Nobody ever takes me seriously."

Leaning back in her seat, Meredith smiled. "You have the main thing a person needs to be a good parent, Ruby. A sense of humor."

"It's either laugh, cry or hit the bottle. Crying screws up my makeup, and drinking comes with its own set of problems. I know that for a fact."

Meredith turned to look at her companion. "This is a side of you I haven't seen before, Ruby."

"Yes, well, you were walking off with somebody I really wanted to be able to say was my man. I knew, of course, that he didn't look at me as wife material. It didn't stop me from hoping I could change his mind. He's the first decent man I've had the hots for. So, you be good to him, you hear?"

Blushing, Meredith turned aside. "I . . . I think you have the wrong impression," she stammered. "We're fellow officers. Nothing more."

"Sure," Ruby drawled, rolling her eyes as she stopped at the gate to show her ID. "You shouldn't lie, Captain St. James. It shows."

"But I'm not," she protested. "You heard us. He's military through and through, while when my uniform comes off I do everything to pretend I'm a civilian. A *female* civilian."

Ruby pulled up and parked outside the building housing legal services. "I don't know this for fact, mind you, but I have a good imagination. I'd guess that beneath Ace Bannister's uniform, he's all-male." She winked.

Because Meredith did know for a fact that what Ruby said was oh-so-true, she nearly fried in her mortification. Recovering minimally, she coughed and said, "Just who's the counselor here, Ruby? I think it's time to forget this silliness. Let's go find out what the post's legal service can do for Blake."

CHAPTER ELEVEN

THE REMAINDER of the week, Meredith managed to avoid Ace. Mornings, she bypassed the office and went straight to class. Afternoons, when he taught, she worked at her desk. The rest of the time she spent bolstering Ruby.

Not a day passed, however, that Meredith wasn't conscious of the fact that she sorely missed contact with Ace. Ruby's needling observation the other day struck closer to home than Meredith cared to acknowledge. Since her feelings were so obvious to an outsider, she had no choice but to place distance between them. Philosophically, they'd never be compatible.

Already she'd let the man get too close. When she thought about the liberties she'd allowed him, her heart went berserk. And if she let herself admit how much she'd enjoyed the experience, she broke out in hives.

No, it was pure folly to spend any time recalling the hours they'd shared in her bed. She *had* to forget his touch, his taste and the feel of his beautiful masculine body.

Yet those were exactly the things Meredith sat at her desk contemplating later that week when Ace walked in from a class and caught her making daisy chains of paper clips.

"Well, well, who's the stranger?" he drawled with a hint of sarcasm. His pride was stung that even after he'd gotten her home phone number and left several messages on her machine, she'd still ignored him. To say nothing of the notes he'd dropped on her desk that were just short of orders to touch base.

Meredith was not pleased that he'd walked in on her like this, but because her thoughts had been centered on him, she was slow scrambling to attention.

"At ease, Captain," he snapped. Ace was hot and tired and short on patience. He'd spent the afternoon on the rifle range with a group of cadets one might think had never seen a rifle. The cammies he wore looked as cruddy as he felt. Not to mention his face, which was streaked with black shoe polish— A smart-assed cadet or group of cadets had found it amusing to use the polish to grease the cinches inside the steel pots of all their instructors' helmets. As if that weren't aggravating enough, the little monsters had also slicked Vaseline on the triggers of every single weapon slated for the demonstration.

Ace was in no mood to pass anything off lightly when Meredith took a good look at him and smothered a laugh.

"Something funny, St. James?"

She dipped her chin and tried to wipe the smile off her face without success.

"Since you obviously find my predicament so entertaining, tomorrow you can take my place on the obstacle course."

That sobered her. "Tomorrow is Blake Tindall's final hearing. I promised Ruby I'd go with her."

"Nice of you to catch me up. I guess you didn't get any of my messages," he said coldly. "Four left on your machine and several more on your desk."

Meredith cleared her throat and sank back into her chair. "You weren't specific about what you wanted. I was busy."

"Busy. Ah. Is that what they teach at the Point? If you're busy you can ignore a summons from a ranking officer?" He disappeared into the washroom. The last of his remark was garbled as he stuck his head under the faucet. It irked him both that she was making excuses and that he was acting petty.

Swamped by guilt, Meredith rose, got a washcloth from the closet and thrust it through the door, and into his hands. After he finished scrubbing most of the black off his face she said, "I didn't know those were summonses . . . exactly."

He stamped out of the bathroom, face buried in a towel. When at last he looked at her, his eyes glittered, warning her that she was treading on dangerous ground.

Backed up against her desk, she stood in the formal manner she'd learned so well at the Point. Heels together, toes at a forty-five degree angle.

"How *exactly*—" he stressed the word as he leaned toward her "—should a request be worded, St. James, in order for you to understand that I want you front and center?" His voice rumbled over her like thunder.

She blanked her features—another trick she'd learned at the Point to get through hazing, an unsanctioned process freely practiced by upperclassmen during the washout phase.

"'Check in' and 'How are things progressing?' did not make me think you required my presence . . . sir." She restrained a sarcastic smile. "Besides, I left notes on your desk twice."

Ace leaned a hip against his desk, looped the towel around his neck and let a reluctant smile touch his lips.

"Technicalities, Meredith. You knew damn well I wanted to see you. Don't tell me you'd have gotten away pulling this kind of crap at the Point."

"If you want to run this office like West Point, you'll have to develop a louder roar." She steepled her fingers. "Plebes don't call West Point 'Hell on the Hudson' for nothing. I didn't realize that was the atmosphere you wanted here. Or is it merely a method of control you've reserved for me?" She glanced up and into his eyes.

Ace read the indictment in her expression, and automatically stiffened in defense. Flustered, he tipped his head forward and massaged the back of his neck. "That's not it," he said quietly. "I really missed you. I didn't want to, but I did. I'd hoped it might be the same for you." His gaze was equally direct.

She was the first to look away. The steeple crumpled and her fingers locked together, knuckles white and strained. Words of denial crowded to the tip of her tongue, but nothing made it past her lips. Lies always got found out.

She sighed. He was right. She'd missed him very much. Although she did her best now to hide the deep feelings that troubled her heart.

His breath escaped in a rush. Her eyes were too easy to read. Oh, he'd won his point and this round, but something told him it was not the time to count coups. A good officer knew when to fall back and regroup, and Ace considered himself a good officer.

"Well," he said, straightening and striding across the room, unbuttoning his cammies as he went, "you mentioned in the note yesterday that you think Blake has a good chance of being probationed into Ruby's custody.

I'd heard from another source that Roy is kicking up a ruckus.''

Meredith felt the tension leave her body. "Ruby put her house on the market. She has affidavits from her parents and other family members saying she and the children have a place to live in Oregon. And she's agreed to counseling. I think Lieutenant Tindall's record speaks for itself. But tomorrow's hearing will tell all.''

Ace opened the closet again and took out another towel. "Think I'll try to clear my calendar. Is it an open hearing?''

"No. In fact, I'll be outside in the waiting room.''

"Oh. Then will you stop back here and give me the verdict?''

She drummed her fingers on the desk.

"Is that a problem?'' he asked lightly. "Got a hot date afterward?'' He really wanted to know. But when he thought about how the question could be misconstrued as subtle harassment, he cursed himself for being such a blockhead. "Sorry, Meredith. It's none of my business. Could you leave a message on my home answering machine? I'd like to know the outcome.''

She leaned back in her chair and smiled. "I don't have a date. Actually I was planning to go to the rodeo straight from the courthouse. I'd suggest we meet there, but a woman gets tired of being turned down. It's not easy working up the courage to ask someone out only to be flatly refused.'' The corners of her mouth lifted impishly.

Ace paused en route to a much-needed shower. She had trapped him neatly with an age-old masculine excuse. "Ahem.'' He cleared his throat. "I, ah, I've been giving that some thought.'' And he had. Each morning he'd told himself there was no way his old man could be riding broncs in this rodeo or any other at his age.

"If the offer's still open," Ace said casually, "I was thinking I might just go out to the arena and eat a little dust with you."

"Really?" Her smile froze.

He nodded briskly, then hurried into the bathroom before she could retract her invitation. Catching the flash of a thin smile in the mirror, he soon altered it to a cocky grin. Now, that hadn't been so hard. In fact it had felt damn good. A man needed to turn the tables once in a while. It wouldn't do to have a woman think he was predictable.

Meredith was still sitting in the same spot when he came out refreshed and whistling his rendition of "Stars and Stripes Forever." "Did I hear you right?" she demanded, interrupting his wobbly high C. "After refusing me twice with about as much tact as a rock crusher, am I to understand you're now willing to lower your entertainment standards—*to watch cowboys fall on their butts?*"

Ace stopped whistling and winced. Damn, but she had a sharp memory. He thought those might have been his exact words. "So what's the big deal? Don't men in Baltimore ever change their minds?"

Her lips twisted wryly. "I've never met a man anywhere who's changed his mind once it's set. I thought you were all bullheaded to the bitter end."

He rolled his wet towel and sweaty cammies into a ball and stuffed them in his duffel before he sat down at his desk. "Well, now you know one who's different. What time and where shall we meet?"

She thought a moment. "Tomorrow I'd planned to visit the craft booths and maybe look in on the midway and the dance. I'm going back Saturday for the rodeo performance. If you really don't want to watch the cowboys, I can do that alone.''

''I'm in for the whole shootin' match, St. James. If you want to climb into jeans after the hearing, I'll stop by the apartment and pick you up. I'm scheduled to take a squad to the obstacle course tomorrow. I'll definitely have to shower afterward.''

''Hmm. I wonder if you'll be alive to pick me up. You looked kind of the worse for wear today after the rifle range. What tricks do you suppose the little charmers will have up their sleeves for you on the obstacle course?''

''Do you know something I don't?''

She laughed. ''No. But I've been on the receiving end at the Point. You wouldn't believe all the things we went through. Upperclassmen perfected physical and psychological torture. Claimed it was intended to weed out the weak and the unworthy.'' She snorted. ''Bunk! If you ask me, every last one was a closet sadist.''

''You don't paint a very pretty picture of West Point. Why does anyone want to go there?''

''Usually one of three reasons.'' She ticked them off on her fingers. ''Family tradition, manly prestige or for the free education.''

''If it was so awful,'' he asked, ''why didn't you quit?''

She lifted a brow. ''Quitting never entered my mind.''

''No? I guess it's easier being passive-aggressive.''

''How so?'' she asked through clenched teeth. She began stacking folders to take with her, hating the way the conversation had turned personal.

He leaned back in his chair. ''Oh... I'm beginning to get feedback from your morning classes.''

"Really?" As if unconcerned, she picked up her stack of folders, shouldered her bag and headed for the door.

"I guess you wouldn't know anything about this garbage I'm hearing—about modern soldiers needing to be diplomats, builders of nations and independent thinkers. Honestly, did you think I wouldn't find out you're slipping your personal ideals into the curriculum?"

"Garbage, is it?" She laughed and opened the door. "I'll have you know that was a direct quote from John F. Kennedy's speech to the graduating class at the Point, June '62. It's public record." She walked out and closed the door quietly but firmly behind her.

Ace snapped forward in his chair. He'd walked right into that one. He shook his head. It seemed a lifetime since he'd been outfoxed so neatly. For sure, he'd never underestimate the lady again.

NOTHING OUT OF the ordinary happened on the obstacle course. However, only the most athletic students performed well. Ace pushed everyone hard and assigned extra wall-drops to those who shirked. Not to be mean, but because he knew what it meant to be dumped unceremoniously into the middle of a civil emergency. Or a war.

He could tell them about being sent to Riyadh, a green captain. After flying all night, the transport had touched down and he'd immediately been put in command of a squad of kids who were bundles of nerves themselves. None of them—including him—had ever seen so much desert. He'd been given a sketchy briefing and told to move tanks and heavy artillery fifteen miles that day— without sleep. Five miles out it hit him. This was real. This enemy was playing for keeps and all those shave-tailed kids expected him to get them back to Fort Bragg alive. Thank God he didn't have one of Meredith's independent thinkers in the lot. Someone had trained them to do exactly as they were told. What could he say to make her understand that discipline was synonymous with survival?

Fortunately puzzling over that problem kept his mind off the rodeo. Oh, he'd seen men and women do dumb things to attract the interest of a special someone. Until now he'd figured himself smarter than that. But here he was, about to do something he detested—just so he could spend a few hours in a woman's company. A woman who didn't seem to give a damn whether he accompanied her or not.

With every minute that passed, his feet got colder. Had he been anywhere near a phone, other than the mobile unit manned by Ron Holmes, Ace would have left a curt message on her machine.

As it was, he got back to town late, and if he wanted to make it to her apartment by 1800, he was going to have to hustle his butt. Being senior officer, he could have left Ron to bring in the stragglers. And he might have if it'd been anyone but Ron. Frankly, he just didn't want to listen to the added griping.

Ace ran through his phone messages as he stripped for the shower. Meredith was the first caller. He could hear the excitement in her low whiskey voice. He dropped a shoe and sat on the bed to listen. Her voice pleased him. It also sent a wave of longing through him.

"The judge ruled in Ruby's favor," she said, obviously thrilled with the verdict.

Ace enjoyed the way she rushed through her explanation as if she was afraid of running out of tape.

"Blake got five years' probation, but they said he could move to Oregon with Ruby. Roy still has to pay full support. He's furious about that." She signed off, saying she'd see him later, and Ace found himself looking forward to the evening, after all.

However, Meredith wasn't the only caller. Impatient as he was to be on his way, Ace stopped when he heard Colonel O'Dell's gruff voice.

"Ace? I missed you at the office. Just wanted to say I've finalized your summer exercise. Frank Loudermilk and I worked a deal with Nellis Air Force Base in Las Vegas. Think of it, m'boy. Joint U.S. Army-Air Force war games at the Nevada proving range. It's a rare opportunity to use some of our newest wire-guided tank missiles. I'll drop the particulars by on Monday. Oh, and, Ace, we've had a request to include Captain St. James. On second thought, consider that an order."

Ace stood rooted to the floor between the bedroom and a shower that was blasting away all his hot water. "Who in hell requested Meredith's inclusion in war games?" he snarled at the blankly whirring machine. Snapping it off, he snatched up the phone and punched out the colonel's home number. Mrs. O'Dell answered and said it was the colonel's poker night.

"That's okay, Mrs. O. I'll see him Monday." Dropping the receiver, Ace stalked into a bathroom filled with steam. Great, all he needed was to keep snot-nosed kids out of the casinos, deal with Frank's paranoia and have Captain Love-Thine-Enemy smack in the middle of level-the-earth warheads.

He cranked on the cold water. Dammit, if she was so hot to go on field maneuvers, why the devil hadn't she said so? Ace scowled. Had she gone over his head, hoping to throw some of her liberal ideas out into the field?

By the time he'd showered and dressed, he'd worked himself into a full-scale burn—to the point that he opened the drawer in his bedside table and tossed in all the little gold packets he'd purchased the day before. It was damned unlikely they'd be spending the night together.

Feeling the way he did about her treachery, they'd be lucky to make it through the evening without killing each other.

Most of his anger dissipated when he pulled into her courtyard and she came tripping down the stairs wearing a pretty fringed Western shirt and a brand-new pair of form fitting jeans. Short though she was, she had the longest legs and a way of walking that made his ears smoke.

It was tough staying mad at someone who could have a man's tongue hanging to his knees.

"Hi," she said in a throaty purr, popping her head inside the car before he could unbuckle his seat belt. Everything about her had Ace cursing his impetuosity at leaving those foil packets behind.

"Did you get my message?" She slid into the passenger seat and slammed the door.

He nodded, unable to manage more as he inhaled a sensuous cloud of her perfume.

"Ruby's folks arrived today. They're helping her move. They seem like nice people. I hope things work out for them. Hey!" She grinned. "You're awfully quiet. You haven't said a word about my spiffy new jeans."

"I, uh . . . They look fine."

"Only fine?" She punched him playfully on the shoulder. "The clerk at the shop where I bought this stuff said I could pass for a cowgirl."

Ace shrugged. "I don't know any bona fide cowgirls."

"And you call yourself a Texan?"

"You're in a good mood," he muttered. "Suppose that's because you're smug about pulling strings."

She turned and gave him a strange look. "If you're talking about Ruby's good fortune," she said quietly, "I didn't have anything to do with it."

His jaw tensed. "I'm talking about... Oh, never mind." What good would it do to fight with her? He didn't even have all the facts yet. "Let's not talk shop." Ace backed carefully out of her courtyard and picked up the street leading to the arena.

Meredith continued to stare at him. Something was eating at him and she wanted to know what. "If you'd prefer Ruby didn't move, I'm sure there's still time to ask her to stay."

He turned to glare at her and almost ran a red light. Slamming on the brakes, he reached out to keep her from being thrown forward. "How many times do I have to tell you? It wasn't that way with us. Ruby was, I guess you could say, comfortable to date."

"Am I comfortable, Ace?"

He thought about the perpetual tightness coiled in his groin. And how he didn't even have to know she was near for the fine hairs on the back of his neck to rise. A glimpse of her in the distance, and his blood pressure shot up twenty points. Ace tipped his head back and laughed.

She eyed him narrowly. "What's so funny? I think I'd rather be comfortable than laughable."

"Meredith, you are silk in a world of cotton. Light in a world of darkness. Brahms in a world of heavy-metal rock. But comfortable? Never!"

The look he sent her shimmered like silver and made her blush. "Well, uh..." She tugged at an earring—new for this outing. A tiny golden horseshoe with diamond chips for nail holes. When his smoldering gaze seemed to lock on her earlobe, Meredith shrugged and turned to look out the side window. "You continually surprise me, Major. First it was the piano, now poetry. I can't help but wonder how you are at soldiering. Oh, you passed the arena two streets back."

Ace hit the brakes and swore. This time Meredith kept herself from being thrown forward.

"Sorry." He looked it, too. "Like I said, you're definitely not comfortable. And if you don't stop calling me Major when we're out of uniform..." He didn't finish the threat. Instead, he checked the street and made a smooth U-turn.

Meredith grinned in satisfaction. "Oh, look!" she exclaimed as he turned down a street behind the arena. "A roller coaster! I haven't been on one in years."

"I might have known you'd be a daredevil," he said as he pulled into the lot and parked. "If you'd joined me on the obstacle course today, I could have saved the money."

"So! You want a date who's not only *comfortable,* but *cheap,* eh? Sorry to disappoint you, Maj—Ace. Tonight's gonna cost you big. Really, really big," she said, clowning around, waggling her eyebrows.

He climbed from the car and sauntered around to open her door. "What's first?" he asked, ignoring her antics. "Food?" he asked hopefully.

She took in everything with the eagerness of a child. "If we do rides first and eat before we visit the crafts, our stomachs won't be so queasy."

He stuffed his keys into a snug front pocket of his jeans and made a face. "Queasy? Sounds wonderful."

Even parked some distance away, they could hear the screams from the midway.

"Where's your sense of adventure?" She gouged his ribs with an elbow.

"Hey, I'm ticklish." He warded her off. "I'm also getting old, St. James. If I'd tied the knot when most of my buddies did, I could have a kid old enough to be bringing his own girl to this clambake."

She turned on him as they approached the ticket booth. "A son? I see. Just like that." She snapped her fingers, her words laced with scorn. "No chance, of course, that a macho guy like you would have a daughter."

Ace, who was retrieving his billfold, heard something in her intensity. Puzzled, he glanced up. "That comparison was off the top of my head, Meredith. When I find a partner to share my life and bear my children, I won't care if we have boys or girls. So long as they're healthy and happy."

He came close to telling her that at the restaurant the day they took the Vanishing River Cruise, he'd envisioned a daughter—a sweet miniature of herself. But from the mutinous expression on her face, Ace doubted she'd jump right up and offer to turn fantasy into fact.

"We're holding up traffic," he said. "If you want to discuss babies, I can think of better places to explore the subject."

She flushed and looked around to see who might have overheard. "This whole conversation is pointless," she said, tossing her head. "Here's money for our tickets. I talked you into this. You shouldn't have to pay."

There were enough people around the booth that her careless words stung his pride. "I think I can manage to pay for a date, St. James. How many rides do you plan on taking?" His tone didn't even suggest that he was open to sharing the cost this time.

Meredith might have pressed the issue had a group of their cadets not ambled up just then. She pretended to study the board listing ride prices and gave him a random figure.

"Hey, Major. And Captain St. James? What a surprise. Are you two together?" Vincent Granelli, never tactful, boomed his question to the world.

Ace turned from the booth, juggling three long curls of tickets and his change. "The surprise," he said dryly, "is that you're here, Vinnie, considering your scores on the rifle range. I figured you'd be practicing this weekend."

Meredith didn't think Ace should take a kid to task in front of his friends. She tried signaling her displeasure, even though Ace's pointed remarks didn't seem to faze the young cadet captain, who grinned and said cheekily, "Didn't notice you hitting too many bull's-eyes, Major."

Ace smiled. "Next time out I won't have Vaseline on my trigger, will I, Cadet?" Satisfied that Vinnie got the message, Ace took Meredith's arm and walked away.

"He *didn't?*"

Ace grimaced. "Someone did. The little gremlins."

"Where do they come up with these things?"

"Probably from supply sergeants who love having a good story to pass around over chow."

"That's awful. Speaking of stories," she said despondently, "I didn't stop to consider that any of the kids might be here. I can just hear the rumors."

"The joy of living in a small town. Everyone and his dog knows your business. All military towns are like that. Maybe you missed that part, living off base and all."

She stopped in the line waiting to board the Tilt-A-Whirl. "Believe me, with a general in the household, gossip lies in wait."

"You don't give the impression that it was much fun growing up an army brat. I've met guys who loved that life."

"*Guys* is the operative word. It's different for girls. Rules for daughters are usually more stringent. So I never got to be a kid—my life was always regimented. No child of mine will ever live by military standards."

Ace might have pursued the subject, but suddenly it was their turn to board the contraption they'd called the Octopus the last time he'd been to a carnival. From the minute they were strapped in and the engine fired, there was no discussing anything. Only now he had reason to cuddle Meredith close. Thereafter he gave himself over to having fun.

Meredith, too, relaxed and squealed along with the teenagers when the bottom dropped out of the centrifuge and when they stalled at the top of the roller coaster. She tucked her face into Ace's shoulder, and as her heart thundered madly, she thought how lucky she was that his shoulder was so firm and broad.

Back on the ground, he urged her to try Texas curly fries and funnel cakes hot from the deep fryer. She closed her eyes to the calories and the cholesterol.

Ace brushed powdered sugar from the funnel cake off her nose and kissed it off her lips. Happy, he looped an arm around her shoulders.

Enjoying the looks of envy she received, Meredith linked her arm around his waist as they wandered out of the midway and through the craft barn. She pretended there were no uniforms back home to make this contentment disappear on Monday.

At the rodeo dance, Ace had to coax her out onto the floor. Western music rocked the rafters, and the floor was a crush of cowboy hats. Double the number of boots shuffled to the rhythmic beat of popular line dances.

"I've never seen so many people all doing the same steps," she whispered, hanging back.

Ace smiled. "I'm afraid I'm not up on the electric slide, but I think I can still manage the Texas two-step."

She insisted on watching a while longer. Finally deciding that all she had to do was follow his lead, she let him sweep her out into the crowd.

They danced until the band announced the last number. Meredith's feet ached. Yet she'd have been hard-pressed to say when she'd had a better time.

She yawned so many times on their walk to the car that Ace teased her. "Past your bedtime, old girl?"

"Who're you calling old? Race you to the car, Bannister." Darting off, she beat him by several feet.

"Sneaky," he accused, panting as he loped around to open her door. Then, because she laughed, he kissed her. Ace knew at once he shouldn't have done that. They were both winded from the run and he took the kiss deeper, faster, than he'd intended.

A series of wolf whistles and catcalls from a group of teens leaving the midway broke them apart. Both their hearts were tripping in four-four time, and Ace found it difficult to let her go and get his feet rooted again.

Neither spoke much on the drive home, but she snuggled close and laid her head on his shoulder.

By the time they reached town, Ace seriously regretted dumping those packets in his bedside table. Maybe he could still salvage the night. "How about coming by my place for a nightcap?'' he suggested in a voice husky with need.

Stifling yet another yawn with her hand, Meredith gazed at him over the tips of her fingers and read exactly what was on his mind. Although she ached with the memory of the pleasure he was capable of giving her, she averted her face and shook her head.

"I don't think that's a good idea, Ace." She sat up, slid over and folded her hands in her lap. "I have a lot of errands tomorrow and laundry to do before the rodeo performance. Are you still interested in going?''

Ace couldn't think of anything that interested him less. He would have agreed to hike Mount Everest to be with her, however. And tomorrow night, he'd damn well be prepared for other activities, too.

''Wild horses couldn't keep me away,'' he murmured as he pulled into her complex, stopped and took her gently into his arms.

She nodded. A few minutes later, she was the one to call a halt. "Ace," she said, touching a finger to his lips, "if we don't stop it's going to be tomorrow."

Reluctantly he walked her to her door. Leaving her there felt like one of the hardest things he'd ever done. He was trembling all over, his whole body screaming for release.

But leave her he did.

Later, at home, as he stepped from a cold shower, not even the prospect of attending the rodeo daunted him. The last thing he did before falling naked into bed was to stuff every empty crevice in his billfold with gold foil packets.

Then, after tossing in the dark a while, he turned on a light and removed half of them. After all, he didn't want to scare her off.

CHAPTER TWELVE

ACE HAD HIS HEAD under a pillow when he was jerked
from a pleasant dream by the shrill ringing of his phone.
Half-asleep, he thrust out an arm and waved blindly
until he connected with the noisy instrument, knocking
it to the floor. The crash brought him fully awake.
Scooping up the receiver, he flopped over on his back
and croaked a hoarse hello.

Colonel O'Dell's no-nonsense voice sent Ace shooting upright to grope for his alarm. O-six-thirty! *Lord,*
Ace thought, rubbing some feeling into his face, *have we
been invaded?* When he blurted out the question, the old
colonel laughed uproariously.

"I called because Mrs. O'Dell gave me your message.
Oh, and my golf partner canceled. We tee off at 0800.
You'll take his place."

"O-eight hundred? Today?" Ace shook the clock and
held it to his ear to see if it was ticking. "But, Colonel,
I'm not dressed and the golf course is across town."

The gist, more or less, of the colonel's reply left Ace
hanging up with a bang, swearing tersely and hitting the
floor running.

A shower revived him considerably. As he toted his set
of clubs out to the car, he actually began to look forward to the day. Unlike many superior officers, Colonel
O'Dell didn't always need to win. He played golf well
and appreciated a challenge.

During the night, Ace had thought a lot about what he would do to while away the hours before his rodeo date. Now he had something that would, if he played his cards right, take him through a nice lunch at the country club.

Luckily traffic was sparse. He made it to the course with time to spare and found the colonel in the players' lounge, breakfasting on beef burritos and a Bloody Mary.

"Ah, Ace," the old man exclaimed, motioning him over. "Come and join me. Can I get you an order of what I'm having?"

Ace smiled on the surface and felt his stomach roll at the thought of hot sauce and liquor hitting his one gulp of orange juice. "No, thanks, Colonel. I'll take coffee, black, if you don't mind. A man's got to have some advantage when he's teeing off against you, sir."

"Hogwash." The old fellow grinned. "But I don't mind eating alone. So, tell me what's on your mind."

"My mind, sir?" Ace thanked the waitress for his coffee and turned a puzzled gaze toward his superior.

"Mrs. O'Dell said you sounded agitated last night. She didn't think I should wait until Monday to see you. In thirty years of marriage, I've rarely found her to be wrong."

"Oh, that call." Ace shook his head. "I was agitated. The change in my summer program surprised me. I'd been looking forward to Arizona, sir."

The colonel stirred his drink vigorously with the celery stick. "I'm sending those cadets to Fort Sill with Captain Holmes. I thought you'd be excited about doing something different, m'boy. When Colonel Loudermilk proposed a joint venture with his air cadets, it sounded like a capital opportunity to me. What's wrong with it?''

"Well," Ace said glumly, "Las Vegas for one thing." He wasn't stupid enough to complain about one colonel to another. It wouldn't do to say Frank Loudermilk was a loose cannon. All colonels were brothers under the insignia. And he'd have to waltz carefully around the other issue.

"Just keep the kids out of town, son. Frankly, I don't see a problem." He waved away Ace's worries with the tines of his fork. "Is that all that's bothering you?"

"No, sir." Ace took the plunge. "There was the bit about Captain St. James. I don't think war games are . . . her thing, Colonel."

The steely-eyed old man ate in silence for a moment.

Ace drank his coffee, feeling uneasier as the silence lengthened. At last the colonel took a big swig of his drink and pursed his lips.

"The captain's father thinks St. James is weak in some areas of soldiering." O'Dell lifted his napkin and touched his lips. "I may have told you. The general likes your war record, Ace. He'd consider it a special favor if you took her under your wing. Toughened her up. I planned to discuss this in more depth on Monday, but we can cover it out on the course." He glanced at his watch, scribbled his name at the bottom of the food ticket, then stood and walked off, apparently assuming Ace would follow.

Ace felt the last of the coffee curdle in his stomach. He knew how Meredith felt about combat. And after last night, he'd pretty well determined how he felt about her. The two didn't gel. In fact they were polar opposites. Unfortunately he also understood the implication in the general's phrase "special favor." When the words came from that high up, it suggested a promotion might be in order if he complied. And if he didn't—he could be dead-ended. Or worse.

Unhappily Ace stood and slowly followed the colonel, who strode out the door. Ace doubted there'd ever been an officer who made it to bird level without doing favors along the way. He wasn't stupid. He'd been mentored and had accepted it as his due. Somehow, though, this was different. This rubbed him wrong.

What's so different about it? his conscience nagged as he went outside to collect his clubs. But Ace knew. Those other times had affected only him. This time the "favor" involved someone he cared about. He wondered what her relationship with her father really was.

He waited to broach the subject again after they'd both teed off. Ace's ball went short and wide.

"Been a while since you've played, son?" the colonel said around a gleeful chuckle.

"I don't want to take St. James on this mission," Ace blurted, although he'd intended to use more tact.

The colonel's smile faded. "It's not your choice." He stormed past Ace's ball, way past, and whacked his own up on the green.

Bile rose in Ace's throat. His feelings showed in his punishment of the ball he sent soaring over the top of the hole and almost off the green on the opposite side.

The two men stalked down the fairway in silence. Both wiped sweat from their brows even though the morning was only pleasantly warm. Each hid his frustration behind sunglasses. At last the colonel spoke again. "Dammit, Ace," he said gruffly, "you know the game." The old man sank his ball easily.

Ace was only too aware they weren't discussing golf. He used two strokes to accomplish what should have taken only one and remained stubbornly mute as the colonel drove his next shot into the rough. His own ball arced up and dropped like a lead sinker into the small pond. By sheer force of will, Ace refrained from swearing.

Colonel O'Dell hurried over, huffing with exertion. "Is St. James a total screwup, Bannister, or what?"

"No, sir!" Ace bristled at the slight against Meredith.

"Ah." The colonel gave a mirthless laugh. "Love. I should have guessed." He spun and marched off toward his ball.

Love. The word bounced around inside Ace's head and for a moment paralyzed him. A group came up behind him, forcing Ace to give himself a mental shake. *It's not love,* he argued against the little voice that continued to plague him. He set a new ball out and proceeded to add so many strokes to his score that the entire game had become pointless.

"Get your personal life in order, Major," the colonel barked when they met on the next green. "Captain St. James is going on this joint mission, and that's an order."

Ace recognized the futility of further argument. And he regretted having let his temper get away. His golf game went from bad to worse. He and the colonel were both so irritable by the time they finished the eighteenth hole that O'Dell didn't bother to claim his hollow victory.

They were heading for the clubhouse when the colonel turned to Ace. "Always considered you a top officer. But if your golf game is any indication of how you let a woman mess up your mind..." The older man shook his head. "Officers are a dime a dozen today,

Bannister. And I'm telling you square. Screw up those field exercises—by that I mean let Frank's side win because you're not on your toes—you can forget any recommendation from me. If I didn't have to go to Fort Riley, I'd beat the pants off Loudermilk and his pantywaist fly-boys myself. I'd put starch in St. James's drawers, too."

On that note, he marched off.

Ace felt a wave of shock run through him, as if he'd been physically struck. He'd anticipated eating a pleasant lunch, maybe sharing a beer and swapping war stories with a man he'd always admired—and suddenly he was being treated like a naughty child.

Fury enveloped Ace and stayed with him the entire way home.

Slamming into the house, he shed his clothes and left them puddled where they fell on the bedroom floor. He yanked on his running shorts and in less than ten minutes had settled into a grueling pace. Over and over the colonel's words battered him with the regularity of his pounding footfalls.

It wasn't as if he were naive. He'd seen this happen plenty of times. It was the army way. Things ran on the "You scratch my back, I'll scratch yours" philosophy.

Sweat ran in his eyes, yet he did nothing to check it as he left the flats and started up a long hill. Wasn't it General MacArthur who'd said the army's mission was fixed and inviolable—to win wars without personal regard? Or words to that effect.

Ace had lived and believed wholeheartedly in the unwritten rules. Or at least he had until Captain Meredith Marshall St. James exploded into his life. He broke stride, fighting a stitch in his side. "Hellfire." He pulled up, bent double and sucked in long drafts of hot dry air.

They were talking about his entire career here. Suddenly he saw everything going down the tubes. And for what? For a woman who didn't like what the uniform stood for. A woman who'd sooner walk over burning coals than get romantically tangled with a man who wore one.

His return was at a much saner pace. On his last lap he decided that the thing to do would be to put her out of his mind. Hadn't she said in plain English that it didn't matter whether or not he went with her to the rodeo? If she didn't give a damn about his company, why shouldn't he order her into the trenches? Make things easy on himself?

Her ideals were just that, ideals. The general was right, dammit. She should toughen up or quit playing at being a soldier.

If only memories of her kisses, her teasing smile and her elusive scent would stop clinging so tenaciously to his brain....

Once Ace had arrived back at the house and spent an extra half hour in a bracing shower, he admitted that he couldn't possibly put her out of his mind—and didn't even want to try.

He counted the minutes until it was time to pick up Meredith. As he dressed with care, he even told himself that he was a disgusting disgrace to the brotherhood of officers. Then he drove to her place.

And from the moment she answered his knock and stood before him in buttery-soft boots and a three-tiered skirt in some Western print, Ace was lost. His gaze swept the blouse belted over her skirt with a slender hammered-silver concho belt. He glanced away, his abdomen tense.

She smiled and stepped outside, donning a flat-crowned hat in the same soft buckskin shade as her boots. Ace could barely remember what his objections to the rodeo were. Likewise, the colonel's orders lay buried far beneath a consuming need to be with this woman.

Seeing his frank admiration, Meredith laughed and did a little pirouette on the landing. "You look pretty snazzy yourself, Bannister," she said lightly, skipping down the first set of steps. It was true, even though he didn't have on one thing that could be considered Western. But his black close-fitting jeans and black T-shirt gave him a lean cowboyish look. A blue linen sport jacket that had surely been tailored to fit his wide shoulders set off the sheen of his dark hair.

The overall picture left Meredith so weak in the knees all she could do was grip the wrought-iron rail and force one foot in front of the other in her mad descent.

Ace caught up with her in the courtyard. "Whoa," he said, grasping her elbow before she could dash ahead to the car. Bending, he dropped a warm kiss on her lips. "I feel like I should be collecting you on a horse, instead of in a car," he murmured. He wanted to ignore the disagreeable event they were about to attend, preferring to imagine how, later that night, he'd divest her piece by piece of this fetching cowgirl rigging.

She stepped back and ran a hand over her blouse and skirt. "Is it too much like a costume? Maybe rodeo fans don't wear this kind of thing."

Ace kissed her again. He couldn't bear it when the excited anticipation in her eyes dulled. "They do," he said firmly, guiding her to his car.

Her laughter returned. "How would you know?" She removed her hat and shook her hair as she climbed in. "You told me you'd never been to a rodeo."

Remembering the times when he was little, times when his mother dragged him from rodeo to rodeo in the vain hope of catching a glimpse of Jarrod Bannister, sobered him at once. "You misunderstood what I said." His voice chilled, warned her off.

Meredith stopped in the act of buckling her seat belt and scanned his face. "I'm sure I didn't. You said you didn't attend rodeos—ever. Ace, what's wrong? Why is the rodeo so painful for you?" She placed a hand on his arm.

He shook it off and peeled out, away from her building. Once they reached the main road, his brain began to automatically chant the dialogue he'd been feeding it all week. *Jarrod Bannister would be over fifty now. No one rode wild broncs at fifty-something. No one!*

When it became clear that he wasn't going to ease her curiosity, Meredith reluctantly turned the conversation to other things. She told herself she didn't want to know anything personal about him.

She lied.

Deep down, his silence hurt. After all, he either didn't trust her or he didn't care enough about her to divulge a part of his past that bothered him very much. The problem wasn't hers, it was his. So, what did that say about Ace Bannister—a man willing to share her bed but not his past?

And what did it say about her, that she kept coming back?

The closer they came to the rodeo grounds, the quieter Ace got. "Fine, be a wet blanket," she snapped when he wheeled into a parking place and set the emergency brake. "This is a new experience for me, and one I've looked forward to since I read my first Western novel. I'm not going to let your surliness ruin it."

Ace wanted to apologize, but the words wouldn't come. The smell of hay and horses grew stronger and more suffocating as they approached the ticket booth. The sight of empty horse trailers brought back snatches of bad memories. He hadn't been subjected to these sights, sounds and odors in many years. Yet he found his stomach too empty, his mouth too dry and his palms sweating as if it was only yesterday that he'd walked into an arena like this, tagging after his mother.

Ironically even the prospect of going to combat in the Gulf hadn't left him feeling this anxious. He wondered what Meredith would say about that. Probably that he needed intense therapy, he thought grimly as he purchased their tickets.

She stood aside and watched him at the ticket window. He looked like a man scheduled to be the major attraction at a hanging. This was no little quirk Ace Bannister had about rodeos. Something bad had happened to him at some time in his life, something that involved cowboys or rodeos or horses or all three. Now she felt terrible for badgering him into coming.

When he hurried toward her carrying the tickets, she moved in close and slid her arm around his waist. "I've changed my mind," she whispered. "Let's return the tickets and leave."

"Changed your mind? What are you talking about? You wanted to see a damn rodeo. We're going to see it."

"Shh." She cast a glance around, disliking the fact that they'd drawn an inordinate amount of interest. People would think they were having a domestic squabble.

She edged over to a less crowded area. "Ace, you don't have to pretend with me. I know this is the last thing in the world you want to do. Did someone you love die in an event? Bull riding, maybe?" She took a stab in the dark.

His lip curled and he laughed scornfully. "I'm not one of your cases, Meredith. Let it alone. You wanted to ogle cowboys in action. Let's hop to it." He locked his fingers around her upper arm and all but dragged her through the automatic entrance. A woman dressed very much like Meredith took their tickets, tore them in half and said, "Enjoy," as she returned the stubs.

Enjoy! Ha! Meredith doubted if Ace realized that tomorrow her arm would very likely bear the imprint of his fingers. She eased out of his hold as discreetly as possible.

He caught her rubbing her arm. "God, Meredith, I'm sorry. I hurt you, didn't I?"

"It's nothing." She made light of it. "Shall we find our seats? Or check the concession booths to see what there is to eat?"

"I'm not hungry. Are you?" he asked anxiously.

She shook her head. "I would like a program, though. I think they're selling them over there with the T-shirts. I'll run get one."

He shifted to the other foot. He didn't want any damn program as a reminder, but she seemed to know that without his telling her. Ace closed his eyes to the sights around him and ran a shaking hand through his hair.

The sound of someone crying sent a jagged lightning bolt through his chest. Damn! His eyes flew open and he looked wildly around, expecting for a moment to see his mother. When he did locate the person shedding tears, he felt stupid. A teenage girl, cradling a bleeding finger.

He overheard someone say she'd caught it in one of the seats. *God.* He had to stop pouncing on every little thing.

Meredith returned about that time clutching a glossy souvenir program. He'd never been so glad to see her. "You want something to drink before we find our seats?"

"Lemonade would be nice." She smiled, relieved to find him more amiable.

"Lemonade does sound good. Let's mosey around the perimeter and find a stand that doesn't have a long line." They did and made their purchases.

"We're up a floor," he said. "They didn't have any seats left on the first level." For which he was thankful. "I hope that's okay."

"Sounds good to me. I'm not wanting to get up close and personal with a Brahma bull."

He laughed. "I thought maybe you did, after all your talk about waiting so long for this experience."

She didn't answer until he'd led her to the row with their numbered seats. "That was big talk because I was peeved at you. Haven't you figured out by now that I'm your typical armchair adventurer?"

"Here." He indicated two seats. "You want the end or inside?" Then he didn't hear which she said. His mind had jumped to the Las Vegas mission. Simulated war in hot mountainous terrain went way beyond armchair adventure.

He remained standing, a blank look on his face. She reached up and tugged on his jacket. "Are you going to sit? I can't see through you, Ace."

"Oh, sorry." He slumped in his seat.

She perched on the edge of hers, trying to see everything at once that was going on below.

"What event is first?" he asked, pulling nervously at the neck of his T-shirt.

"I don't know," she murmured. "Hey, look!" She grabbed his arm. "The clowns have come out."

Indulgently he wriggled from her grasp and touched a finger to her silver earring. "These look nice on you."

She didn't pull her gaze away from the antics of the clowns. "Oh, thanks," she said absently.

"Are you going to tell me which event is first?" He spoke louder to jog her memory. "You have the program."

"So I do." She took it from the side pocket of her purse and smoothed it out. "Calf roping. Then steer wrestling, followed by bull riding and barrel racing." A roar of laughter from the crowd made her stop to see what was happening. One of the clowns had climbed into a barrel and a gangly calf had wandered into the arena and tipped it over. The other clowns were trying to draw the calf away as if they were matadors, but he was having none of it and continued to chase the colorful barrel. Meredith closed the program, stood to see better and laughed in delight.

"When's bronc riding?" Ace asked nonchalantly the moment she sat down.

"What?" She wasn't listening.

"Bronc riding." He leaned close to her ear. "Is it after barrel racing or what?" Ace didn't know how long each event lasted, but he figured bronc riding would be a good time to take a break. Maybe by then he'd feel like eating. Meredith, too.

She thrust the program into his hands. "For goodness' sake, you look up it up. I want to watch. This is hilarious!"

"Um. Page one says clowns are the most important part of the rodeo. Wow, out of the four hundred participants here more than half have had their lives saved by the clowns." Ace let the program fall to his lap. "I wonder if that's how our cadets see themselves. As comic relief for the brass."

She choked on her lemonade. "Don't make me laugh when I'm drinking." She saw he wasn't smiling. "Surely you're not serious. I don't think they plan beyond the moment."

"You're probably right. This year's cadre is just full of the devil."

She nodded. "Oh, by the way, do you know why Colonel O'Dell wants to see me?"

He catapulted from his seat and the program fell to the floor.

"Well, do you?" she repeated, stooping to retrieve the booklet. "I was out doing errands when he called. He left a message."

Ace was very glad a team of riders presenting the flags came into the arena, distracting Meredith's attention. He wouldn't lie to her, but as far as he was concerned, the colonel could do his own dirty work. Ace didn't think she was going to be happy with the order for simulated war. And he didn't intend to take flak for something *he* wasn't at all happy about. Mock battle was both serious and necessary, but Meredith didn't see it that way.

She craned her neck to watch the riders circle and weave a figure eight in the ring. "Oh, Ace, look at those gorgeous palominos!"

He leaned back and slung an arm over the back of her seat to watch her, enjoying the light that danced in her eyes. Ace touched her cheek and her earlobe with a finger. His lips quirked in a smile as she unconsciously rubbed against his hand.

The last horse had barely cleared the ring when the gates opened and a calf raced out of the chute, a roper hot on his heels. Meredith bounced up and down and clapped when the rider overthrew his rope and the calf went free.

"Some cowgirl you are," Ace whispered, dropping a kiss near her ear.

She grinned. "I'm always for the underdog. Or undercalf, in this case." She was delighted when the other calves proved equally wily.

Steer wrestlers fared little better. Meredith watched the last two through fingers splayed across her eyes. "Ouch," she said, hiding her eyes completely as the last steer all but plowed a furrow with his wrestler.

Ace managed his first laugh for a group of youngsters participating in the calf-scramble. Some of the kids weighed less than the calves they were trying to grab and pull back across a chalk line. He and Meredith both cheered a pug-nosed pigtailed girl who held on to a black calf with a determined half nelson. They clapped when she made it over the line.

Bull riding was a different story. Meredith practically climbed into Ace's lap. Twice she hid her face against his shirt.

"I think I could get to like this," he teased, doing his best to take advantage of the situation.

He'd finally loosened up enough to look forward to barrel racing, when the loudspeaker crackled, cleared and the announcer called for cowboys to take the chutes for bronc riding. Ace straightened so abruptly he nearly dumped Meredith on the floor.

"What is it?" she asked, seeing him go from relaxed to tense in a heartbeat.

He stood. His jaw tightened. "I need a break," he said.

She squinted up at him. He no more needed a break than she needed a talking dog, but it was obvious he was taking one.

"If you want something to eat, tell me now," he said curtly.

Hurt by his brusque manner, she snapped back. "Go. I wouldn't want to keep you."

By this time, a disembodied voice was reading the names of the contestants. Ace bolted, but not before Meredith caught a glimpse of the panic in his eyes. The minute he was out of sight, she grabbed the program and thumbed through to the section on bronc riding. The names listed didn't mean a thing.

She started to worry as the bronc riding wound down, and Ace still hadn't returned. Had he left her? she wondered. No. She was being silly. He was too considerate a man to do that. She folded the program into halves, then fourths. How well did she really know him? She realized sadly that only on rare occasions had he allowed her a glimpse of the private man—the man beneath the major's uniform.

Yet had she been any more forthcoming? How could she sit here and condemn him? The answer was that she couldn't.

Bronc riding was over and a crew had set up for the barrel racing when Ace finally returned. He handed her a wrapped burger and a soft drink as if that were all he'd gone for. As if he hadn't been away more than thirty minutes.

Meredith accepted the gift. "Feeling better?" she asked, knowing she should let well enough alone.

"I'm fine." He sounded mildly surprised that she should ask. "It's stuffy and noisy in here. I went outside for a walk. Ran into an old buddy at the beer shed. He insisted on buying me one."

"Ah." She opened the hamburger and decided it was too greasy, rewrapped it and tucked it under her seat, sipping the soft drink instead.

"Something wrong with the burger?" he asked, brows knitted. "Did I put on the wrong condiments?"

"You did fine. It was floating in grease."

"Sorry."

She shrugged. "It's not your fault." It wasn't the burger she wanted him to apologize for. And judging by his stony expression, he knew it, too.

All at once the announcer asked for their attention. A hush fell over the crowd, and everyone leaned forward to see who was walking into the center ring.

A new voice boomed out. "The Rodeo Association would like to take this opportunity to introduce former bronc riding champion and longtime stock provider, Jarrod Bannister and his lovely wife, Cheryl. The C & J Ranch raises some of the orneriest bulls and the buckingest horses a cowboy ever tossed a leg over." The announcer paused and the audience clapped. "Tonight, the C & J brings us two very special fillies—and I'm not talking horses, men. The Bannisters' twin daughters, Letty and Meg, are about to treat us to a trick-riding performance I guarantee you'll never forget."

Meredith leaned over and listened as intently as the rest of the audience. All at once she realized Ace had gone rigid at her side. She glanced at him, then back at the handsome dark-haired man with a touch of silver at his temples who was lifting his white cowboy hat. She didn't look at the man's wife—not when she saw how closely Ace resembled the nattily dressed cowboy. She grabbed his arm, but the question died on her lips as Ace leapt to his feet, yanked her up and strode angrily toward the exit. "Wait." She panted. "Ace, stop. You just made me spill my drink."

But it was as if he hadn't heard. Her objections sailed into infinity as he stormed out of the arena and all but dragged her through the parking lot to his car. He let go of her wrist long enough to unlock the passenger door.

"Who was that?" she asked, her voice shaking. A streetlight revealed the tight lines of his face and the harsh set of his lips. She ached to ease his pain, but hadn't a clue how to go about it.

"Get in," he ordered.

She didn't argue. Before her trembling hands could buckle the seat belt, he'd revved the engine and roared out of the lot.

"Ace, is he a brother?" Her query was met with silence. "I can see you're hurting. Wait—not your father? Oh, Ace, that's it, isn't it? Don't you think you should talk about it?"

"Keep out of this, Meredith," he warned icily. "You don't know a damn thing about how I feel. The last thing I need is your psychoanalytical crap."

She smoldered. Here she sat, wet skirt plastered to her knees, thanks to the rude way he'd upended her drink. She didn't deserve his fury. But when a person was in pain... She sighed. Maybe when he calmed down, he'd realize he was taking it out on the wrong person and be more reasonable.

ACE FELT GUILTY for venting his rage on Meredith. She was innocent. Just happened to be in the wrong place at the wrong time.

Unfortunately his rage was the result of too many years of suppressed hatred for that cowboy. How often had he planned what he'd do if ever he did meet Jarrod Bannister face-to-face? The actions Ace envisioned had changed appreciably with maturity. Yet in reality, he'd just taken the route of the hurt child. He'd run away.

As a teenager, he'd dreamed of rearranging Jarrod Bannister's face. As a man, Ace saw himself laughing in his father's face and walking off. Not that someone like Jarrod Bannister would give a damn that his illegitimate son had made it to manhood, let alone managed to pull himself out of the poverty the SOB had left him in and actually make something of himself. Something he risked losing if he didn't play ball with General Harding Addison St. James.

His old man and hers were both pig slop. Fathers in general were no damned good. The army wasn't so perfect, either.

Seething, Ace darted Meredith a covert glance. Had she known who the rodeo's stock provider was? But how could she? No, the only thing she was guilty of was having a daddy powerful enough to make poor devils like Ace dance on a string.

Well, let her find some other puppet for Papa to manipulate.

ACE WHEELED the Lexus into her courtyard and ground it to a halt beside the stairway.

"Ace?" His odd behavior drew a frown from her. It worried Meredith that he sat there gripping the steering wheel, making no move to get out. "Why don't you come up for coffee and maybe a sandwich?'' she said quietly. "You'll feel better if you eat something."

"Stay out of my head," he snarled, wanting to hurt her—feeling unreasonably irritated at her continued rationality. It was partly, he realized, because of how he'd envisioned this night ending. He'd dreamed of losing himself in her softness. In spite of everything, he still wanted that.

But now, considering what had happened, it would be hazardous for him. For her. Ace knew of one sure way to break off this explosion of feeling between them—to hurt her as much as *he* hurt.

"Not only do I want you to stay out of my head, Captain St. James," he said viciously, "from here on, stay out of my life."

Meredith could see he was more upset than she'd ever seen a man. But that didn't give him the right to take that tone with her. Lifting her chin to a proud angle, she sent him the most withering look she could muster, threw open the door and climbed from his car. Furious, she ran headlong up the stairs without once looking back.

Ace bit his lip so hard he tasted blood. So, he was a bastard in more ways than one. If this didn't prove to the whole world that he was his father's son, he didn't know what did.

Still, he sat watching her windows until he saw a light come on. Then he backed out, headed for the O-club. He had some thinking to do, starting now. She certainly didn't need *two* bastards in her life—not her manipulative father and not a coward like him.

And *he* didn't need a bastard like Jarrod Bannister. He'd done just fine all these years without a father, thank you very much.

He didn't need Meredith Marshall St. James, either.

He'd plan his schedule for the next few weeks so there was absolutely no chance of their paths crossing.

The O-club's parking lot was in sight when Ace suddenly slowed the Lexus, made a U-turn and swung back toward the arena. God! He had two half sisters he'd never met. How could he let that go?

CHAPTER THIRTEEN

ACE SHIFTED uncomfortably in his seat. The engines of the C-130 transport seemed to drone on forever, although it was just a short flight from Fort Freeman to Nellis Air Force Base in Las Vegas.

This was the first time he'd seen Meredith except at a distance in more than three weeks, and he was disturbed to find that what he felt for her hadn't diminished. First thing he noticed now was that her ears were bare. Second, her perfume was the same, and it provoked images he needed to forget.

He had expected her to balk at being forced to come on this mission. When she didn't, it left him wondering if she and her father had planned it together. A scheme to let her try her agenda out in the field, perhaps?

If that was true, he was glad he hadn't dropped by to see her the day after the rodeo—to let her know he'd gone back to see his louse of a father. Jarrod Bannister didn't want his precious daughters to hear what a skunk he'd been in his younger years. Nor would he accept any blame for what he claimed were raging hormones and a willing whore. Ace was proud of himself for not breaking that handsome nose. But he'd discovered he was the better man. He wouldn't waste another moment's regret. Not even for the sake of his mother, who'd really loved the bastard. Funny, for the first time in thirty-five years, Ace felt truly free of the man.

Meredith—peace-loving, live-in-harmony Meredith— wouldn't understand that. It was just as well he'd avoided her at work. Otherwise he might have told her exactly what he thought of *her* old man, too.

Ace just wished the cadets weren't so aware of their feud. It might affect how they performed against Frank's team. He and Meredith should try to forge some sort of truce, at least for the next two weeks.

He'd worked up to suggesting it when the copilot stepped to the door of the cockpit and requested Ace come forward. Sighing, he unfolded his long legs from the low-slung seat.

Meredith glanced up as he stood, but when their eyes met she quickly averted hers and feigned interest in the endless blue sky.

The moment she felt him pass, she turned back to study him, gazing with detached appreciation at his wide shoulders and narrow hips. His lack of trust had hurt her terribly—even if, over the last strained weeks, she'd come to understand that the actual cause of their rift had nothing to do with her and everything to do with the cowboy. Ace's father. She'd found out that much by digging through personnel files.

Despondently she let her eyes feast on Ace's lean body until he disappeared into the cockpit. She'd have done anything to help him cope with the shock of seeing his father. Instead, he'd avoided her. Not only that, he'd scheduled her for this mission out of spite. She hadn't expected that of Ace. The pain had been so acute Meredith had done something she'd sworn never to do. She'd asked her father for a favor. All but begged the general to use his influence to get her out of this assignment. Of course, she hadn't let on that her heart was involved.

Surprisingly the general hadn't made her grovel. Perhaps he was mellowing in his old age. He'd even called her back himself to say that local command wouldn't budge. At first Meredith thought he meant Colonel O'Dell, but she'd cornered him and the poor man had seemed embarrassed to admit the decision belonged to Ace. Then she remembered Ace's saying the colonel let him run the program.

Meredith sighed heavily.

"I'm sorry you and the major are fighting," Corporal Betsy Larson murmured in an undertone.

Her statement caught Meredith off guard. She coughed. "Excuse me, did you ask about the fighting, Betsy? It's all fake. Rocky terrain, I understand, and we'll have to dig in. Not quite as much fun as camping. Especially with the air force trying to root us out. Uh...did that cover your question? If not, I'll know more tonight after we bivouac."

Betsy's blue eyes blinked owlishly.

Meredith felt badly about giving the poor girl double-talk, but she wasn't about to admit to squabbling with the major. Rumors and gossip were running rampant, as it was.

"Uh, I think you about covered it, Captain." Betsy sat back and smiled.

Just then Ace walked back into the body of the craft. He didn't look pleased. "Listen up," he said, assuming a wide-legged stance as the plane dropped and forced him to brace one hand on the wall behind Meredith.

She stared at his belt buckle, licked her lips and turned away.

Her action didn't escape Ace. He all but snarled what he had to say. "The area around Nellis is experiencing unusual thunderstorms. We've got heavy lightning below," he said. "Apparently the base commander doesn't want to truck us out to set up our tents until it blows over. All air-force barracks are full, and so are the hooches at Indian Springs. For the time being, we'll bunk in a hotel on the edge of town."

A cheer went up from the cadets, and Ace's scowl darkened.

At first Meredith sided with the cadets. She'd never been to Las Vegas and wouldn't mind seeing what all the fuss was about. Her enthusiasm waned when she noticed the gleam in the eyes of their friskiest cadets. Keeping this bunch corralled held about as much appeal as mud wrestling a tiger.

She set aside her differences with Ace and shot him a commiserating glance.

He saw her empathy and took it as a good sign. "St. James," he said, grabbing the opportunity, "after we land, you and I need to reconnoiter."

That term produced a sudden wicked connotation in Meredith's mind. Lord, if only he'd move his hand. Those long suntanned fingers that had once elicited such a delicious response from her body....

The sinful thought, along with a curious silence that fell over the cadets within earshot, prompted Meredith's frosty reply. "Is that an order, Major? Surely you don't need my psychoanalytical crap. That *is* how you phrased what I have to offer, I believe. Incidentally it'd be *socio*analytical crap."

Ace figured he'd obviously misread her look. When the plane hit an air pocket and took another drop, he tensed to keep from touching her. If that was the way she wanted to play, so be it.

"It's not an order," he said curtly. "By the time we land I'll have a list of cadets who'll be under your command throughout the exercise. How you keep them out of bars and on task is up to you.''

A hush fell over the entire core of cadets as he strode angrily back to his seat.

Meredith tucked in her chin and balled her fists—bracing, they called it at the Point. It allowed her to block out the many covert glances darted her way. She could tell the young men thought she'd made a tactical error in ticking the major off. The women, at least, seemed sympathetic.

Inside, Meredith felt sick. Her reaction had been inexcusable. Lashing back like that in front of the students was immature. Unprofessional. Not to mention that it slammed the door on further communication between her and Ace—something she believed to be of paramount importance. And it drove home the fact that, deep down, she wanted more from Ace Bannister—more than just a workplace truce. Rocked though she was by the realization, Meredith knew she owed him an apology. Her behavior just now was the antithesis of everything she believed.

Unfortunately events changed so quickly there didn't seem to be a good time to attempt a reconciliation. The copilot called Ace again, advising him they were about to land.

No sooner had the craft touched down than Ace was whisked off to meet with Colonel Loudermilk and two officers from Nellis. Meredith was not included.

On returning an hour later, Ace placed two fingers between his lips and whistled to get their attention. "We have a change in plans. The storm has abated for the moment. We have four-bys outside ready to take the Green Geese—that's us—to Skull Mountain. It's a long bumpy ride. We'll stop along the way for sack lunches and milk. Enjoy. Because starting tonight, we'll be on MREs."

Ignoring the groans and long faces at the idea of having nothing but "Meals Ready to Eat," Ace gave his ranking cadets handouts of the game plan for the next fourteen days.

Again Meredith wasn't included. She had to request a copy, which didn't sit well with her.

Ace seemed nonplussed. "We'll scope out a good place to pitch our pup tents tonight and set up field headquarters. Tomorrow the colonel's fly-babies will parachute into the hills above us. We wear green arm bands, they wear blue. Our first goal will be to capture and interrogate. Anyone captured gets tagged with a yellow band and held for trade. Anyone marked by our artillery will be banded black. Captain St. James and I will decide on wounded and issue red crosses. I see some of you grinning. The air force has the same rules, guys. Bands will be tallied at the end of two weeks. The team with the most points wins."

Hands on hips, he frowned around the circle. "Need I say that it had better be us?"

Subdued, the cadets, as if on cue, all shook their heads.

"Where are the rules for interrogation and pickup of wounded?" Meredith asked. "I don't see them attached."

Ace paused. "Rules?"

She pursed her lips. "Yes. The rules for humane treatment of prisoners and set hours for cease-fire to pick up wounded."

Ace blinked. "We're using blanks, Captain."

"Yes, but—"

"Could we discuss this later?" he asked, lips taut. "I'd like to dig in during daylight." What was she trying to do?

Meredith nodded, imagining they'd ride in the same vehicle. They'd be able to discuss the rules then; it would also give her a chance to apologize. As it turned out, Cadet Captain Granelli, put in charge of loading, pointed Meredith toward the last truck in the convoy. Ace had already climbed aboard another.

Nor did she have an opportunity to speak with him when they stopped to pick up lunches. The ride had become so rough Meredith had her hands full keeping their gear intact. The only plus she saw was that they'd left behind the dark menacing clouds hanging over the city.

Meredith ate her turkey sandwich and peanut-butter cookie in silence and read about the operation. One paragraph in, and she knew this had been drawn up by seasoned militarists. Terms like *battle dress, perimeter patrol guards and ground aggressors* were definite clues. Not to mention *cold-water showers* and *chemical toilets*. In bold letters someone had typed that women were not to be treated differently from men on this mission.

It irritated her that someone, Ace most likely, thought he had to spell it out. She didn't want special favors, only across-the-board fair treatment. Since the women were all in the one vehicle, Meredith elected to give a little pep talk of her own. "Ladies, I get the feeling someone doesn't think we measure up. I'm a firm believer in teamwork, but it's obvious our buddies don't want to play ball with us. Let's show them we can do the job as well as any man."

"All right. You bet!" Like toppling dominoes, high fives passed down the row. Enthusiasm ebbed a bit on arrival, though, once they got a good look at the desolate granite mountain.

They moment they'd climbed from the truck, Ace gave another of his shrill whistles. Those whistles were beginning to grate on Meredith's nerves.

"The trucks are leaving in five minutes," Ace shouted. "Anyone who doesn't have all his or her gear out will suffer the consequences, since we have none to spare. First, we set up tents. You're each responsible for locating a spot you deem enemy safe. When you're finished, I want all cadet captains to report to me. We'll select a site for our command post. Except for a small green flag on that tent, everything gets camouflaged. Remember, the first wave of enemy will come in from overhead. Okay, let's move."

Meredith chafed inwardly. He acted as if she didn't exist. Well, two could play his game. She wouldn't apologize now if her life depended on it.

Perversely, or so it seemed, the sandy soil came with a hard crust that did not lend itself to setting tent stakes.

Meredith watched two young men who had a degree of success in hoisting their tent. She stole their method, but soon discovered she'd have to haul in rocks to block her tent spikes. Because the rocks were heavy and unwieldy, she decided the smartest thing would be to set up nearer the rock bed.

The spot she chose wasn't deep enough to be called a canyon. Once she cleared out the largest stones and set her tent close to one slope, it would be simple to string camouflage netting over the scrub.

Feeling pretty darned smug, Meredith threw her muscle into finishing. She'd show Ace Bannister what a woman could do.

Some of the women, though, had real problems. So did a few of the men. Cadet Sergeant Jefferson, one of the efficient ones, offered to lend a hand to the women and got yelled at by Ace.

"Jefferson, didn't you hear my order? These women may end up in combat zones after they're commissioned. Don't you think they'll need to know how to pitch a tent?"

The chivalrous student saluted smartly and retreated.

Meredith stood with her hands on her hips and glared at Ace. *Macho ape!* She took back every nice thing she'd ever thought about him. She was too incensed to admit she'd already bloodied two fingers and smashed a third between some rocks. But she'd get her tent up alone, by God, or die trying.

Eventually it *was* up—sort of. The structure leaned a little to the east, but if she propped her pack inside against that wall it looked level. "This whole business is stupid," she muttered, standing to brush her hands together as she surveyed her work.

"What's stupid, St. James?" Ace asked silkily from behind her. "Isn't it more stupid to send green kids into war without preparing them first? That's what happened in 'Nam, you know. To plenty of West Point grads, too."

"If I had my way, Major, we wouldn't send anyone to war."

"I forgot. You wear the uniform but you believe in shaking hands with the enemy."

"I only propose that we learn not to go off half-cocked," she said indignantly. "There *is* a difference. Besides, I happen to think that if our leaders send armed troops into starving nations to keep the peace, those soldiers should have at least a passing acquaintance with the concept of humanitarianism."

His eyes narrowed. "Is that a fact? Are you saying I'm a warmonger because I believe in being combat trained? What about your father?"

"What about him? He's one of the worst. The man has little conscience and no heart."

Ace laughed bitterly. "Come off it, Captain. I know what lengths he's gone to in order to get you in the thick of it."

Her brow puckered. "What do you mean? I begged him to pull strings to get me out of this trip! I should think you'd have applauded his efforts."

His eyes blazed. "How you can lie so convincingly is beyond me, St. James. You think I don't know your old man resorted to threats to get you on this mission? Colonel O'Dell made it only too plain—take St. James or my career hits a brick wall. Incidentally, I decided you weren't worth throwing away seventeen years." Whirling, he left her, without sparing time to inspect her tent.

It took Meredith a moment to digest his angry words. She ran after him, grabbed his arm and spun him around. "I don't have the faintest idea what you're talking about."

"I'll just bet you don't. Well, you can cut the innocent act. I'm telling you in plain English—the only damn reason you're here is because General St. James ordered it. You tell me why he'd do that if you don't want to be here."

She folded in on herself. "I don't know. I gave up trying to second-guess him long ago."

Ace frowned. "A few weeks ago, O'Dell mentioned that your father wanted you toughened up. But when you didn't throw a fit about coming, I thought it was a scheme you two cooked to get your nutty theories out in the field."

Meredith's laugh was strained. "A lot you know. The biggest fight I had with the general was over my 'nutty theories,' as you call them. He claimed I was dead-ended in this field. I said I didn't care about gaining rank. Next thing I know, I'm winging my way to your ROTC program. Go figure."

A cadet ran up and asked Ace a question about camouflage. He answered automatically, then turned back to Meredith. "The only thing I can think—and it's pretty farfetched..." He paused and rubbed his jaw. "The only promotions coming down now are in combat units. Surely he wouldn't send his only child—his daughter— into a known hot spot."

She looked so bleak Ace wished he could get his hands on General St. James.

"He just might," she said in little more than a whisper. "If I got killed, at least he'd have another medal for the St. James memorial wall."

"God, Meredith, you can't be serious!"

"Think what you will," she said wearily. "Until I finish my active-duty requirement, he has the power to send me anywhere."

Ace didn't know what to say. Generals did have the ultimate power, that of autonomy. "Meredith, I'm sorry. I wish I'd known. I swear to you, I would have told him to take a flying leap." Which he planned to do in any event, once the mission ended.

"No, Ace. You were right. I'm nothing to you. Certainly not worth throwing away seventeen years."

Ace would have told her what she meant to him except that a group of cadets converged on him, claiming to have found the perfect site for the command post. He knew if he didn't go, darkness would overtake them. Since there wasn't anything else he could do at the moment, he intended to walk away from this mission a winner.

"Table our discussion for now," he said.

Meredith watched him stride away. Perhaps she shouldn't have been so quick to believe the worst of Ace. All the same, she'd have to see that the major didn't do anything foolish. Her father had the power to destroy a man. Damn him for causing all this trouble! And for lying to her again . . .

Resignedly she went to look in on her cadre of men and women and to settle them for the night.

Ace and his crew worked feverishly to erect the command post before dark. It didn't help that the black clouds they thought they'd left behind in Vegas rolled in and shortened the daylight hours. As a result, Ace stayed busy until bed check. When he went to touch base with Meredith, he was disappointed to see that she had retired, too.

Keyed up as he was, Ace wandered out to check on his sentries. They were fine, so he went back to take one last look at tomorrow's mock battle plan before turning in. By the time he finally hit the sack, he was asleep the moment his head touched the ground.

He awakened once and thought he heard rain, but couldn't quite drag himself out of the cobwebs of sleep. A colonel from Nellis said these little squalls never amounted to much and nearly always blew over by morning. Content with that, Ace drifted off again.

The next thing he knew a bomb exploded overhead. Awake in an instant, he yanked on his pants and crawled out of his tent to see what Frank thought he was pulling. No bomb, he found, only thunder. And lightning like none he'd ever witnessed. Jagged bolts bisected heaven and earth, burying themselves deep in the ground.

Sleepy cadets scrambled out into the mud to see what was happening.

Ace tried his best to allay their fears, but his voice was drowned out by a distant roar, sounding like a freight train heading full throttle into a tunnel.

Cadet Larson ran up. Her freckles stood out individually in a sudden burst of lightning. "We've got ourselves a real gully washer, Major. The last time I heard a flash flood anywhere near as powerful, Pop lost a bull, ten heifers and twenty or so steers. We don't have anybody camped in that draw, do we?" She jerked a thumb in the direction of Meredith's tent.

Ace swore succinctly. She'd bedded down in a dry wash. He started running. Why hadn't he realized it before? Mud lapped at his bare feet. Sharp rocks slowed his progress. His heart went on a rampage when another bolt of lightning reflected off a boiling, raging river thundering toward them down the dry creek bed.

Meredith lifted her head once and heard rain pounding on her tent. She smiled and snuggled back into her bag—to recapture a dream. Oh, how she loved a good spring rain. It made everything so green and fresh smelling. Would Ace be the kind of man who liked to hold hands and walk in the rain? she wondered.

Ace hit the once-dry creek bed the same instant a great foaming dragon of water struck Meredith's small tent and swept it away. A hoarse cry spilled from his throat, rivaling the thunder that rolled overhead.

Lightning split the sky, affording the small group of cadets, who'd arrived on his heels, a clear look at their leader's dangerous plunge into the crazed stream.

The major thought he heard Meredith scream. But he couldn't answer because the impact of the floodwaters stole his breath and wrenched away his strength. Another burst of lightning struck a tree on the west bank. Ace, who rode a crest of water, was trying too hard to spot her tent to worry about the prospect of being killed himself. From his momentary vantage point, he glimpsed her tumbling a few feet away like a rag doll. Then he got sucked down in a trough of water and she was gone again.

HAVING BEEN TORN wickedly from her sleeping bag and her dream, Meredith awoke in the black of night. Instinctively she knew she had to get out. Water—gallons of it swarmed around her. Had a water main broken? Had the Chesapeake overflowed its banks? Then reason returned. She wasn't in Baltimore. Seconds later, she was too busy choking on the water she inhaled to care precisely what had caused the problem. If she didn't make it to solid ground, she'd surely be killed by the rocks that battered her from all sides.

Or she'd be struck by lightning. It cracked all around—and that last bolt struck close by. She was normally a strong swimmer, but her efforts had little effect in this current. Suddenly she smacked up against a bush or a small tree that seemed firmly entrenched. Flinging her arms around it, heedless of the way it scratched her face and arms, she hung on for all she was worth.

Strange things went through her mind. She thought about the wind chime Ace had given her—imagined she heard it tinkling. She worried that she'd never actually apologized to him. Was this a prelude to death?

ACE WAS THROWN about willy-nilly. He'd never thought he would pray for lightning, but he did. And when the next bolt shattered the sky, he realized Meredith was caught on something in the middle of this madness, less than a foot away.

Then his light was gone. Desperate, his lungs screaming for air, he flung out an arm and closed his fingers around soft material. Of what—her T-shirt? He felt the material stretch.

In the yawning blackness, all the things they'd shared and some they hadn't hurtled through his brain. Crying out in protest against the force doing its best to rip her from his grasp, Ace wrapped the fabric around and around his hand and hung on.

CHAPTER FOURTEEN

THE FRANTIC BEAT of Meredith's heart against his chest was strangely comforting. It was enough for the moment to know she was alive. He murmured nonsense in her ear and prayed that the bush was strong enough to hold them until the water receded.

Fortunately it was.

In the way of flash floods, the water rose and swirled around them, then dropped and sped into the night, sucking greedily at the bone-dry land.

Soon, twenty or so cadets waving flashlights stumbled along the bank. "Major, how can we help?" they yelled.

"A rope," Ace shouted. "Tie it to a boulder and throw me the other end."

Meredith listened as if detached. She was shaking with cold, with fear, with shock. All the same, she trusted Ace to keep her safe. His arms were solid and reassuring.

"I feel foolish," she gasped, when he'd caught the rope and secured it around them.

"It's my fault." He grunted. "I should have double-checked everyone's location. That's a rule from basic training. I blew it."

The temperature had fallen markedly with the onset of the storm and once they landed on the bank, Meredith still couldn't control her shivers.

She seemed to be uninjured, but Ace wanted to run his hands over every inch of her body to satisfy himself that she was indeed all right. His first duty, however, was to check on everyone else. "Let's get you back to camp." He tossed the rope to one of the cadets and scooped her up in his arms.

"Put me down. I can walk." Probably not true, but for some insane reason Meredith didn't want the cadets to see her looking helpless.

"Shh. You're barefoot."

"So are you," she pointed out as he stepped on a rock and winced. Something else Meredith realized—his chest was bare. How many times since their one-sided love-making had she dreamed of touching him again? Too many. She knew that surviving a close brush with death often led to erotic urges—to a need to reaffirm life. But her reaction to the major was attributable to more. It went even deeper.

When they reached camp, they found themselves ringed by young cadets with anxious faces. Meredith thought it best to lighten things up.

"Well." She made a face as she struggled to get down. "I certainly hope you guys paid close attention to how *not* to pitch a tent," she drawled.

"Get us two blankets," Ace barked, "and start a fire. I want an inventory of loss. Who's your size?" he demanded. "Instead of clowning, Captain, you might worry about the fact that your gear's washed halfway to Arizona."

"Gear? Is that what's important here? *Things* are easily replaced."

Ace was furious with her. "If I hadn't seen you in that brief spurt of lightning, you'd be standing at the pearly gates cracking bad jokes." He plunked her down none too gently and shoved a blanket into her hands. His were unsteady.

She wrapped herself as best she could, not understanding why he was yelling. They had survived. Couldn't he see the kids were shaken? "Easy for Major Cool to say. He didn't come out looking like Biggy Rat." Spiking her muddy hair out in a wild halo, she crossed her eyes and stuck out her tongue. As she'd anticipated, everyone laughed.

Everyone except Ace.

"Stop it." He grabbed her arm and hauled her across the clearing to where two cadets had started a small blaze inside a circle of rocks. "These kids are too young to remember that silly cartoon rat. What's with you? You might have been killed tonight. And me, too! Where would the mission be then?"

His chest tightened. Somehow that hadn't come out right. He couldn't have stood it if something had happened to Meredith through his negligence. Didn't she know that?

She sank down on a rock one of the cadets had rolled over. "Heaven forbid. How dare Mother Nature forget your precious mission?"

His brows nearly met over the bridge of his nose. "That's not what I mean and you know it. Oh, hell. Forget it. I'm hunting up some dry clothes and I suggest you do the same." He stalked off into the night, angry with her. And angrier with himself.

She huddled in her blanket, hardly noticing the light rain that was still falling. What *did* he mean, then? Duty first. Before people. Always duty.

Betsy Larson interrupted Meredith's black thoughts to bring her a stack of clothes and supplies. "Some of these belong to the men," Betsy said. "But shirts, jackets and pants are pretty much generic. Private Jefferson had two packs—don't ask me why. Maureen had an extra first-aid kit. We've scrounged a flashlight, canteen and a weapon. Only thing we couldn't find was a tent.''

"This is great," Meredith praised the young woman. "If our dauntless leader doesn't object, maybe I'll bunk at headquarters." She stood, her knees still quaking, and looked around at the somber faces. "I made a gross error, okay?" she said, accepting full blame. "The major is right to be upset."

It was the correct thing to say, even though she felt Ace should have been more understanding of the cadets' feelings. And hers. "Hey." She smiled weakly. "You ladies had better turn in. I'll feel worse if we don't make a good showing against the air force in a few hours."

Betsy grinned. "Don't worry, Captain. We've dated some of those nerds. They couldn't find their way down the mountain if the colonel dropped a trail of iridescent bread crumbs."

Meredith tried to look stern as she gathered the gear they'd given her. "It never pays to get too cocky. See you at sunrise for the briefing."

They left her, and Meredith wandered off in search of Ace. She found him crawling out of his tent.

He stood to snap his jacket. "You still in those wet things, Baltimore? I've got a flash for you. They don't give medals if you die of pneumonia. You'll have to think of some other way to get one for Daddy's wall."

"You think I did this on purpose? Is that why you're acting like the butt end of a donkey?"

Reaching out, he gripped her, blanket and all, and yanked her up against him so hard she dropped her things. Their eyes clashed and their breaths fused in the

cool night air. All the worry and frustration that had
torn at Ace when he saw her being swept away pooled in
his throat, choking him. He wanted to kiss her senseless. He wanted to wring her neck. He wanted to make
slow, delicious love to her throughout the night.

Because the sentry came running in just then to
breathlessly report enemy activity on the mountain, Ace
was forced to release her without doing any of those
things. "What in hell is Frank trying to pull?" He swore.
"St. James, get dressed. Alert your division. That
sneaky, no g-good... He never intended to parachute
in."

She blinked.

"Meredith!" Ace shook her. "Move. Assemble your
team at command post in three minutes. And tell somebody to douse that fire. Leaves us sitting ducks."

Ace shrugged into his pack, then buckled on his pis-
tol belt, ammunition pouch and canteen. Last, he picked
up his M-16. "Full battle dress," he reminded her
tersely. "On the double, Captain St. James. On the
double."

Still dazed by the rapid change in events, Meredith
stooped and slowly gathered the items she'd dropped.
What happened to the man who'd been about to kiss
her? Moments ago his eyes had been soft. Loving. Now
they were steely, like two more pieces of his precious
military equipment. Apparently he expected her to be a
robot, too.

She shuddered and did as he asked—told someone to
put out the fire, then rousted her cadets. But her fingers
shook as she crept into Ace's tent to change out of her
wet clothes. At first she tried frantically to scrub the mud
from her body with her wet T-shirt. Wincing when she
hit a huge bruise on her leg, she gave up. Who cared if

she was filthy or, for that matter, if she was one massive bruise? Apparently not Ace.

What came across loud and clear as Meredith went through the motions of dressing was that he belonged in this simulated combat zone. She didn't. Obviously, she could no longer separate her feelings from the job. Not like she'd done at West Point, when she hadn't felt anything for those who made the rules.

It changed everything. What she felt for Ace Bannister displayed all the signs of love. But because she wasn't up to dealing with the full implications of that, Meredith shoved all thought of him to the back of her mind. Right now, she had a group of young people depending on her, no matter how limited her combat skills might be.

Ace was pacing, wearing a hole in the dirt floor, when at last she rushed into the command tent. Without so much as a smile of welcome, he jumped right into blackout procedures and handed his cadet leaders the few night-vision goggles they'd been asked to try out. Brusquely Ace laid out their counterattack.

"Any questions?" he asked when he'd finished, although his tone insinuated that none was warranted.

Meredith wished she were half as confident.

"By the way," he added as he folded his map and tucked it inside his shirt, "the original outline called for us to be shelled with blanks at dawn. I have no reason to believe that will change. I just want you to be prepared for any variation or modification. Try not to get tagged. But anyone who does, follow the rules. Don't talk to anyone from either side when you're released. Some of you may be taken for interrogation. You'll be freed when the exercise ends at 1700 hours. Tomorrow we'll be handed a new drill. Dismissed." He popped off a salute.

After returning his salute, Meredith glanced at the huddle of half-scared kids. "What?" she demanded suddenly. "No good-luck wishes, Major?"

His cold gaze skewered her. "This isn't a civilized game of volleyball, Captain. This is imitation war. Tagged represents capture, and capture very often means torture and death. I want the Green Geese to rely on things learned in military science—not on luck. There's a right way, a wrong way, and the army way. Do it the army way."

She clamped her teeth on the urge to call him a jackass. Wheeling, she led her cadets away. Into darkness and the unknown.

There was no denying that Ace knew more about combat than she. In the midst of the *rat-tat-tat* of artillery fire, she realized he'd spoken the truth. Each one of her baby-faced charges owed at least four more years to active military duty. They might not all be lucky enough to avoid combat. Some would be sent to hot spots, where survival would take a solid melding of strong hearts and cool heads.

This was the first time since she'd been forced to attend West Point that Meredith had given credence to her father's philosophy. It was Ace's philosophy, too. *Give 'em your worst to separate the wheat from the chaff. Then knuckle down and give 'em hell.*

"We've all read the books," she whispered softly, giving the hand signal to spread out. "Now let's put those words into practice."

By the end of the day, when a neutral helicopter circled overhead, its bullhorn announcing the workout was over, Meredith's team had suffered only two wounded.

She was proud of her cadets, whose performance was exemplary. All in all, they'd tagged a fair number of opponents and had no casualties.

The sun hung hot in the west again. It looked as if the storm had blown over. They were all dirty and tired after covering some rough terrain. Meredith's group met at the river so they could march back to camp together. The river had receded appreciably but still bubbled down the wash. Although a few of the cadets were out of water in their canteens, Meredith reminded them not to drink from the polluted stream. They griped, but settled good-naturedly for soaking their feet, instead.

"Is this everyone?" she asked Betsy when fifteen minutes had passed and no one else showed up.

"Yes." Betsy nodded. Then she shook her head. "Where's Mouse?"

Captain St. James looked around for Maureen Porter—the only woman in the outfit shorter than herself. She frowned. "Did anyone see her get tagged?"

Someone near the back of the line spoke up. "I ate lunch with her. She drank too much water afterward and threw up."

"Why didn't you tell me?" Meredith demanded.

"You know Mouse. She made me promise I wouldn't."

"If she was sick," Betsy offered, "maybe she went back to camp."

"Yes, maybe," Meredith agreed, scanning the ravines one more time before she moved them out.

In camp a quick check didn't turn up the girl, either. Ace was lecturing his squad when Meredith slipped past him into the tent to call Colonel Loudermilk's unit on the base radio. "Are you still holding a Green Goose captive?" she asked. The code name had caused much dissension at first because the air force was coded with the more macho name of Blue Boars.

"Negative on prisoners," someone answered, and Meredith stifled a shiver of fear. She was answerable for that young woman.

Ace walked in just as she clicked off the set. "Great showing, Captain," he said, beaming at her. "I mean really great."

"Don't be so hasty with your praise. I seem to have lost a cadet." In spite of being tired, she squared her shoulders to await his dressing down.

He dropped his pack. "I can see you're worried. Not just a straggler?"

Meredith bit her lip. "She might be sick. One of my cadets says Maureen threw up after lunch."

"Tell me approximately where that was and I'll go take a look," he said without hesitation. "You look beat. Why don't you get dinner organized? I've stashed some real grub in my tent. I want everyone to eat a hot meal tonight. They'll need all their strength tomorrow. We get shelled for sure, or so I'm told."

"Mouse is my responsibility, Ace. I'm going after her. You didn't have any more sleep than I did, and you climbed the mountain face today."

"We'll both go," he said quickly. "If she's sick, she may have fallen asleep. This crew can handle dinner on their own." He smiled. "I'll wager they're too dog tired to get into mischief tonight."

"I'll let Betsy in on the plan and check again with the last person to see Maureen. Meet you at the big pine tree by the river?"

He nodded.

Meredith refilled her canteen and shed everything from her pack except one small survival tarp and her first-aid kit. When she met Ace, he'd stripped down to summer shorts, a T-shirt and cap, as if headed on a pleasure jaunt. "You're going to melt," he said as Meredith walked up. "Why don't you go back and change?"

"My lightweight stuff washed away, remember? I'm fine. The sooner we find Mouse, the sooner we'll get back and both of us can rest."

"Suit yourself. What are our coordinates?"

She gave them and followed as he led the way. The ground went steadily uphill. It was also filled with blind switchbacks and afforded almost no shade except for a few boulders here and there. They both kept an eye on a row of pine trees where the two young women had reportedly shared lunch. Because Ace and Meredith were close to exhaustion, they talked little.

Well into the second hour, Meredith stopped to catch her breath and fan herself with her cap. "What if we don't find her before dark?" she asked, casting a worried glance at the sun that was fast slipping behind a layer of low clouds.

Ace answered over his shoulder as he rounded an outcrop of rocks several yards ahead of her. His response was muffled, but Meredith thought he said the trip back would be a cinch. The next thing she heard was his harshly expelled *"God!"*, followed by a host of unrepeatable words. Then silence.

Panicked that he'd found the girl and something terrible was wrong, Meredith ran. Never mind that her legs felt as spongy as foam rubber. Circling the mound, she discovered not Mouse, but Ace in trouble. He sat in the middle of the rocky trail, clasping his leg with both hands about two inches above his boot top. His face was pale and contorted in pain.

"What is it?" she asked, bending, placing her palms on her knees to catch her breath. "Did you slip on a rock? Your leg's not broken, is it?" He just looked at her and began whipping off his belt. "I didn't slip. I surprised a rattler. See, there he goes." He pointed.

She saw. The snake was a good size. That meant a greater risk, or so she'd read. The larger the rattler, the stronger the venom. "Wait," she shouted as he started to wrap his belt around his thigh. "Don't do that! Let me get the snake-bite kit out of my first-aid box." She wriggled out of her pack and fumbled with the buckles. Her fingers didn't want to work.

"How do you know so much about snakes?" he asked around a grimace when she finally hauled out the kit.

"I don't. I read a bit last week when I heard where we were headed. Okay. Hold still." She peeled out the directions. "This sounds simple. Place this gadget over the wound and depress the bulb."

He jerked when the device broke through his skin. Then he was silent while she suctioned. Tension radiated as hot and humid as the air.

Meredith glanced over once and saw he'd turned white around the mouth and appeared to be sweating. From the sun, she hoped, using half the water in her canteen to wash his wound. "The directions say to apply ice. As if people hiking in the desert carried ice."

"Finished?" he asked weakly when she offered him a drink of water.

"Yes. It's as good as I can manage. Let's scoot you under that overhang to wait out the symptoms."

"Wait? I'm not waiting. I need to get back to base camp right away. To get some medical care for this and to request help finding Maureen."

"Ace, that's foolish. The directions clearly say for the victim to stay quiet."

"Well, this victim's not going to wait around for that fellow's mate. I've heard rattlers travel in pairs. Slap a bandage on it and help me up."

She gazed at him unhappily, but did as she was ordered, wrapping gauze around his leg and securing it with the adhesive tape. They hadn't gone a mile, however, when he started having chills and his skin got clammy.

"If you pass out and fall down a ravine," Meredith warned in her toughest voice, "it'll take five men and a mule to haul you out. Sit down, lean against that cliff and don't give me any flak."

"Yes, ma'am," he said weakly, slumping forward the moment he sat.

A pit seemed to open in Meredith's stomach when she went to bathe his wound. The leg was badly discolored below the knee and had swollen to twice its normal size. She thought his eyes looked glassy. About then, he clutched his stomach and started vomiting.

"I think it's curtains for me," he mumbled, voice slurred. "Don't blame yourself. You tried. You came prepared. Fine soldier I am—walking out with nothing."

She placed a hand on either side of his face and made him look her in the eye. "You listen to me, Ace Bannister. No one's died from a rattlesnake bite in a long time, and you aren't going to be the first to break the record. Do you hear me?"

But he didn't. His eyes rolled back in his head and he passed out.

CHAPTER FIFTEEN

MEREDITH BATHED his face with water from her canteen. He roused, but from the wild look in his eyes, she knew he wasn't seeing her.

When his teeth began to chatter and he started raving about her in ways that would have been embarrassing if others had been around, Meredith began to think seriously about getting help. But how? Darkness was creeping in, and in his present condition he couldn't be trusted not to do something foolish. She pulled the survival blanket out of her pack and tucked it around him. It seemed to settle him for the moment.

Lord, they'd made a mess of things. And what about poor Mouse? Meredith was almost sick with worry. She really wasn't cut out for the rigors of command. She'd much rather be home baking bread or playing her piano. Or raising children. Her hands stilled. Where had that thought come from?

Ace thrashed his head from side to side and tried to sit up. Meredith failed to get him to lie back. Finally she tackled him, and although she weighed less by far, she did force him into a reclining position. Panting, she lay over him to hold him down—which proved to be a mistake. He moved his hands over her back and said erotic things about how she'd look in nothing but a pair of topaz earrings.

The ravings of a madman. She didn't own topaz earrings. After the things he said, though, she wished she did. He had a vivid imagination—vivid enough to make her blush. Was there any validity in a temporarily deranged person's rantings? Probably not.

He moved on to things that weren't nearly so exciting. Meredith found them riveting just the same. But sad. He was clearly reliving his childhood. She recalled Ruby saying it hadn't been good.

Night closed in. Automatically her arms tightened around him. It wasn't the adult she was trying to shield, but the lonely boy who'd obviously never had anyone to love him. "I love you," she whispered fiercely, tucking her head beneath his chin. Shocked, she realized it was deeply true.

Right after that, he grew strangely still. She lifted her head, wishing she could see his expression. She sat up and snapped on the flashlight. He muttered nonsense— said his mother was *delicate,* not weak.

Meredith trained the light on his wound. Was it more discolored than it had been? She bathed it again, and this time her hands shook. Putting the vague feelings that had been building for weeks into words—saying *I love you*—brought a sense of rightness she'd been quick to deny before. It made her ministrations more tender and less sure.

When had the differences in their beliefs stopped being an issue? she wondered. But she knew. It had been a gradual thing. No matter how she'd tried to convince herself otherwise, Ace was a more sensitive leader than men like the general and Colonel Loudermilk. He cared about what happened to kids like Jefferson, Larson, Porter and Granelli, and he could have sent someone else to look for Mouse. But he didn't. He went himself.

Over the next half hour, Ace revealed some harsh facts about his parents. Meredith wished she'd known all this earlier. Oh, how she detested his father. No wonder Ace loathed rodeos. If only his mother had seen through the jerk and made a life for herself and her son.

Sometime after midnight, Ace sat up abruptly and asked groggily for a drink of water. He dislodged Meredith.

Blinking, she rubbed sleep from her eyes and groped for the canteen. Did his skin seem warmer? Less clammy? "How are you feeling? Better?" she murmured, guiding the canteen to his lips.

"Better than what?" he asked hoarsely. "I'm nauseated and weaker than a newborn pup." He thrust the canteen into her hands again and fell back. "What time is it?"

"It's 0300," she said after checking her watch.

Leaning on one elbow, he brushed an unsteady hand over his face. "In two hours this area becomes a rifle pop-up course. If Mouse hasn't found her way back we'll cancel the exercise and get search teams out. You'd better leave me now or help me back to camp."

"I'm not leaving you." She turned the flashlight on and took another look at his leg. It was hot. Splotchy red and purple.

Sluggish as he was, Ace saw determination in the jut of her jaw before she plunged them into darkness again.

"I'll defer to you, Captain," he said. "You call the shots. You've done the right things so far."

Meredith's heart skipped at the unexpected praise.

"Funny," she said, "I've been thinking I'm not cut out for this."

He found her in the dark and pulled her into his arms. "Where would I be if not for you?" He framed her face a moment, his fingers trembling.

She cupped one of his hands and closed her eyes. "Tonight, sitting here, I realized I'd rather be home raising my own children than maybe just confusing a bunch of kids who'll ultimately get thrown into some tough situations. Benevolence and the military mind-set don't mix," she said sadly.

Her admission touched something in Ace. He wanted her home raising *his* children. But what made him think she'd have him? She didn't like *anything* about the military. Including military men.

"You figure to settle in Baltimore?" he asked, wishing they could have this conversation when his head didn't feel so disconnected.

"I doubt it." She glanced away and lost the warmth of his hand. "Maybe I'll pick up a few more psychology classes and see about being a civilian consultant at the fort. I need a new start," she said wistfully. "Like Ruby."

If only he could think. Ace closed his eyes. Might she be willing to stay in Texas? Then he thought of something else. "If you resign, you'll have deal with your father, you know."

She tensed suddenly and gripped his hand. "Speaking of fathers...Ace, why didn't you go down that night at the rodeo and slug Jarrod Bannister? He deserved it for the abominable way he treated you and your mother."

Ace tried to sit, but gave up and waved a hand. "Violence from Captain Temperance?" he mumbled. "Anyway, who said he's my father?"

Monday, she'd checked his file. Tonight he'd filled in the blanks during his delirium, and she told him so. "No wonder you don't want to be called Austin Cody Bannister," she burst out indignantly.

His voice was fading. "I went back, you know—kept thinking about how you said a man's enemy is human. We started off wrong. He blamed my mother, said she was unstable and obsessed. Claimed she tried to trap him by getting pregnant. I got mad again. He left me—his own flesh and blood." Ace sucked in a long uneven breath. "That wife of his swore he looked for me—once. After they heard my mother had died." He sat up and sighed, his voice raspy. "They wouldn't let me see my half sisters. Said I had no right to ruin his image in their eyes. I walked off and left the bastard begging me to keep his miserable secret."

"I'm sorry, Ace. Family can be—" She was going to say disappointing, but broke off when he struggled to stand. "Ace, what are you doing? That leg looks awful!"

He managed to lean on the cliff wall until the dizziness passed. "Don't be sorry for me, Meredith. It's over with Jarrod Bannister. For good." It took almost more willpower than he could muster to move up the trail away from her. Thank God he hadn't foolishly declared his love. How could he have forgotten how proudly she wore those lofty family names? *Meredith Marshall St. James.*

Meredith tried sorting through the pain she'd detected in his caustic speech before she raced after him. "You didn't let me finish. No matter whose genes a person shares, each one of us has his or her own unique makeup. Ruby told me how you wouldn't let a woman close because you were afraid of being like your father. Is that the reason you let her walk out of your life?''

He stopped and turned. She was right below him. Even after all this time in the wilderness he could smell her perfume. It invaded his pores and weakened his determination to drive her away once and for all. It made him dizzy.

"What in hell are you talking about?" he shouted when the wooziness passed. "*You're* the one I let get too close. You, a woman who's probably in every social register in the country, while I don't even have a legitimate right to my last name. Damn laughable, isn't it?" The effort it took Ace to make that speech sent him reeling.

Meredith grabbed his wrists to steady him. She could feel his pulse galloping. When hers matched, she fought for control. Carefully she slipped beneath his arm on the side with his bad leg. "Lean on me," she commanded. "Now," she continued, wanting to amuse him once they'd developed a pattern of hobbling, "were you— with customary masculine inadequacy—trying to say that you feel affectionate inclinations for *moi?*" she teased. Had his leg not looked so bad, she would never have had courage to joke about such a thing.

"If you're asking do I love you, Baltimore . . . the answer is yes." Sounding sad, he said, "Without a thesaurus and your fancy French, tell me what in hell I'm supposed to do about it."

Meredith drew in a shaky breath. She ran through the possibilities, beginning with *a* for affair and skipping directly to *m* for marriage, when up ahead among the boulders, lights bobbed.

"Yo!" Ace whispered. "Who goes?"

Too soon, in Meredith's opinion, they were surrounded by a group of cadets led by Granelli and Larson—bless their little hearts. Everyone talked at once, until Ace tried one of his famous whistles and failed.

"Before we worry about me," he rasped, "what about Mouse?"

Betsy stepped forward. "Sir, Mouse came in on her own. We think it was the heat that made her sick."

Vincent Granelli elbowed his way past Betsy. "Did you fall, sir?"

"I tangled with a rattlesnake and he won." Ace laughed self-consciously. "I don't recommend it for sport. Captain St. James tells me the venom works like sodium Pentothal. As well as spilling the family secrets, I've lost track of time. What's the ETA on the invasion?"

Meredith kissed the prospect of continuing any personal conversation goodbye as two husky cadets took over helping Ace. She was left to trail behind, wondering if she'd imagined he said he loved her.

On the perimeter of the campsite, they were halted by a sentry, identified and passed on into camp, where the rest of the unit had begun to stir.

Meredith wished the whole Nevada test site would blow away in the stiff wind that had risen out of nowhere. But Skull Mountain had withstood centuries of wind and rain and a host of mock invasions. Wishing wouldn't turn it into a nice deserted island for two.

There was nothing Meredith could do but hang in and bide her time. Before this was over, she vowed to lead a clearheaded Ace back to the subject of *them,* even if she had to steal one of Colonel Loudermilk's jets and sky-write, "I love you, Ace Bannister," for all the army and air force to see.

Once they were in camp, the major stubbornly refused to let anyone call a medic. "I'll do the briefing first," he insisted. So for fifteen minutes he sat on a box that served as a makeshift desk and drilled them on the upcoming maneuver.

Meredith's thoughts strayed to what it had been like lying next to him on the sandy slope. She imagined how it would feel to wake up next to him every day for the rest of her life. In the midst of her fantasy he called her name.

"Captain St. James. Stay a minute after the others leave, will you?"

She didn't like the dark circles ringing his eyes or the pinched look to his mouth. Instinctively she knew he didn't want the cadets to learn how much pain he was in. She figured that was what he wanted to discuss.

The last thing she expected from a man who looked half-dead was a kiss that nearly knocked her combat boots off.

The tent flap still waved from the last cadet out when Ace pulled her into the cradle of his thighs and settled his mouth over hers. Her lips were soft and mobile—and a different part of his anatomy was rock hard—before he moved on to plant moist kisses down her neck. "Damn," he murmured. "You drive me crazy, Baltimore."

Meredith shivered and clung to his broad shoulders. She thought he must be out of his head again. "I . . . I need to go call a corpsman."

Ace rested his damp forehead on hers and smiled. "My leg hurts like hell or I'd say forget the corpsman and get a chaplain up here, instead."

"A chaplain?" She drew back. "Oh, my God. You feel that bad?"

"Meredith." He kissed her softly. "Chaplains do things other than administer last rites."

She frowned. "Yes. So?" Her hands fluttered.

He gripped both of her hands to hold her still. "I've tried not to, but I can't help loving you. I am, with—how did you put that?—with customary masculine inadequacy... asking you to marry me, Captain St. James."

When she continued to gape, he pulled her close and put every last ounce of energy into a kiss. Breaking for air, he swayed against her. "I really hate...to do this...but I'm afraid you're going to have to take over for me, sweetheart." Without warning, he slid from the box.

Meredith froze. Fear ripped at her heart. She dropped to her knees and checked his pulse with a shaking hand. His pulse was fast and irregular. *"Yes,"* she whispered with relief, he was alive. And she intended to keep him that way. Why hadn't she noticed that he'd been running on guts and adrenaline? If anything happened to him...

He moaned, and Meredith ran to the flap to call for Mouse. Then she hoisted the emergency flag and dashed to the base radio to call Nellis. An airman at the other end promised to send a corpsman and a chopper within ten minutes. He told her Colonel Loudermilk's team had yet to board their craft and asked if she wanted to abort the mission.

Meredith glanced at Ace. A scratch meant lost points. Wasn't this what he taught his cadets—to reach down and pull out superhuman strength in the face of adversity? Could she?

"We won't scratch," she said. "I have a cadet student nurse who can stay with the major." She had confidence in Mouse, who had already placed a cool compress on Ace's leg. "You get that chopper here on the double."

The minute he called back to confirm that they were airborne, Meredith explained the situation to Mouse. The soft-spoken girl with the somber brown eyes had lost her father in Vietnam. Meredith trusted her implicitly with Ace's life.

She intended to leave him a note. A simple *I love you*, tucked into his shirt pocket. Or maybe it should be bold, block letters stating, *yes, yes, yes!* to his question of marriage. But before she got the chance, Captain Granelli stuck his head through the flap and said two strange planes had shown up on radar.

Meredith made herself act like a good soldier, blanking all thought of Ace from her mind as she stepped outside and into his role.

Squinting, she thought the planes darting through the clouds were A-10 Warthogs, most likely on their way to another mission. Dismissing them, she hiked up the mountain to check the depth of the foxholes as Ace would have done.

Stopping only long enough to give suggestions for better camouflage, she quickly deployed her ground forces to counter the blank shells Loudermilk's team had just begun lobbing into the ridge.

But wait! Something wasn't right! Those weren't blanks ripping the ridge to smithereens. "Holy smoke! Live ammo!

"Keep your heads down," she shouted in her toughest voice, "and don't move a muscle until I give the word. Get those helmets on and keep 'em on."

Meredith scrambled toward the command post on her hands and knees, paying no attention to the rocks that bit into her flesh or the horrendous *kaboom*s that slammed through her head.

The planes dropping the shells flew out of sight again, leaving only the echo of explosions, along with the whir of the helicopter coming to get Ace. God, she had to get down there and ask someone for help.

Then, before she picked her way through the boulders, the helicopter lifted off again and took off for Nellis.

Mouse stood in the clearing, eyes shaded, watching its progress. Out of breath, Meredith was still four feet or so away when she again caught the flash of silver sliding out of the west, coming in low—with purpose. She hit Mouse hard, tumbling them both into a ditch as the planes banked, rolled and blew the army headquarters tent clean off the map. At the speed they traveled, the planes disappeared over Skull Mountain almost before Meredith had a chance to pin them with her binoculars. Air force A-10s, all right. What in hell were they doing? Sweat mixed with grit pooled between her breasts as she thought how recently Ace and Mouse had been in that tent. Involuntary shudders attacked her knees, making it next to impossible to stand.

Grabbing the portable radio from Cadet Private Jefferson, who was huddled over it shaking like a leaf, Meredith beeped Nellis. "This is Green Goose. I've got two Warthogs dropping hot rocks to heck and gone out here. Tell Colonel Loudermilk if it's his idea of a joke, it's not funny."

"Live ammo?" The airman laughed. "Impossible."

"Believe it," she snapped. "Twice. And me with inexperienced ROTCs spread over hell's half acre. I want those pilots' heads on a chopping block. ASAP."

"I show a couple of A-10s on a bombing run to Frenchman Flat. Maybe they dropped a load too soon. We'll evaluate. Put your team leader on the horn. Loudermilk's ETA is two minutes out."

"This is Captain St. James. I *am* team leader, you jerk. I suggest you make that the fastest evaluation in history. And, buster, the air force owes me a tent and a base radio unit. Over and out."

It was amazing how quickly she'd gone from temperate to tigress. Wouldn't Ace love that, Meredith thought as she scanned the sky for a return of the planes. Following a period of blessed silence, she heard the drone of a transport. All at once the sky overhead blossomed with parachutes, and the still-smoking ridge swarmed with activity. Several shots rang out before Meredith realized that not one member of her team had moved.

But of course, she'd told them to stay put. She might have laughed if she hadn't been shaking in her boots. Wait until she told Ace how everyone had followed orders to the letter.

"Move 'em out," she shouted at Granelli. "To steal a line from an old movie—let's win this one for the Gipper."

Vinnie gaped at her as if she'd lost her mind. Meredith shrugged and put it in terms he understood. Didn't these kids know old movies?

Thank God there was no reappearance of renegade planes. It took all day, but the army won by a narrow margin. That evening, they were all too exhausted to discuss their success—or their close call.

A no-name colonel said two Warthogs out on maneuvers *might* have dumped on the wrong green target, and wasn't it lucky no one was hurt? He insinuated it was Meredith's fault that her tent was marked with a green flag. "I don't know if it *was* green," she snapped. "There's nothing left to check." But she did know. They were the green team, for pity's sake, and had the flag to run up in case of emergency.

He hung up and she cursed Ace. Damn him. She longed to hear his voice. Where was he?

How was he?

She buzzed Colonel Loudermilk. He was in a surly mood. All he said was that Ace wouldn't be returning to the field. Frank had taken the liberty of calling Colonel O'Dell, who had decided to bring in a replacement. Captain Harper couldn't get there from Fort Huachuca until late tomorrow. Loudermilk suggested Meredith take a wash on the artillery scramble.

"In a pig's eye," she told him, and signed off. All night she worried about Ace as she plotted and replotted strategy.

Next day, bleary-eyed, she carried out the briefing alone and tried not to think of him. Standing virtually in his shoes, she found him impossible to forget. Especially when Vinnie fessed up to having "requisitioned" five mortar launchers from regular army infantry on maneuvers below them on the flats. Meredith thought she handled it well—in an appropriately firm but low-key manner. Granelli was the type who was either going to end up a hero or in the brig. And darn it, her team needed those mortar launchers.

Their operation went smoothly from the start. All the cadets carried out her every order. They deserved to crow over the win that night. What would have made their victory even sweeter would have been a call from Ace. Not a peep, however. Meredith couldn't reach Frank and didn't know who else to ask about him.

So far, Colonel Loudermilk had been her only source of information for updates on Ace's condition, and he'd all but told her it was none of her business.

Next day, when the new captain blew in, his cammies clean and his boots spit-polished, Meredith found herself resenting him for no good reason.

Captain Harper considered himself in command from the outset. His sole justification for this, as far as Meredith could tell, was that he was a man. And his idea of commanding was directing from inside his tent.

The cadets disliked him, too, and Meredith understood why. Harper didn't believe in getting his hands dirty. The results were twofold. First, the teams did poorly in exercises, and second, the kids went out of their way to make the captain's life miserable. The best and funniest, to Meredith's way of thinking, was when someone, Granelli probably—because he looked so smug following the incident—put green dye or food coloring in the makeshift shower Harper had spent hours rigging for his personal use.

The cadets thought that since Harper was supposed to be leading the Green Geese, it was only fitting he look the part. Needless to say, Harper was livid. His tantrum put Colonel Loudermilk's tirades to shame.

Meredith gained a deeper respect for Ace's lazy, easy style of leadership. Although she'd have felt better if she could share that observation with him directly. His continued silence concerned her more than she let on. Her concern deepened day by day, even though some nights she fell into the tent she'd inherited from him too exhausted to eat her evening MREs.

When the sun rose on the last day of exercises and there'd still been no word from the major, Meredith actually began to fear that he'd died and no one had the guts to tell her.

Her momentary depression was diverted by the arrival of three unscheduled helicopters. For a moment she was thrown into panic, afraid it might be a sneak attack from Loudermilk. They turned out to be army helicopters, though, and this was a surprise visit from army brass. Meredith almost fell over in a dead faint when her father climbed out of the lead craft.

The silence his appearance invoked among the students was one of reverence. Few of them had ever met a man with four stars and that many medals. And why was he in full-dress uniform? Although she had to admit the general wore his rank well. Tall and broad-shouldered, he exuded power. She hated the fact that her ragtag group was thirteen days into a two-week mission and looked every sweaty minute of it.

"Captain St. James." Formal as always, the general singled her out.

"Sir!" She came to attention, unable to conceal her annoyance.

He arched a brow. "At ease, Captain." His tone was gruff. "Let's take a walk."

"As you wish, sir," she said stiffly, falling in beside him.

"Dammit, Meredith," he said when they were out of earshot of the others, "what's this I hear from Bannister? I positively forbid you to leave the army."

Her hands balled at her sides. She lifted her chin. "I am resigning my commission," she said, meeting his chilly hazel gaze. "What else did Ace say?" Nothing that would hurt his career, she hoped, her heart stepping up its speed.

"Enough to make me very disappointed in the boy."

"Ace is hardly a boy. He's a man."

Again the general's brow shot up. "Yes, well . . . he's a stupid one. His record was spotless before . . . Nobody disobeys my orders. I'm on my way to Fort Freeman to invoke court-martial proceedings. When I finish with Ace Bannister, he'll be lucky to end up a buck private."

She had turned to look out over the camp. Now she whirled to face him. "On what grounds will you court-martial an exemplary officer?"

"Keep your voice down," he said coldly. "I ordered him to toughen you up. Instead, he talks you into re-signing. I'll have his rank, by God. And I demand that you reconsider. Think of the St. James name. Think of your mother and the Marshalls. She's the *only* reason we're having this conversation. If that young scoundrel poisoned your mind, rest assured, he won't influence anyone for long."

She took a step closer. "I'm going to marry him, Father. I don't care how far back you break him."

They were standing toe-to-toe, and both knew how long it had been since she'd called him "Father" in a conversation. "The St. James name be damned. I'm going to be Mrs. Ace Bannister." Reading hesitancy in his normally intractable eyes, she played her trump card. "He's going to father your grandchildren, General," she said softly. "If you do this, so help me, I'll never speak to you again."

She left him then and walked away.

"Meredith!" he shouted. "Stop this minute. You aren't thinking like an officer. You're thinking like a woman."

She stopped and settled a sad look on him. "That's something you never understood. I *am* a woman."

Fighting a yawning emptiness in her heart, she returned to camp. Had she unwittingly lied? Was the tender, passionate, funny, brave man she loved with all her heart wishing he'd never met her?

Grabbing her pack, she gathered her cadets and led them up the mountain to meet Colonel Loudermilk's final assault. She threw her all into winning for Ace. Only for Ace.

The mission couldn't end too soon for Meredith. She no longer wondered why Ace hadn't called. She had to get back before he did something irrevocably foolish—like letting the love they held for each other slip away forever.

CHAPTER SIXTEEN

ON THE FLIGHT HOME, Meredith had difficulty entering into the cadets' celebratory mood. She was still upset with them. Forced by foul weather to spend a night in Vegas, the kids had run wild. No wonder Ace had had reservations. But rascals or not, they had earned Meredith's like and respect. And once they arrived back in Texas, it hit her that this was a final farewell. She would be leaving the service before classes started again in the fall. These bright, mischievous kids would go on to graduate and proudly receive their second lieutenants' bars, but her time to guide and influence them was over.

As she apprised them of her plans, tears were shed on both sides. Betsy, Mouse and even Granelli begged her to reconsider. Her heart, however, had already led her in another direction. Toward Ace, marriage and motherhood.

If he still wanted her.

Entering her apartment later, Meredith immediately telephoned Ace. They had so much to discuss. She was extremely disappointed to connect with his answering machine again—the same as when she'd called from Vegas. That time she hadn't left a message. This time she did, then took the phone into the bathroom so as not to miss his call while she indulged in a long scented soak.

In afterthought, she checked her own answering machine. Three messages from her mother—none from

Ace. Not significant, she told herself. Colonel Louder-milk had confirmed, albeit reluctantly, that Ace had re-turned to active duty.

Fairly certain he knew when they were due back, Meredith began to worry in earnest when an hour passed and he hadn't called. After several more tries to reach him by phone, she gave up with a sigh.

Maybe he was at the office. There were no summer ROTC classes, but he might expect her to stop by and file her reports. Ugh! A chore she still had to face. As she donned her uniform for the official task, Meredith wondered if Ace had heard about the trouble she'd stirred up over the A-10s. Would he believe it if he had?

She grinned. He'd have been shocked by her unchar-acteristic behavior. Fear for her cadets had made her furious enough to want to grab those pilots by the neck and make them pay. She understood a little better now how one might feel when facing an enemy. Because those jerks at the air-force base wanted to sweep the incident under the rug. Well, they'd learned she was no push-over.

Blast. The silver Lexus wasn't at the office. Only Ser-geant Sutton's car. Maybe he knew where to find Ace.

When Meredith walked in, the sergeant glanced up, then jumped to his feet. "Captain, sir!" His chin was all but buried in his chest.

She smiled. He'd called her sir the first time they'd met, too—which seemed so long ago. "At ease, Ser-geant. I know I lost weight bypassing all those gourmet MREs, but I'm not a ghost."

"It's...well, I thought you'd be on your way to D.C." He waved a hand toward her old desk. "The major had me box and label your things."

Meredith felt as if someone had ripped out her most vital organ. "Box my things? Wh-why?"

Sutton scratched his head. "Dunno. The other day—the major's first out of the hospital, I think—he looked pretty rocky, too. I guess you know about his reaction to the antivenin that laid him low for so long."

Meredith hadn't known. Although just now she wanted to shake the old man to get him back on track. "About my going to D.C....," she prompted.

He nodded. "Right. As I was saying, the major told me he'd talked with General St. James. Then he said to clean out your desk and label it for transfer. Come to think of it, that's all he said. He tossed out that folder." The sergeant pointed. "Then he helped himself to a couple of your red poppies and left." Sutton frowned. "Say, did something happen between you two?"

Meredith swallowed a lump and plucked the indicated folder from Ace's trash. It bore her name and contained the forms she would need to resign. *Curious. And why take flowers he'd never liked?*

"You haven't talked to him since?" she asked.

"Nope. We're officially closed, you know."

"Are Captains Caldwell and Holmes still on mission?"

"Yep."

"And Colonel O'Dell?" Meredith thought the commander might be able to shed some light.

"I ran into Mrs. O'Dell at the PX Friday. The colonel's sitting in review on a court-martial at the fort. Came up sudden, she said."

Meredith couldn't breathe. Pain knifed through her body. What had made her think her father would listen to her after all these years? He probably knew Ace wouldn't marry her if he was stripped of rank. She'd always felt manipulated; now she felt betrayed.

Sick at heart, she fled, not even trusting herself to salute. After tumbling into her car, she drove, heedless of direction.

The sun was sinking when she realized the car was almost out of gas. Not surprising, as her every thought had been consumed by Ace.

Suddenly it struck her. If she was to be of any help to him, she had to get a grip. Only, what if he refused to see her? No. She wouldn't consider the possibility.

First, she made a U-turn and found a gas station. Filling the tank and getting her bearings, she headed home, still wrestling with the problem. Should she try appealing to her father again? What if she promised to stay in the army? Would he back off? She'd do it for Ace. Not to preserve the general's precious tradition, but she'd stay to save the career of the only man she'd ever love.

Driving through town, Meredith felt nothing. Frankly, she doubted she'd ever feel anything again. She smoothed a lock of hair behind her ear. A strand caught on her earring. In freeing it, Meredith realized she had donned the opals. The earrings she'd worn the night Ace came to dinner. The night they'd . . .

Lord, but she had to stop thinking of him in terms of *them*. An angry tear slipped down her cheek. Dashing it away, she wondered where the general might have taken a room. It was best to focus on what she could do for Ace.

One way to check on her father's whereabouts would be to call her mother. Meredith almost felt sorry for the woman who'd spent half a lifetime with such a heartless man. Except that her sorrow would be misplaced. She doubted anything mattered to her mother but the social status that came with being *Mrs. General St. James.*

Home again, Meredith snatched up the phone and dialed. Then she paced impatiently, waiting for her mother to pick up on her end. Mrs. St. James's abrupt response to Meredith's dull "Hello" shocked the daughter to silence.

"Shame. Shame on you, Meredith. I simply can not believe that you discussed your marriage plans with the general, without so much as a peep to me. Have you no idea what's involved in putting on a wedding?"

Meredith had stalled on the word *marriage.* And Mrs. St. James didn't wait for a response. "All Marshalls and St. Jameses get married in the cathedral. Don't you know how far ahead they book? You won't get a decent date now until spring. Well, you'll just have to wait. Which may be a blessing in disguise. Baltimore is prettiest in the spring."

Meredith put a hand to her head. The room threatened to spin out of control.

"Why are you so quiet?" her mother demanded. "You haven't made other plans, have you?"

Meredith cleared her throat, but the older woman swept on like a steamroller, naming people she said absolutely must be included on a guest list. Before she progressed to caterers, Meredith blurted, "Stop! Where is the general right this minute?"

"Working in his study. Why? All week he's been setting up scholarship funds for our grandchildren. Meredith, dear, you aren't pregnant, are you? Tell me you're not. It would be so awkward."

Meredith almost dropped the phone. "Mother! I am not pregnant. I have to find Ace," she muttered. "Don't you dare plan our wedding, do you hear?"

"You wouldn't elope! No one in our family has ever eloped."

Strangely Meredith felt like laughing. "Now that's a thought, Mother. Please do me a favor. Tell the general to stop with the scholarships. No child of mine will ever be coerced into attending West Point. I want my children to be whatever they want to be." Slamming the phone back into its cradle, Meredith threw out her arms and spun in a circle. Now that both of her parents knew how she felt, it was as if a giant burden had been lifted.

Snatching up the phone again, she dialed Ace. This time his line was busy. Good. She smiled at nothing. He wasn't embroiled in a senseless court-martial. He was home. Then it dawned—he hadn't returned her calls. And he'd had the sergeant pack her things. Did that mean he'd changed his mind about loving her? Fear gripped her chest.

There was really only one way to find out. If the general's forcing her to go on that Nevada mission had done nothing else, it had toughened her up. Ace Bannister would find it hard to avoid her when she showed up at his house.

On the drive across town, Meredith's mind leap-frogged from one subject to another, but always returned to Ace's proposal.

Men often got cold feet at the thought of weddings. Or so she'd heard. It could be that simple. Then again...

When she actually arrived and parked outside his home, the butterflies she thought she'd banished returned and flapped so hard inside her stomach, she wanted to leave. But no St. James had ever been a coward. And Ace had said he loved her. Twice!

Clinging to that, she slowly climbed from the car and took a moment to straighten her uniform skirt. Oh, why hadn't she changed? Well, too late to worry about that now.

Meredith walked slowly toward the house. Overhead, a new moon was rising. That was a good sign. A new moon meant new beginnings. If ever two people needed to shed their pasts and start anew, it was she and Ace. Resolute, Meredith hammered on his door.

An eternity seemed to pass before he opened it.

Mouth dry as summer dust, she soaked up the sight of him. After a moment, it registered—he hadn't thrown the door wide and scooped her into his arms. In fact, he seemed hesitant. Maybe even reluctant to see her.

She dug deep for a smile and stepped forward. Their uniforms brushed. Because he frowned and moved back, Meredith might have lost her nerve had she not chanced to see a large 3-D picture on his wall. And beside his lamp, a vase filled with bright red poppies. *Her* poppies. It was the most promising sign yet.

Ace stared at the woman who hovered on his threshold. Too numbed at seeing her to speak, he felt like a drowning man going down for the third time. He'd run through his phone messages and knew, of course, that she was in town, however temporarily.

He certainly hadn't expected her to come by. Considering her brilliant performance in the field, he assumed the general would have her on the first flight out of town. Glory bound. And rightly so. She deserved it. But, Lord, he had no idea wanting her to stay could hurt so bad.

After a long silence, Ace collected himself enough to manage a civil greeting. "Meredith, what a surprise. I didn't suppose you'd come all this way to say good-bye."

She frowned. Goodbye? In a gnat's eye! "Aren't you going to invite me in?" she asked, taking several steps, forcing him a few inches back into the room.

Ace felt the murky waters close over his head as she lifted her chin in that special saucy way, and the fiery opals flashed at her ears. He cleared his throat, recalling vividly the small box on his dresser that held a pair of topaz studs. What did it say about him that, after he'd called her father and the general had set him straight about how selfishly he stood in the way of Meredith's promotion, he'd kept those stupid earrings?

Scowling, he clung to the doorknob. "Don't let me keep you. Flying standby?" he asked politely, casting a quick glance at his watch. "Of course. Why else would you be in uniform? Guess it's goodbye Texas, hello D.C." The statement held a slight edge. So he was a sore loser. And he detested goodbyes. But he'd been wrong about her father. The man was proud of her and only wanted to keep his family together. Not easy in the military, Ace knew. The nicest thing he could do was to let her speak her piece from the doorway and leave.

Meredith was getting hot under the collar of that uniform he seemed to be so focused on. After all the worry she'd been through—after the way she'd raced over here to declare her love, expecting him to say he loved her, too—all he could talk about was her leaving.

Placing the flat of her hand on his chest, she pushed him inside. "You're so keen on this uniform, Bannister, I think you should have it." Ripping off her tie, she threw it in his face.

They both watched it flutter to the floor and curl over his shoe. Her perfume engulfed Ace, bringing with it sweet memories. Memories he swallowed back. "Such drama isn't called for, St. James. You think I haven't heard how you whipped the pants off Frank and his fly-boys? How you've become a regular chip off the old block?" Ace started to touch one of the insignia on her jacket, then caught himself and drew back.

She found his attitude infuriating. So infuriating, in fact, that she kicked the front door closed and reached behind her to engage the lock. So help her, if she had to cram this uniform down his throat one piece at a time to make him listen, that was what she'd do.

Stepping onto the carpet, Meredith began to unfasten the brass buttons down the front of her regulation shirt.

"Meredith, what are you doing?" Ace asked, nervously fingering his tie.

"You figure it out, Major."

He caught a glimpse of hot orange lace as the last button fell away, and his breath lodged in his throat. "Uh…" Ace licked his lips. "I had a lot of time to think while I was in the hospital. You have a good point—a little tact and diplomacy never hurt anyone."

Her eyes blazed. "Diplomacy? Or lies? You said—"

"I said a lot of things. Sometimes a man's got to eat his words. Did you hear that Roy Tindall trashed Ruby's new place in Oregon? At his court-martial, half the brass said to toss him in the brig and throw away the key. I suggested counseling. Me, would you believe?" God, why was he babbling?

She moved and the lace flashed again. Ace scooted his tie a notch closer to his Adam's apple and moved back into the room. She had an unholy gleam in her eye. It made him doubt she'd heard a word he said.

Meredith followed his retreat. "Bah!" She kicked off her pumps. One sailed past his ear. "You taught me that nice doesn't always pay."

Ace began to sweat. As she moved in on him, he narrowed his eyes.

She rose on tiptoe and grasped the points of his collar.

He almost strangled on a single word. "Ca...ptain..."

Meredith eased back, smiled and ripped off her insignia. Eyes locked on his, she scattered them at his feet. "No stars, no bars, Major A period, C period, Bannister. So tell me what you think of that."

Ace gasped her name. "Meridith! What happened to all your ideas about the military needing a higher consciousness level?"

"War is hell, soldier."

For the first time since she'd appeared at his door, Ace let a smile flicker. Until his conscience nudged him again and he shook his head. "This role reversal—it's clever, but it won't wash. Your father... The general—"

"—has a choice," she murmured, circling her finger seductively around his gold oak leaf. "He can change his ways or never see his grandchildren."

"You don't mean that." Ace drew in a sharp breath. "I know what living without family is like. I won't be a party to that."

Meredith's heart plunged. It was over. She'd run a bluff and now she felt foolish. Foolish and exposed. The general had won, after all. Blindly she bent to gather her shoes and her tie.

Ace knelt and gripped her arm. "God, Meredith, don't do this to me. You filled my boots out there and did a fantastic job. The general can and will get you promoted. You should have heard him. You're wrong about him, Meredith. He loves you." His fingers bit deep into her flesh.

She tried shrugging loose. "My father wants a son. Let me go. How do you know what kind of job I did?"

He eased his hold, but helped her to stand. "Vinnie called me from Las Vegas. Told me about the incident with the Warthogs. The kid said you're one helluva leader. Don't you see? You don't have to wait for anyone to build a new army. Your methods work. Go on now and lead."

"I don't want to lead!" she shouted. "I want a home. A family." Her voice faltered as suddenly his eyes flared, going from charcoal to hot smoke.

Perhaps things weren't hopeless. Her heart slammed against her ribs.

Ace caught her around the back of the neck and stared into her eyes. "You never once called to see if I'd lived or died."

"I asked Frank every day—and you didn't check on me, either."

"I did. I always got Harper. You were off mapping out strategy, or leading assaults up the mountain. He called you gung ho. That wasn't the Meredith I knew. Anyway, the way I see it, I'd had my say. You're the one who's big on communication. How would you read silence?"

Meredith studied the man and saw pride and vulnerability. The pain of having been a throwaway child hovered in the depths of his gray eyes.

Look at him.

Look at her.

A moment ago she'd been quick, once again, to feel rejection where apparently none existed.

"I haven't changed my ideals," she said quietly. "War is barbaric. But what I learned in filling your shoes, Ace, is that I can defend my home, my country and the people I love if push comes to shove. Most especially, the people I love.''

He gazed at her from beneath hooded lids. "Those people—who might they be?"

Mischief sparkled in her eyes again. "Well, they say you only nag the ones you love. From the day we met, I set out to hone all your rough edges."

"That'd take a while." He tugged his ear. "You'd have to stick around, you know. Be a camp follower."

"I know." She beamed.

He ran a finger softly down her cheek, along her jaw. "If I recall, I offered you a crack at the job, twenty-four hours a day, 365 days a year."

Meredith flattened her palms against his chest, then ran her hands up over his shoulders. In a firm voice, so there could be no misunderstanding this time, she said, "My answer was then, and still is, *yes*, Ace Bannister."

He smiled. "I hear military social work is exciting. And flexible."

"You mean, retain my commission?"

He pulled her fully into his arms. "I think it's your patriotic duty, Captain. At least until we start that family."

"You drive a hard bargain, Major. I'll give it some thought. But if you don't kiss me in two seconds, I swear all bets are off."

Since the army rarely promotes fools to the rank of major, Ace followed her orders to the letter. To the letter and beyond. He was, after all, dealing with a lady who set great store by officers being independent thinkers.

As his lips claimed hers in a deep satisfying kiss, his mind jogged ahead—to his king-size bed, to the two of them touching skin to skin, and to topaz earrings. For a fleeting moment it crossed his mind that he just might go broke buying earrings.

Or toys for a certain tough old general's grandchildren. In his way, the old buzzard did love his daughter. She'd see. And he'd learn sons-in-law were important, too.

But that would come later, after he and Meredith got the art of compromise down to a science.

Meredith's fingers worked to unknot his perfect tie. She sighed when it slipped loose and joined hers on the floor. As she freed the buttons on his shirt, a vision soared before her eyes—baskets filled with brilliant flowers and this man standing beside her at the altar, proud and handsome in his dress greens.

Or, if it suited him better, she'd go before a chaplain at the fort tonight with nothing but a single red poppy.

Following a second lengthy kiss, Ace picked her up and carried her down the hall to his bedroom. He didn't need words to tell her the pleasure would be mutual this time.

Somehow she knew it would be morning before the subject of marriage surfaced again. But they'd get around to it.

She had something else to do first. Because in all the ways that counted, Meredith Marshall St. James was very much a chip off the old block. And perhaps the most admirable trait of St. James men and women was that they always, *always,* finished what they started.

HARLEQUIN SUPERROMANCE®

WOMEN WHO DARE
They take chances, make changes
and follow their hearts!

Dangerous to Love
by Carol Duncan Perry

Vicki Winslow refuses to do the sensible thing—enter the
witness protection program. She's done nothing wrong and
she isn't going to cut herself off from her family. So now she's
hiding out, protected only by secrecy and her own wits—if
you don't count her eighty-seven-year-old great-aunt, her
poetry-quoting cousin, two large dogs, one rifle and a pet
skunk named Sweetpea.

Caine Alexander aims to change this situation. Not that
Caine's any knight in shining armor. *Hell, no.* A man could get
killed playing hero. Still, he's promised to protect Vicki, and if
any man can make good on such a promise, Caine's the man.
Too bad Vicki doesn't want his protection…. Because she's
stuck with it.

Watch for *Dangerous to Love*
by Carol Duncan Perry.

Available in July 1995 wherever
Harlequin books are sold.

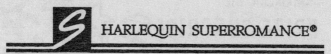

HARLEQUIN SUPERROMANCE®

presents

Big Luke, Little Luke
by Dawn Stewardson

This July, meet the third of our Four Strong Men:

Mike Alexander was the best friend Navy pilot Luke Dakota ever had. So when Luke received a letter from Mike's wife, Caitlyn, he wasn't too concerned—until he opened it. In the letter, Caitlyn told him about Mike's death and the birth of their son, Luke. His namesake.

Drawn by a sense of responsibility to Mike, Luke arranged for a leave of absence and set off for Arizona.

Once there, his life was sent into a tailspin. He learned that Caitlyn's business was in the red, military intelligence wouldn't leave her alone and, worst of all, she was convinced that Mike's death was the result of foul play. Luke became determined to help Caitlyn fight her unseen enemies. But he soon found himself up against an enemy he couldn't conquer—himself. Because Luke Dakota was falling in love with his best friend's wife....

**Look for *Big Luke, Little Luke* in July 1995
wherever Harlequin books are sold.**

ANNOUNCING THE

PRIZE SURPRISE SWEEPSTAKES!

This month's prize:

L-A-R-G-E—SCREEN PANASONIC TV!

This month, as a special surprise, we're giving away a fabulous FREE TV!

Imagine how delighted you and your family will be to own this brand-new 31" Panasonic** television! It comes with all the latest high-tech features, like a SuperFlat picture tube for a clear, crisp picture...unified remote control...closed-caption decoder...clock and sleep timer, and much more!

The facing page contains two Entry Coupons (as does every book you received this shipment). Complete and return *all* the entry coupons; **the more times you enter, the better your chances of winning the TV!**

Then keep your fingers crossed, because you'll find out by July 15, 1995 if you're the winner!

Remember: The more times you enter, the better your chances of winning!*

PTV KAL

PRIZE SURPRISE
SWEEPSTAKES
OFFICIAL ENTRY COUPON

This entry must be received by: JUNE 30, 1995
This month's winner will be notified by: JULY 15, 1995

YES, I want to win the Panasonic 31" TV! Please enter me in the drawing and let me know if I've won!

Name_____

Address _____ Apt. _____

City   State/Prov.   Zip/Postal Code

Account #_____

Return entry with invoice in reply envelope.

© 1995 HARLEQUIN ENTERPRISES LTD.

CTV KAL

PRIZE SURPRISE
SWEEPSTAKES
OFFICIAL ENTRY COUPON

This entry must be received by: JUNE 30, 1995
This month's winner will be notified by: JULY 15, 1995

YES, I want to win the Panasonic 31" TV! Please enter me in the drawing and let me know if I've won!

Name_____

Address _____ Apt. _____

City   State/Prov.   Zip/Postal Code

Account #_____

Return entry with invoice in reply envelope.

© 1995 HARLEQUIN ENTERPRISES LTD.

CTV KAL